BEAST
of the
NORTH WOODS

BEAST
of the
NORTH WOODS

~

ANNELISE RYAN

BERKLEY PRIME CRIME · NEW YORK

BERKLEY PRIME CRIME
Published by Berkley
An imprint of Penguin Random House LLC
penguinrandomhouse.com

Book design by Elke Sigal

Library of Congress Cataloging-in-Publication Data

Names: Ryan, Annelise, author.
Title: Beast of the north woods / Annelise Ryan.
Description: New York: Berkley Prime Crime, 2025.
Identifiers: LCCN 2024033548 (print) | LCCN 2024033549 (ebook) |
ISBN 9780593816059 (hardcover) | ISBN 9780593816073 (ebook)
Subjects: LCGFT: Detective and mystery fiction. | Novels.
Classification: LCC PS3568.Y2614 B43 2025 (print) |
LCC PS3568.Y2614 (ebook) | DDC 813/.54—dc23/eng/20240724
LC record available at https://lccn.loc.gov/2024033548
LC ebook record available at https://lccn.loc.gov/2024033549

Printed in the United States of America
1st Printing

*To all the kindly people of
Rhinelander who work to keep the legend of
the Hodag alive.*

BEAST
of the
NORTH WOODS

PROLOGUE

Andy Bosworth slogged his way through a snowdrift sculpted between two large conifers, tugging his loaded sled behind him. His fishing equipment, including a tent, a gas heater, and an ice auger, made for a heavy haul, yet the sled they were on glided over the uneven snow with little more than a whisper. He, on the other hand, emitted loud whistling breaths and the occasional strenuous grunt as he made plodding progress through two-foot-high drifts skirting the deeper three-foot piles on the windward side of the trees. He'd gone only about a hundred yards from the cabin before he was winded and had to halt to catch his breath. He was rethinking his decision to forgo buying new snowshoes after his last pair had given up the ghost. He'd forgotten how taxing it could be trudging through deep snow, and it served as a reminder of his promise to himself to get back into the gym.

As he sucked frigid morning air into his lungs—air so cold it burned—his misery wasn't enough to detract from the beauty surrounding him. The sky overhead was the color of a fresh bruise, though it faded to a pale blue on the horizon and grew lighter with each passing minute. Branches on the surrounding trees—some of them iced bits of bare wood, others bowed down with the weight of snow piled on evergreen needles—glistened with crystalline whiteness. The snow sparkled and glittered in the rays of the morning sun like facets on a diamond. Aside from the sounds of Andy's own stertorous breathing, a sepulchral silence surrounded him. His breath created clouds of mist as he exhaled, and his beard bore tiny crystals of ice, making it look bejeweled in the morning light.

When he finally took off again, an eerie, creaking noise broke the silence. Andy recognized it as the sound the ice floes made in the partially frozen river as the sun warmed the surface and things began to move and rub together. He was well bundled and, aside from the sting he felt in his nose and throat with each breath, the cold was of little consequence to him. In fact, his exertions had him sweating slightly and he was considering undoing the zipper of the jacket he had on over his bibs when the morning's relative quiet was shattered by a short, bloodcurdling scream.

Andy froze in place, his brain scrambling to analyze the noise. It had sounded scarily human, but he knew the cries of eagles and hawks in the area could mimic a human scream. Plus, his own heavy breathing had layered itself over the sound, obscuring it just enough that he couldn't be sure of what he'd heard. Might it have come from a wild animal or bird? He tilted his head one way, then another, waiting to see if the sound would repeat.

Seconds later, it did, not as loud, yet somehow more desperate and definitely human. It imbued Andy with an urgent need to move, to act, but where? How? The sound had echoed through the trees and over the snow in a way that made it seem to come from multiple directions at once. Then he heard a grunting noise followed by odd, guttural sounds as if someone, or something, was struggling. He thought it was coming from the direction of the river. Had something fallen through the ice?

He dropped the rope attached to his sled and headed toward the sound, taking high, lurching steps through the snowdrifts. Though he tried to hurry, both the depth and the slipperiness of the snow made him nearly fall several times and, at one point, he went down on his knees. Winded, he stayed in this supplicating position for a moment, listening, belatedly realizing he should have grabbed the pack on his sled that held several tools, including a knife. And oh yeah, his frigging bear spray. What the hell was he going to do if he encountered someone being attacked by a bear? He mentally berated himself.

Some great first responder you are.

He briefly considered going back, but then a meager cry of "Help me" triggered a new sense of urgency. He got to his feet and plunged ahead. As he rounded a large tree trunk, he halted in his tracks, momentarily stunned by what he saw.

Beneath a quartet of trees about twenty feet away, a man's body lay sprawled on the ground, his arms crossed over his torso where his jacket had been ripped open, the white stuffing inside the garment spilling out and stained red. The man's feet were clad in a pair of worn snowshoes and a walking pole lay half buried in the snow beside him. Though the man's face was largely hidden beneath a dark ski mask speckled with gore, the bit of facial skin Andy could see beneath the mask was as white as the snow. The man's eyes stared skyward, unseeing.

The snow around the body was stained dark and red and a coppery, meaty smell in the air made Andy gag and nearly toss up the eggs and bacon he'd had for breakfast. He saw one leg of the man's snow pants was torn along the thigh and there was a long, ragged gash in the flesh beneath the material. From that wound a tiny fountain of blood spewed out, spattering the snow pants and running down into the snow. Andy knew instantly the bleed must have been bigger before he'd arrived because the snow all around the man was a spreading red halo of death.

Andy pulled off his gloves with his teeth, stuffing them into his pockets as he knelt beside the man. He grabbed a handful of the leaked stuffing from the torn parka, wincing when he caught a glimpse of glistening viscera beneath, and pushed it into the leg wound hard to try to stem the arterial flow.

"I gotcha, pal," he said. But there was no reply, no movement, not even a wince as Andy pushed hard into the leg wound.

With his other hand, Andy reached in under the lower part of the ski mask near a tear, exposing a thick, wiry beard. He dug his fingers into the man's neck to try to find a pulse but what he found instead was yet another gash. No, wait, not a gash but rather a hole where that tear in the mask had been.

Instinctively, Andy pulled away, shaking off the blood and gore clinging to his hand. Just then the guy gasped, and Andy felt a fine spray hit his face, making him lean back.

Change of plans, he thought. No need to check for a pulse. The leg wound had been spurting, meaning the guy had a heartbeat.

Except the operative word there was "had," because even as Andy thought this, he realized the slight pulsation he'd initially felt beneath the stuffing on the leg wound had now disappeared. Lifting the wad, he saw there was no more fountain of blood, just a slow, oozing trickle with bits of the fibrous stuffing sticking to it. Andy thought he might need to do CPR but knew he had to get help first; otherwise this guy was a goner.

He's a goner anyway, Andy thought as he fished his phone out of his pocket and held it aloft, not surprised to see he had no service. Cursing to himself, he stood and turned in a circle, holding the phone as high as he could.

There was a rustling sound behind him, and he whirled around, eyes wide with panic. Inanely, a childhood ditty he'd learned raced through his mind:

If the bear is brown, lie down. If the bear is black, fight back.

Andy looked around frantically—which was it, black or brown? In these parts, most likely black. The rising sun cast the trunks of the trees in long, gray shadows, shadows that appeared to move at times when a wind gust blew the powdery surface snow around. A reflective glint caught his eye on the other side of the man's prostrate body.

A knife!

It was bloodied and lying on the snow not far from the victim's right hand, suggesting the man had been trying to defend himself against—

Against what, exactly? Black or brown?

Andy trudged around the dead man's feet to get to the knife, but his boot caught on something, sending him sprawling into blood-soaked snow. When he sat up and looked, he saw a second ski pole partially buried beneath the man's body, the business end of it sticking out just beyond his snowshoes. Andy scrambled onto his hands and knees and crawled over to the knife, snatching it up and holding it at the ready. He scanned the shadows again, but all had grown quiet. The lack of sound was somehow scarier than the desperate noises he'd heard earlier.

Andy knew cell reception would be better by the river and it was closer than his cabin, so he got to his feet and headed in that direction, stopping every few steps to check for service. Minutes later he broke out of the trees and onto the steep, narrow banks of the river. He saw two bars on his phone and started to dial but then froze when he heard something crashing through the underbrush to his right, heading toward him at a rapid pace with heaving, grunting breaths.

Black or brown?

Seconds later a beast burst out of some nearby bushes, startling Andy so badly he jumped and instinctively turned away. His feet slipped on the wet snow and he pinwheeled his arms in an effort to stay upright, but gravity won out. The snow cushioned his fall, but his phone disappeared into a drift and the hand holding the knife slid down the handle and over the blade, slicing into his fingers and palm. He yelped in pain and yanked his hand back, causing the knife to fly out onto the breaking ice of the river, where it skittered across the surface and dropped into the water through an open area.

Andy spun himself around on his butt, knowing he was vulnerable as he sat in the snow without a weapon, but prepared to defend himself the best he could. He was stunned to see the creature standing and staring at him a mere twenty feet away, its sides heaving, its heavy grunting exhalations creating tiny clouds of mist in the air. Andy stared back and blinked hard, not sure he could trust his own eyes.

Seconds later, the creature turned and ran down the riverbank onto an area of solid, shaded ice, navigating the frozen surface with surprising ease. When it reached the other side, it scrambled onto shore and melted into the thick woods.

Andy stared stunned and disbelieving at the spot where he'd last seen the creature, afraid it might reemerge and come back across the river. He shook his head as his logical mind struggled to accept what he had clearly seen: the spiny ridge along the back; the red eyes in a frog-like face that was spattered with blood; two nasty-looking horns above long, tusklike teeth; and clawed feet.

A Hodag. Holy mother of God, it was a freaking Hodag!

Andy shook his head again, refusing to give in to the idea.

It couldn't be. They don't exist. They aren't real.

If only he could've snapped a picture with his phone.

Damn! My phone.

Andy tore his eyes from the spot across the river and examined the snowdrift where he'd dropped his phone. He spotted a small opening and started digging through the snow until he found the device, wet but still turned on and showing—*thank God!*—two bars of service.

The wind picked up as he dialed 911 and fat flakes began drifting down from the sky. He explained his dilemma to the operator who answered, providing the location of the injured man—though not committing to declaring the victim dead—and instructions on the best way for first responders to get to him. Prompted by the operator to explain what had happened to the injured man, Andy hesitated for a few seconds, reluctant to say what his eyes had clearly seen, afraid they'd think his call was a hoax. In the end, he told her the victim had apparently been attacked by an animal.

The call ended following Andy's explanation of the meager cell service he had available to him in the woods, and he took a moment to ponder the situation. He needed to prepare himself for the arrival of the authorities. What was he going to tell them? Had the Hodag killed the man? Andy couldn't say for sure, because he hadn't seen the attack happen, but his gut said yes. The creature had had blood on it, though he supposed it could have been sniffing around the victim after some other animal, like a bear, had attacked and left.

Andy headed back toward the victim, but instead of following his own trail—a series of deep footprint holes in the snow—he spotted the more tamped-down and trampled trail the creature had been on, a trail speckled with drops of blood. He followed it, thinking it might get him back to the victim quicker. The blood droplets increased in both number and size the farther Andy went, and the trail ended where the man's body still lay at the base of the tree. There was no other bloody trail leading away from the victim, no other areas of disturbed snow. In fact, the expanse beyond the tree at the man's head was pristine.

A brief glance at the exposed portion of the man's face told Andy there would be no point in doing CPR. The eyes looked upward, dead and lifeless. The marble whiteness of the surrounding skin beneath the specks of gore made Andy shudder. He turned his gaze to the trees instead, alert and watching for any movement. The silence that had seemed so magical and wondrous to him earlier now felt ominous.

He feared the animal might return. Would it be ramped up with bloodlust? Would it gore him to death the way it had this poor man? No sooner had this terrifying possibility crossed Andy's mind than he heard a snort from off to his left . . . or was it? The combination of snow, wind, and trees made sound bounce around him crazily. A horrifying thought came to him. Could there be more than one of those things in the woods? The possibility scared the bejesus out of him, and he prayed the first responders would hurry up and get there.

Every nerve in his body was telling him to get the hell out of there, to head back to the cabin, where there was warmth and safety. But as uncomfortable as he was, he didn't want to leave the dead man alone. His right hand throbbed and when he looked down he realized his own blood was now staining the snow from where the knife had sliced into his palm. Both of his hands were freezing and when he reached into his pockets, he realized he'd lost his gloves somewhere. He looked around and saw them half buried in the snow near the feet of the dead man. They'd be frozen, he realized, and he jammed his hands into his pockets to warm them instead.

It was hours later—after help had finally arrived, after Andy saw the skeptical looks on the faces of the police, after he realized that telling the cops the victim might have been attacked by a Hodag sounded far-fetched and desperate, after the man's wallet had been removed from a pocket and his identity revealed—that Andy realized the man's death would be classified not as an accident or animal attack, but as a homicide.

It was also when Andy learned he was the number one suspect.

CHAPTER 1

I carefully removed a glass orb from a carton stuffed with wood shavings and held it aloft in one hand, eyeing it in the overhead light of the store.

My employee Rita Bosworth came up behind me in the aisle and peered at the orb over the top of her glasses. "What did you order now, Morgan?"

I noted the light chastising tone in her voice. It was mid-January and with the holidays over, sales in the store would be slow. It wasn't the best time to add inventory, but I hadn't been able to resist.

I glanced from the orb in my hand to Rita and noticed how her typically messy bun of snow-white hair looked surprisingly neat this morning. She was wearing the light blue angora cardigan I'd given her for Christmas, and it really heightened the blue of her eyes.

"It's a crystal ball," I told her, stating the obvious. I reached back into the box with my free hand and pulled out an ornate brass base with two skeletal hands rising up on either side. After shaking loose a few clinging pieces of wood shavings, I set it on a nearby shelf and then carefully nestled the glass ball in between the hands. Once I knew it was secure, I stepped back and eyed it critically, my head tipped to one side.

"What do you think?" I asked, expecting practical Rita to tell me how impractical an item it was and then giving it a week before someone knocked the glass ball loose and broke it. Maybe it was impractical, but I'd bought a crystal ball for my other employee, Devon Thibodeaux, for Christmas, knowing one of his Cajun relatives in New Orleans not only had a similar one but operated a successful fortune-telling business centered around it. I'd heard Devon wax on wistfully about the orb on more than one occasion, saying that while he knew the thing possessed no magical powers, he still found it mesmerizing.

Once I saw the one I got for Devon, I realized it was, indeed, mesmerizing and decided then and there to get another for the store. It was precisely the sort of thing my store was known for— that and mystery books. The store name said it all: Odds and Ends. The oddities were what fascinated me the most, whereas the mysteries, in which someone typically comes to their end, fell more in Rita's wheelhouse.

When I turned to look at Rita, I saw she was no longer focused on the crystal ball but instead had her back to me, looking at something, or as it turned out, someone who had been hidden behind her. I eyed a tall—though an inch or two shy of Rita's six feet—slender fellow dressed in a tailored suit and tie beneath a dark gray, herringbone overcoat. He held a briefcase clutched close to his chest, and in contrast to his otherwise neatly pressed self, he had an unruly mop of graying brown hair. The expensive suit and coat and the briefcase suggested he wasn't my typical customer, but my store is in Door County, a vacation mecca located in Wisconsin, and as such it attracts all types of people. I didn't want to jump to any conclusions. Besides, the store was closed today, and our only sales would be either online or by phone. I wondered how this man had gotten in.

"May I help you?" I asked him, my tone a bit frosty.

"He's with me," Rita said, giving me a tenuous smile. "I let him in through the back door."

That answered one question. I had several more.

"Morgan Carter, meet Roger Bosworth, my brother-in-law," Rita said.

"Technically, I'm a step-brother-in-law," Roger corrected.

"Yeah, okay." Rita turned slightly so that I could see her face and Roger couldn't and she rolled her eyes.

"I didn't know you were having family visit, Rita," I said. "If you need time off, you know it's not a problem. Things are slow this time of year."

This was an understatement. Even though there's plenty of fun stuff to do in Door County in the wintertime, things tend to slow down and freeze up, both figuratively and literally. Lots of local business owners head for warmer climes in the winter, shutting down completely. Others, like me, stay open but with reduced hours and more of a focus on phone and online sales. Thanks to

Devon, I have an excellent online store with displays of some of my more interesting wares.

Roger stepped up beside Rita and she glanced at him briefly before turning her laser stare back my way, clearly trying to communicate something to me. My dog, Newt, sat beside me and he must have been trying to pick up on Rita's nonverbal cues, too, because he tipped his head to one side, then to the other, and let out a little whine as he watched her.

Roger eyed Newt nervously, a common reaction when people meet him for the first time. He's a big dog, and his stare can be intimidating, but that's because he's mostly blind, not because he's a threat. He's a sweet boy and wouldn't hurt a soul unless they were trying to hurt me.

"Well, yes, I might need some time off," Rita said, "but not for the reason you think. Roger wants to hire you."

Something else I should mention: in addition to owning my store, Odds and Ends, I'm a cryptozoologist available for hire. In case you don't know what a cryptozoologist does, let me explain. I hunt for legendary creatures that may or may not exist, like the Loch Ness Monster and Bigfoot. It's not a job in high demand, at least not usually, though things have picked up for me lately. Go figure.

Roger retrieved a business card from his coat pocket and handed it to me. It was made of heavy stock and the name *Roger Bosworth, Esq.* was embossed on it in thick, black letters. Underneath this, written in gold: *Bosworth & Crown, Attorneys at Law,* and an address in Rhinelander, Wisconsin.

"Roger's a lawyer," Rita said.

"I see that."

Why would an attorney want to hire me? And why did Rita seem so out of sorts? I wondered if I was about to be sued. My paternal grandfather made millions in the Great Lakes shipping business and thanks to his smart investment choices, I'm comfortably situated moneywise after inheriting the family fortune. This can make me a target for lawsuits when certain types find out. I don't advertise my wealth and live a relatively modest lifestyle for the most part, but the Carter family name is well known in the area and word gets around.

"It's my nephew, Andy," Rita said, an odd hitch in her voice. "He's a suspect in a murder case and I'm hoping you can help him."

This only confused me more. "I'm not sure I understand."

Roger clarified. "My son, Andrew, has been arrested for the murder of a young man found in the woods north of Rhinelander. The victim was nearly disemboweled and had severe wounds to his face, neck, and one leg, the latter proving fatal as his femoral artery was severed."

Even spoken in the matter-of-fact, terse, and lawyerly voice of Roger, these facts took me aback. "Oh, my," I said, feeling my throat tighten. My heart picked up its pace and I recognized what was happening right away; I was on the verge of a panic attack. Newt realized it, too, and he immediately thrust his head into my hand, leaning into me. I stroked the fur along the back of his neck and it calmed me. A little.

"Andrew swears the man was killed by a Hodag," Roger continued in a tone one might use to order dessert. "He saw the creature leave the scene."

His claim was absurd, so much so that I felt my tension begin to ease. This had to be a practical joke Rita was playing on me. I tilted my head to one side and smiled at her. "Good one," I said with a sly wink.

Rita opened her mouth to say something, but Roger got there first.

"Rita says you're a renowned cryptid hunter. I need you to prove a Hodag, not my son, killed this man."

I bit my lip while trying to figure out my response to this. After a few seconds, I said, "I don't know how renowned I am, but I'm a serious cryptozoologist who knows the Hodag is a made-up creature."

Roger cocked his head and narrowed his eyes. "Is it? Are you one hundred percent sure?" He looked around at my inventory, making a sweeping gesture toward some of the displays. "I see lots of extraordinary things here in your store, some of them real, some of them fake, many of them fascinating and out of the realm of normal. You even have a mummified mascot sitting up front by the door. Rita tells me the fellow was once a forty-niner."

"Henry," Rita tossed out, nervously picking at her skirt. "His name is Henry."

"Mr. Bosworth," I said, "I'm interested in cryptids of all types, but I have to say, the Hodag is at the bottom of my list. The creature was a manufactured hoax perpetrated by a logger back at the turn of the twentieth century. He eventually confessed to the deception."

"While that may be true," Roger said, "the fellow came up with the idea of a Hodag because there were plenty of legends surrounding the creatures already. Who's to say those rumors weren't based on some truth? Tales of similar creatures can be found in folklore all around the world."

Well, he had me there.

He paused and gave me a little smile. "I understand your skepticism, and it's your reputation for thorough and honest research I want. To be honest, if anyone other than my Andrew had come to me claiming a Hodag had killed someone, I would have dismissed it without a second thought. But Andrew is not someone prone to confabulation."

"Even when he's up against a murder charge?" I asked. "Most people are capable of manufacturing all sorts of wild stories under much less life-altering circumstances."

"I get your point," Roger admitted grudgingly. "But I know my son."

"And I know Andy, too," Rita said. "He spent a lot of time with me and George when he was little because Roger lived in Milwaukee until Andy was thirteen. Andy's mother died when he was only two and we often helped Roger with childcare. Andy spent plenty of time in our bookstore and our house. I know him. He's not a killer." She paused and gave me a pleading look before adding, "You have to help him, Morgan. Please."

This pleading version of Rita, so unlike her usual reserved and composed persona, unsettled me.

"At least meet Andrew and talk to him," Roger said. "See what you think. If after you've talked to him, you don't want to help, I'll understand."

"I won't," Rita muttered, making me wonder if she'd intended for me to hear her or not.

"Okay," I said. "I'm willing to look into it. But I'm not making any promises."

"Thank you," Rita said, the words coming out in a rushed sigh of relief.

"Help me understand this better," I said. "Why do the police think Andy killed this fellow? Couldn't it have been someone else? Or some*thing* else?"

Rita and Roger exchanged looks before Roger said, "There is some history between Andy and the victim, history that could be interpreted as motive."

Now we were getting into the nitty-gritty, but before I could ask for more details, Roger said, "You'll want to come check out the scene of the crime as soon as possible. They're calling for snow off and on starting in a couple of days and it will alter things. Andy was denied bail, so he's currently housed in the Oneida County Jail, and I assume you'll want to talk to him soon, as well."

"Okay," I said slowly, resisting an urge to slap back at Roger's assumptions.

"I'm coming, too," Rita said. "Devon can manage the store for a bit, can't he?"

This was essentially a rhetorical question. We both knew Devon was more than capable of handling things, especially since we were currently open from Thursday to Sunday, and it was only Monday. I knew he would love the chance to manage things on his own, not to mention the guaranteed hours.

I looked down at Newt and ran a hand over his big head. "Looks like we're taking another road trip," I said. He thumped his tail with happy excitement.

Rita stepped up and wrapped me in an awkward hug, her tall, bony body stiff against mine. "Thank you, Morgan," she whispered. "I won't forget this." When she pulled back, she smiled at Roger. "I told you she'd do it."

"Very good," Roger said. "Thank you. I appreciate your help."

He bowed and it struck me as comically decorous. Then again, everything about Roger was overly formal, from his way of talking to his posture and the clothes he wore. Despite this, I saw hope bloom in his eyes, and it worried me. I didn't want to elevate his expectations, because a big part of me believed this was going to be a fool's errand.

"Don't thank me yet," I said.

"Can you be in Rhinelander tomorrow?" Roger asked, savvily ignoring my caution.

"I suppose." I was starting to feel a bit out of sorts with the speed of it all. "I'll need to find a place to stay."

"Already taken care of," Rita said. "I took the liberty of booking rooms for both of us at a motel in town. It's nothing fancy, but it's clean and allows dogs."

I arched my brows at her presumptiveness, and she had the good grace to blush and look away.

Roger cleared his throat, said, "I'll see you tomorrow, then," and made a hasty retreat. Seconds later I heard the back door open and close.

Rita said, "I'll drive my own car, in case one of us wants to come back sooner than the other. I left the motel info on the desk in your office. I need to go home and pack." She whirled around and, like Roger, disappeared out the back door moments later.

I looked down at my dog and shook my head. "Looks like we've been played, Newt." He whined back at me but thumped his tail, seeming unsure if he should be worried or happy. "Best get to it, I suppose."

I started to head for my office, a tiny space tucked beneath the stairs that lead to my apartment on the floor above, but detoured and went toward the front door instead. There, seated in a large chair, was Henry, the mummified forty-niner Roger had referred to. The poor fellow had fallen into an ice crevasse during the gold rush and was found by some Native Americans years later. They further preserved his already mummified body and kept him for years at a store on their reservation. My father acquired him back when I was in my late teens, brought him home, stuck an Indiana Jones–style hat onto his head, and named him Henry. He's been something of a store mascot ever since and, along with Newt, he's also my confidant. Henry is a great listener and really good at keeping secrets.

I adjusted his hat to a jauntier angle and then stood back and eyed him critically. He'd suffered some trauma recently, but I'd had him repaired and he looked none the worse for it.

"What do you think, Henry?" I said. "Have I stepped out of the frying pan into the proverbial fire with this one?" He stared back at me. "It's not like I have a choice, really. Rita is like a mother to me. I can't tell her no."

Henry remained reticent. I sighed, turned around, and looked about the store. With everyone gone and the place closed for the day, it was deathly quiet. In retrospect, I probably should have recognized this for the ominous sign it was.

CHAPTER 2

I went to my office because I needed to make some phone calls. My first one was to Devon.

"Hey, boss. What's up?"

"How would you like to manage the store on your own for a while?"

"How long of a while?"

"Not sure. I need to head up to Rhinelander and Rita is going, too. I don't know how long either one of us will be there."

"Are you going monster hunting?"

"Sort of."

"With Rita?"

The blatant disbelief in his voice made me laugh out loud. After giving him a brief summary of the situation, I said, "I may well be back before the store opens to foot traffic on Thursday because, to be honest, this is one situation where I feel confident of the outcome. The Hodag is a completely fictional creature born out of folktales, local legends, and a prankster's con. The only monster likely to be involved in this death will be of the human type. My biggest challenge may be trying to convince Rita and her brother-in-law of the fact."

"You think Rita's nephew murdered this guy?"

"Occam's razor."

"Ah, but empirical data can be altered by statistical noise and it's not always easy to identify which set of data contains the noise. Therefore—"

"While I love our philosophical debates, you're losing me already," I said, interrupting him. "I only meant the idea of someone committing homicide is a far more likely scenario than a mythical creature doing so. I'll talk to Rita's nephew and see what he has to say. I may not be able to absolve the man of the murder, but I'll at least be able to rule out an attack by a Hodag."

"You know," Devon said in a thoughtful tone that told me I was about to have my horizons further broadened, "growing up in New Orleans, I often heard about a similar creature called the Grunch Road Monster, or sometimes just the Grunch. It's been described as a cross between canine and reptilian chupacabras, which is broad and vague enough to basically allow folks to come up with any characteristics they want. But when I moved up here and heard about the Hodag, I was struck by how similar they are."

"I vaguely recall my parents once talking about the Grunch," I said. "But I don't remember the details and I don't think they ever brought it up again, at least not in my presence."

"It's a localized thing among the voodoo/hoodoo crowd,"

Devon explained. "And I don't think anyone has claimed a sighting in decades. But even though the Grunch and the Hodag are both localized legends separated by hundreds of miles, there are some striking similarities. And your mom always used to say those kinds of similarities added up to—"

"Plausible existability," I said, finishing his thought. I could practically hear him smiling over the phone. "Okay. I hear you. I'll keep an open mind."

"And I'll keep the store running smooth as ever. You head up nort', as they say in these parts, and see what you can find. Don't worry about things here. And let me know if you need my help with anything while you're there. My computer is always at your beck and call."

I thanked him and then placed my next call, this one to Jon Flanders, the chief of police on Washington Island and someone I was slowly building a relationship with. Very slowly. Slower than the movement of the ice floes currently damming up the shoreline.

He answered with, "Hey, Morgan."

"Hey back. I'm calling to apologize because I need to cancel our dinner plans for tomorrow evening."

"Bummer. Can I ask why?"

"It seems I have another monster to hunt down."

"Oh."

While Jon is largely supportive of my efforts as a cryptozoologist, he hasn't been too crazy about the recent consults I've had, because they exposed me to some serious risks.

"Don't worry," I said. "This monster is not known for being vicious, violent, or real for that matter."

"Sorry?"

"I've been hired to find a homicidal Hodag. Have you heard of it?"

"Can't say that I have."

"I'm not surprised," I said, forgiving him his ignorance. Jon moved here from Colorado a year ago and the Hodag is a regional legend. "It's a Wisconsin-based cryptid, and a very beloved one," I explained. "It's mainly associated with Rhinelander. In fact, it's their city mascot. There's even a statue of one outside the city's chamber of commerce."

"What does it look like?"

"A hot mess," I said with a laugh. "It's said to have the face of a frog, red eyes, a spiny back, a spiked tail, and sharp horns. There's an interesting history associated with it, including some brazen hoaxes that were staged a hundred and some years ago. Google it and you'll find all you need to know."

"I'm confused," Jon said. "If this creature is totally made up, why are you getting involved?"

I explained the situation to him, concluding with, "Maybe you can help. Is there any way you can get me information about the charges Rita's nephew is facing and what evidence they have? I know I can ask Roger since he's presumably his son's lawyer, but there's bound to be some bias there given the family connection. I need something less subjective, or maybe differently subjective, like law enforcement gossip about the case. Though an official police report would be nice, too."

"You don't ask for much," Jon said with a chuckle. "I don't have any connections in Rhinelander, but one of my officers used to work for the department there. I'll see what I can do. Give me the name of Rita's nephew and what you know so far."

I did so, adding, "I imagine I'll get more of a lowdown once I arrive in Rhinelander. I'll update you after that. I'm heading there first thing in the morning."

"I assume you're taking Newt?"

"Of course. Rita will be there, too. I'm leaving Devon totally in charge of the store for the first time ever."

"He'll be fine," Jon said in a dismissive tone. "He's a freaking genius."

"He is, as long as his girlfriend isn't around. He tends to get a bit stupid when he's with Anne."

"Ah yes, the dumbing-down effect of raging hormones. I can check on him while you're gone if you want."

"Thanks, but there's no need. For the next few days, it will only be online stuff to manage, something Devon can do in his sleep. I'm thinking I'll be back by the time the store opens on Thursday."

"Really? Won't Rita be upset if you come back too soon?"

"Possibly, but I can't imagine taking more than a day or two given the circumstances. I'll just have to deal with Rita the best I can. I owe it to her to try, but beyond that I offer no guarantees."

Jon let out a long, slow sigh. "Okay. Just promise me you'll be careful."

"Of course, though I don't foresee any direct threat to me. My involvement in the case will be minimal."

Famous last words, and ones I would come to dwell on later that day when I dug out the letter I'd received a few weeks before, not long after I'd returned home from a visit to Bayfield, Wisconsin, to look for a Bigfoot. I opened my desk drawer, shoved aside the random bits of paperwork piled on top, and removed the envelope I had buried at the bottom. The postmark was for Minneapolis, a five-and-a-half-hour drive away—too close for comfort in my opinion. My name and address on the envelope had been created by what appeared to be an inkjet-style printer because the ink in my last name had smeared slightly where it had gotten wet when the mail carrier delivered it. There was no return address, and the envelope was the type with a self-adhesive strip you can peel off. I knew they could be found in any store selling stationery supplies and, in fact, I had a box of the same ones in my desk. The letter inside the envelope was printed on a single sheet of cheap copy paper, the kind you can buy for a few bucks a ream, the kind I used in my own copier. I took the letter out and read it for the hundredth time:

> *Did you catch your Bigfoot, Morgan? I miss you, though it*
> *helps that I can still watch you.*

There was no signature. I was willing to bet there'd be no fingerprints found on it either, should anyone fancy a look. And while there was no way to know for sure who sent it, I had little doubt. It had to be from my ex-fiancé and the man who had murdered my parents, David.

Irritated, I hastily folded the letter back up and stuffed it inside the envelope. I started to shove it back into the drawer but changed my mind at the last minute and carried it upstairs to the apartment instead, stashing it in my computer bag. Why I felt the need to bring it with me I'll never know.

As I packed for the trip, I hoped my time in Rhinelander would take my mind off David and the letter for a while. But as it turned out, I couldn't have been more wrong.

Dead wrong, in fact.

CHAPTER 3

I got an early start the next morning, leaving at a little after six. The drive would take me three and a half to four hours, depending on road conditions, and I wanted to get there before lunch. I considered chartering a flight but quickly ruled it out as Newt doesn't like planes much. Besides, I like driving because it gives me time to sort my thoughts and I wanted my own wheels while I was in Rhinelander.

Winters in this part of Wisconsin tend to be cold and snowy and the day of my trip was no exception. Two hours into my journey, snow began slowly drifting down from the sky in fat, fluffy flakes that blew over the roads and provided a fresh, white coverlet for the three-foot-high berm of dirty, plowed snow along the sides of the roads, detritus left over from a major winter storm that had blown through most of the state the week before. There was a peaceful hush to the countryside, and as I neared town, I had the car's heater going full blast and a back window down so Newt could sniff the air.

I arrived in Rhinelander just after ten. It's a city of around eighty-three hundred souls, more than a third of whom are of German ancestry. Much of the local architecture, culture, and place names are reflective of these early settlers. That is, if you ignore the Potawatomi, Ojibwe, and Ottawa tribes that were there first.

The Wisconsin River cuts Rhinelander in half and branches off into dozens of streams and lakes all around the city, contributing to its title as the Ice Fishing Capital of the World. The area is thickly wooded, and this combination of waterways and trees made Rhinelander a perfect location for the lumber trade.

The history of the Hodag was loosely connected to this industry because it was a Wisconsin land surveyor and timber cruiser named Eugene Shepard who first engineered a prank about the creature in 1893. Shepard and a small group of locals came into town one day claiming they had not only captured and killed a nearly extinct animal called a Hodag, but they had photographic proof to back up their story. Shepard described the creature as having the face of a frog, long tusks and horns, a spiked tail, huge claws, and a spiny body like a dinosaur's. People clamored to see the picture of this hideous beast; however, the men claimed the creature was so ferocious, they'd had to use dynamite to kill it. This proved rather convenient given the nondescript nature of the charred bits in the photo, supposedly the only remains left of the animal.

Not one to take rampant skepticism lying down, three years

later Shepard claimed to have captured another Hodag—this one alive—by using chloroform to sedate it. What he really had wasn't anything alive but rather a mess of cobbled-together body parts, wooden carvings, and smelly skins from several animals. By displaying this mishmash in a dimly lit corner of the county fair and having his sons use a series of thin, nearly invisible wires to manipulate the creature so that it appeared to be moving, Shepard drew in the crowds. Toss in the occasional moaning sound emanating from the exhibit, also courtesy of Shepard's sons, and it had the effect of keeping the already skittish crowds at a distance, thereby preventing them from looking too closely.

The story of the captured, living Hodag was big news in Rhinelander and eventually it hit the national rags. When Shepard got word the Smithsonian was planning to send inspectors to Rhinelander to catalog this newly discovered creature, he was forced to admit the whole thing was a hoax. But rather than feeling embarrassed about being duped by this bit of chicanery, the good-natured folks of Rhinelander adopted the Hodag as their official mascot.

I drove past the motel Rita had arranged, which was on the outskirts of town, because I wanted to get a feel for the city proper. Given the Eugene Shepard history, it came as no surprise that one of the first things I saw was a large fiberglass sculpture of a grinning, colorful Hodag sitting in a snow-covered expanse of lawn outside the chamber of commerce. The sculpture looked like a friendly creature from a children's picture book rather than a homicidal monster, making Roger's son's claim even more ludicrous.

I followed signs and my GPS to the downtown area, spotting plenty of Hodag signs, Hodag business names, and Hodag pictures, including another large sculpture outside the beautiful Oneida

County Courthouse building, a neoclassical structure topped off with a large green dome. It seemed everywhere I looked, I saw a Hodag. It was undoubtedly a significant part of the city's culture and history, a fact that might make my job harder.

When I was done exploring the town, I drove back to the motel, hitting up the drive-through at the Culver's restaurant across the road first to grab some chicken tenders for myself and Newt. It was only a little after noon when I entered the motel lobby, and I didn't know if they'd let me check in this early. Turned out, it wasn't a problem and everything went off without a hitch. I was informed by the rosy-cheeked young lady working the desk that Rita had arrived already. Rita must have been watching for me because after I unloaded my car and ventured down the hallways to the back of the building where my room was located, she met me at my door with a coffee cup in each hand. Newt greeted her with more enthusiasm than I did since I was hoping for a little time to get settled and organize my thoughts, though I had to admit the coffee sounded and smelled mighty good. The woman knew me too well.

"Come on in," I said, once I had the door open and had wheeled my suitcase inside. Newt nearly knocked her over squeezing past her to join me, but Rita took it in good stride. She walked past the two beds in the room and set the coffee cups onto a small table in the far corner. Then she slipped off her coat, hanging it on the back of one of two chairs there.

"When did you get here?" I asked.

"Last night. I wanted to beat the snow."

I had my doubts about this explanation. Rita has lived in Wisconsin most of her life and a mild snowfall like the current one wouldn't phase her in the least. You can't live in the climes of Wisconsin if you're afraid of snow.

Seeming to sense my skepticism, Rita turned away and then quickly added, "And I wanted to be here to show my support for Andy." There was the tiniest hitch in her voice, the barest hint of emotion, a rare thing for staid and stolid Rita.

"You two are close," I said, an observation rather than a question.

She shrugged. "Like I told you, we spent a lot of time with Andy when he was growing up. George was sixteen when his stepmother gave birth to Roger, and their mutual father died a few years after that. Then Roger's mother died when Roger was eighteen. He got married two years later, they had Andy, and then his wife was killed in a car accident, leaving Roger in the middle of law school with a two-year-old kid. He turned to us for help, and we ended up caring for Andy as much as, if not more than, Roger did." She looked at me then, her eyes beseeching. "Andy's a good kid, Morgan." She gave me a reflective smile. "Except he's in his thirties, so not a kid anymore. Still, he's much too young to be facing murder charges."

I didn't think age restrictions applied to such things, but Rita's point was one I could relate to. A few years ago, when I was thirty, I'd faced a similarly troubling scenario because I became the primary suspect in the horrific murder of my parents. It made me wonder if Rita's mention of Andrew's age had been intentional on her part. Wily fox that she was, she might be trying to tender an emotional connection between me and her nephew, to get me to vest more thoroughly in his case. And damn if it hadn't worked to some degree.

Rita took a deep breath and let it out in a long, slow sigh, giving me plenty of time to pick up on her not-so-subtle innuendo. She took a sip of her coffee, set down her own cup resolutely, and then leaned across the table toward me. "I really need your help with this, Morgan."

"I'm here, aren't I?" It came out snippier than I'd meant it to, and Rita drew back into her chair, a hurt expression on her face.

"Look, Rita, you need to understand something. I won't disguise or ignore any truths I discover, no matter what they reveal or point to."

"Of course. I would expect nothing less from you," Rita said with a faint jut of her chin. "Just promise me you'll do everything you can because you need to understand something, too. I know there's no way Andy did what they're accusing him of. I know that boy."

"He's not a boy anymore," I reminded her. "People change as they grow. Even Roger admitted Andy has motive."

Rita dismissed this with a loud *pfft* and an irritated wave of her hand, as if the idea were nothing more than a pesky gnat. "Just because he had history with the victim doesn't mean he killed him."

"Yeah, about that history," I said, getting up and removing a notebook and pen from an outer pocket of my suitcase. I settled back into my seat, took a sip of coffee, and clicked the pen into readiness. "Give me the deets."

Rita looked confused. "The what?"

"The deets. The details."

"Oh, right." She frowned, shaking her head. "I don't care for the way proper English is getting pruned away these days. Is it really so hard to use a two-syllable word? And don't get me started on some of these texting shortcuts. Honestly, it's abysmal, the end of society as we know it."

"Absolute Armageddon," I teased.

This earned me a chastising look. "Don't make fun of me, Morgan."

"Sorry," I said with a half-hearted shrug. After a split second of thought, I added something I hoped would ease some of the lingering tension between us. "Though I must admit, I find your attitude on the matter somewhat rhadamanthine."

I saw the corners of Rita's mouth twitch upward and knew my ruse had worked. She and I often engaged in a friendly game of obscure word usage, trying to outdo each other by slipping them into our everyday conversations. "Rhadamanthine" was my offering and, not coincidentally, it had also been the word of the day on the desk calendar Rita had given me for Christmas.

"Good one," Rita conceded. "As for the details, I think it will be best if you talk to Andy and get it straight from the horse's mouth, so to speak, but I'll tell you what I've heard. Just know it's all secondhand information."

"Understood."

"Okay." She tugged her sweater into smooth submission, patted the sides of her head in an unsuccessful effort to restrain some of her flyaways, and straightened her already rigid posture even more. She was about to speak when her phone dinged for a new message, and she dug it out of her sweater pocket. "Just a sec," she said as she typed out a quick reply.

"No problem."

"Have you had lunch?" she asked while she was still typing.

"I have. We hit up the Culver's across the road right before checking in."

"Good." She set her phone onto the table with the screen facing down and once more went through the ritual of sweater tug, hair taming, and back straightening. It was a quirk I'd seen before, one she went through when she was about to tackle a difficult subject.

"So," she began, smiling at me. "Roger owns this place in the woods just outside town. It's near but not on the Wisconsin River, and Andy likes to go there in the winter and ice fish. He uses a sled to haul his stuff through the woods to the river's edge. Roger said Andy was there this past weekend and he was making his way through the woods when he heard a strange noise. He said it sounded like something, or someone, in distress. At first he thought it might have been an animal but then he clearly heard someone hollering for help.

"Andy told Roger he abandoned his sled and slogged through the snow toward the sound as fast as he could, but it was hard for him to tell what direction the noise was coming from. Eventually he found the source: a man with his belly and leg ripped open. Andy tried to phone for help, but he had no service. The leg wound on the man was pumping blood, so Andy tried to put pressure on it. Unfortunately, he was too late, and the man died."

"How awful," I said, suppressing a shudder as I flashed back to the day I'd found my parents' bodies with both of their throats slashed.

Rita nodded. "I can only imagine. But Andy has EMT training, so I think he may be more inured to such things than the rest of us. Anyway, he knew he could get a phone signal by the river, and it was closer than his dad's cabin, so he headed in that direction. And when he finally got there, this animal burst out of some nearby bushes, scaring him half to death."

Rita clapped a hand to her chest and let out a tiny gasp, as if she had seen the animal herself. "I'll let Andy describe the creature in detail for you. He said it crossed the river ice to the other side, where it then disappeared into some trees. Andy made his 911 call and then returned to the victim, backtracking along a path the creature had used to see if it did, in fact, lead back to the body. It did. When the police got there, they saw Andy covered in blood. It was on his boots, his parka, his snow pants, and his hands were caked in it. And then they ID'd the victim as Brandon Kluver."

Rita leaned back, blew out a deep breath, and had another swallow of coffee. I could tell this wasn't easy for her, so I just kept writing my notes, giving her time to gather her thoughts and emotions before she continued.

"Andy hadn't recognized him," she finally went on. "Brandon was wearing a ski mask and had grown a full beard since the two of them had last seen each other. Between that and the blood on Brandon's face, the distraction of the injuries . . . well, Andy had no idea who it was until the authorities showed up and found Brandon's ID in his pocket."

I nodded. This was the first time anyone had mentioned the victim's name. "Tell me about this history between Andy and Brandon," I said.

Rita winced. "It's complicated," she said. "Brandon grew up here in Rhinelander. He and Andy met when Roger decided to leave Milwaukee and move here to get away from big-city life and crime. He wanted Andy to be somewhere without all the drugs, gangs, and other bad influences." Rita paused, scoffing. "Kind of ironic, in a way," she said with a slow, sad shake of her head.

"Anyway, they moved here when Andy was a freshman in high school and Andy and Brandon were both on the high school football team. They were friends until their senior year when a girl named Willow entered the picture. She was a cheerleader who had dated Brandon off and on during his sophomore and junior years. Apparently their relationship was an explosive one, and they broke up often. It became a predictable pattern until their senior year. They'd blow up with the fury and volatility of a summer thunderstorm, retreat to their respective corners, lick their wounds, and then make up and get back together again, all in a matter of days."

"Wow, you're really mixing your metaphors there," I teased, hoping to get Rita to relax a little. She was wringing her hands, and her right foot had been tapping on the floor, picking up in both cadence and tempo. It worried me. While Rita appeared to be as healthy as a horse, she was not a young woman.

Rita frowned and appeared to think back on her words. "I suppose I am," she said with a chuckle. Her foot ceased its drumming, and she took another sip of coffee.

Mission accomplished.

"Anyway," she went on, "as I was saying, the dynamic changed during their senior year. Willow broke things off with Brandon for the umpteenth time, but instead of her usual rebound, she started dating Andy. Not surprisingly, Brandon didn't take it very well, and several confrontations followed. Initially they were merely heated word exchanges, but over time things escalated."

I sipped my coffee, waiting on tenterhooks to hear the rest of the story. I suspected, judging from Rita's facial expression, that it was going to be a doozy.

"Not long after Willow started dating Andy, she discovered she was pregnant, and thankfully she was far enough along to know the baby had to be Brandon's. Lord knows how much worse things might have been if there had been a question about paternity."

It was hard for me to imagine how it could have been worse for either man, given the ultimate outcome. One was dead, the other in jail accused of murder. But I let it go.

"Willow was torn about what to do since her deeply religious parents had raised her to believe abortion was a sin," Rita went on. "Back then women still had rights over their own bodies here in Wisconsin, but Willow decided against it. I don't know if it was her decision alone or the result of pressure from her parents and others. Either way, it created some tension between her and Andy and when Brandon found out about the pregnancy, he tried to use it as a way to persuade Willow to come back to him."

Rita paused and gave a woeful shake of her head. "Andy and I were always close, and I talked to him a couple of times during all this drama. I'm sure you can imagine how complicated the situation must have been for an eighteen-year-old boy who thought he was in love with a girl carrying someone else's baby."

I could and nodded.

"Andy told me he was confused about where the relationship with Willow would go and unsure if he wanted to be embroiled in the mess that would undoubtedly follow. Willow swore she was in love with Andy and begged him to stay with her, but while she rebuffed any amorous moves from Brandon, she couldn't keep him out of her life completely because he was the baby's father. There was the issue of support, both financial and otherwise. Both sets of prospective grandparents were compelled to weigh in, too, of course, putting Willow under a huge amount of pressure."

"It's nice Andy had you to talk to through all of that," I said.

Rita nodded, looking off to the side as tears welled in her eyes. "It all became moot a couple of weeks later when Andy was driving Willow to a prenatal doctor's appointment and a bus hit their car at an intersection. The bus driver apparently had a heart attack, lost consciousness, and went through a red light, hitting Andy's car broadside on the passenger side. Willow was killed instantly."

I hadn't seen that one coming and my mouth dropped open.

Rita flashed a feeble smile and swiped her palms over her cheeks before continuing. "Of course, everyone was devastated. Brandon blamed Andy for the death of both Willow and his unborn child. A lot of folks hoped things between the two might cool off once they graduated from high school, but as luck would have it, both of them ended up working at the paper mill here in town. One day they crossed paths, heated words were exchanged, and the next thing you know they were engaged in a brawl right there on the job. They were both fired on the spot and, as young men are wont to do, they each decided to try to drown their sorrows at a local bar. Unfortunately, they picked the same one—like there aren't enough bars in Wisconsin to go around, right?"

Clearly this was a rhetorical question on Rita's part. About a decade ago there was a study showing Wisconsin had almost three times as many bars as it had grocery stores and there was no reason to think this had changed.

"Things got ugly at the bar, and they picked up their fight where they'd left off. The cops were called and both Andy and Brandon were arrested. They got off with a slap on the wrist that time, but when the two boys ran into each other at another bar a few years later, things escalated, and once again the cops were called. After breaking up the two of them, the cops let them go home and sober up. No charges were filed, though I understand restitution had to be paid to the bar for damages."

"How long ago was this?" I asked.

Rita shrugged. "I don't know . . . five, maybe six years ago? After that first fight they had at work, Andy found another job within a few weeks of getting fired, but Brandon wasn't so lucky. He got into the drink hard and heavy, lost his house, couldn't find a job except seasonal farmwork, and blamed Andy for it all. Roger told me there were some heated exchanges between the two men on social media, and being that Rhinelander is a small town, they have crossed paths a few more times over the years. Each time there was a lot of yelling and threats, sometimes some shoving, all of it resulting in calls to the police. One night, just a year ago, Brandon got himself good and pissed and drove to Andy's apartment, where the two of them got into it yet again, first verbally and then physically. The police were called and by now they were well aware of the history between the two men. So you can imagine what they thought when they learned the dead man in the woods Andy had called about was Brandon."

"I can," I said with a troubled sigh. I scribbled down a couple more notes, and then said, "I'd really like to get a look at the spot where Brandon died. Do you know the exact location?"

Rita wagged her head from side to side. "Sort of. I can take you to Roger's cabin and you can trudge through the woods between it and the river if you like, but Roger will have a better bead on the spots in question."

"It would also help if I could get my hands on the official police report."

"Roger should be able to help with that, too. For the moment, he's Andy's defense attorney of record, though he said he plans to bring in someone else to be the primary. If there's anything you need that Roger can't get, maybe Devon or Jon can help."

I found Rita's current level of investment in my investigation amusing. Normally she would have been cautioning me to mind my own business, stay home, and tend to the store. Instead, here she was all up in it with an anything-goes attitude.

I glanced at my watch and saw it was after one. With the current cloud cover, it would be dark before five. "Maybe the site visit would be better left for first thing tomorrow," I said. "When do you suppose I might be able to talk to Andy?"

Rita picked up her phone, glanced at the screen, and said, "Will imminently do?"

CHAPTER 4

⌒

I was a bit taken aback by Rita's answer.

"Roger added your name to Andy's visitor list last night and it was approved this morning. He's on his way here now to pick you up. Visiting hours are until six but the sooner the better, no?" She paused, glancing apologetically at Newt lying on the floor. "I'm afraid you won't be able to take him," she said with a sideways nod of her head. Newt, who wasn't fooled by her attempt at subterfuge, let out a little whine. "They don't allow animals to be left in cars in the parking lot at the jail. But I'm happy to stay here with him while you and Roger go. I'm no substitute for you, but I think we'll survive."

Newt sighed, apparently resigned.

"I see," I said hesitantly, not as obliging as my dog yet. "I wasn't expecting to talk to Andy so soon and I don't have all my questions sorted yet, though I suppose I can pull something together."

Rita at least managed to look chagrined. "Oh, good," she said, ignoring my objections. "Roger will be here any minute now."

Clearly plans had been made behind the scenes and, frankly, I was a smidge annoyed at the presumptuousness. "I should take Newt for a quick walk," I said, though I needed to walk more than my dog did. I had some tension to get rid of.

"I'll do it." Rita stood, swept her coat from the back of the chair, slipped it on, did a quick look around, and grabbed Newt's leash. My dog hopped up, tail wagging excitedly, and hustled to the door of the room, where he waited impatiently. I was too stunned by all this quick action—and frankly a little hurt at Newt's rapid defection—to formulate an objection. As the two of them stepped out of my room and into the hallway, Rita said, "Oh, look. Here's Roger now." Then, as Newt looked back at me and let out another little whine—scant consolation at that point—they were gone, and Roger appeared, stopping in the doorway.

So much for prep time. This level of manipulation was extreme, even for Rita.

"You're okay with going to visit Andy now?" Roger said, eyebrows raised.

I got the distinct impression the question was rhetorical, so I said, "Apparently." Then I grabbed my coat and dutifully followed Roger down the hallway to a side exit and then to his car. It had stopped snowing since I'd arrived and there was only a dusting on the ground. Rita and Newt were nowhere in sight, which was probably just as well. I hated sneaking off on Newt like this and if he caught sight of me, he'd probably come running, dragging Rita behind him.

"It's a bit of a process getting into the jail," Roger warned as he drove. "You'll have to leave your cell phone in the car, and they might want to search you."

"Got it."

"You'll need to tell them you're my assistant. Otherwise, you won't be let in. They allow only video visitations. We'll be allowed one hour."

"That should be more than enough time."

Roger shot me a worried look. "You sound like you've already made your decision regarding his guilt."

"No, but I would have preferred to have more time to look at the evidence against him before talking to him."

"I promise you'll get it," he assured me. "In the meantime, keep an open mind. Andy didn't kill Brandon so there must be another explanation for what happened."

"I appreciate your conviction, Roger, but you're hardly an objective character witness. And as far as alternate explanations go, I can think of several that don't involve a mythical monster born out of a hoax."

"I'm sure anyone could," Roger said. "Which begs the question of why Andy would come up with something so . . . out there."

"Maybe it was all he could think of at the time. And once he told the story, he couldn't very well change it if he thought of something better, could he?"

Roger sighed heavily and shot me a pained look. He didn't answer my question—I'm not sure there was an answer for it—and the rest of our drive was silent, though there remained a distinct underlying current of tension in the car.

Roger had been right about one thing. It was a process getting into the jail. After a metal detector, several electronic doors, and a disturbingly intense scan from the guards, who asked in a robotic monotone if I had any phone, photographic equipment, weapons, or other contraband on my person, we were led to a private room with a table and chairs.

We waited in awkward silence for a good ten minutes before a handcuffed Andy, dressed in an orange jumpsuit, was brought into the room by a guard.

"This is privileged," Roger said, eyeing the guard challengingly. "I'm his lawyer." The guard's gaze slid toward me. "She's my assistant," Roger added hastily.

The guard shrugged and left the room, though I doubted he'd gone far.

Andy Bosworth was a handsome, somewhat muscular man with pale blue eyes, a square jaw, and a strong, patrician nose, though the dark circles under his eyes and the gaunt draw to his cheeks were a testament to the rigors of his time in jail and the stress of his current situation. I guessed he favored his mother because aside from his height, he bore little resemblance to Roger. Like his father, Andy had a full head of hair, but Andy's was neat and better behaved. He eyed me with unabashed curiosity.

"How are you doing, son?" Roger asked, his voice softer than I'd ever heard it. It gave me a little hitch in my chest.

Andy forced a smile. "I'm managing." He nodded toward me. "Who is this? She's not your assistant."

I jumped in before Roger could answer. "I'm Morgan Carter. I'm a cryptozoologist and your father has asked me to talk to you about what happened."

Andy leaned back and looked askance at his father. "I thought you were bringing in another lawyer," he said. "You told me you had a friend who was willing to help you represent me."

"I am. I do," Roger said. "I've already spoken to him, and he'll be here tomorrow. He was away on vacation. Morgan here is a good friend of your aunt Rita's and I want you to tell her your side of things, about the Hodag."

Andy's gaze shifted from his father to me and then back again. His shoulders dropped as he slumped in his chair. "Nobody believes it was a Hodag," he said miserably. "I know how it looks to the cops, but they're misinterpreting things. It's obvious they have their own agenda." He paused and sighed. "No one is going to believe me."

"I know the Hodag is supposed to be a fictional creature," I said. "But I'm open to the possibilities."

Like the possibility you're lying through your teeth.

The thought raced through my mind before I could stop it and I mentally shut it down.

"Do you think it's possible that what you saw was another type of animal, like a wild boar perhaps?" I asked.

Andy shook his head vehemently, his lips set in a determined line. "I've seen wild boars before." He leaned toward me, locking eyes. "This . . . this *thing* was different," he went on. "It had bloodred eyes, tusks, and horns, and its face was all . . . bulbous looking. There was a spiny ridge down its back and rather than a hoof, it had these . . ." He trailed off and his left hand formed into a talon-like shape. "It had claws," he concluded. He stared at me, gauging my reaction. I forced myself to maintain a noncommittal expression and after a few seconds, his hand fell back into his lap.

"Look," he said wearily. "I didn't attack Brandon. I didn't see this creature attack him either, but it must have been what took him down because it had blood all over it. I swear to you, I didn't do anything to Brandon. Hell, I didn't even know it was him until the cops told me."

Andy's description of the creature fit the classic image of a Hodag to a tee, at least the ones I'd seen in pictures, signage, and the statues about town. Plus, his demeanor, tone, facial expressions, and body language lacked any of the key signs of deception. The world of cryptid hunting is rife with practical jokers, con artists, liars, and attention seekers, and my father had taught me early on how to suss out the lies, truth stretching, and exaggerations. So far, I'd determined Andy was either an excellent liar or telling the truth—or at least what he believed to be the truth. Therein lay my problem.

"I understand you backtracked along a trail left by the animal?" Andy nodded. "Why?"

"Honestly, it was mostly out of simple convenience. The snow was already tromped on and tamped down, as if multiple animals had been over it, so it made for easier going. And I wanted to see if it led back to the body."

"That could explain blood on your boots and bloody footprints in the snow, but I was told you were covered in blood. How did that happen?"

"When I first came upon the victim . . . Brandon, I checked for a pulse." He squeezed his eyes closed, looking genuinely pained when he uttered Brandon's name. Horror or remorse?

"Where did you check for the pulse?" I asked.

Andy raised a hand and placed two fingers on his own neck. There was something robotic and detached about his movements. "The carotid," he said. "But I discovered a deep neck wound there, so I pulled back. Besides, he had a pulsating bleed in his leg, telling me his heart was still pumping. I put pressure on the leg wound, but then the guy coughed up a bunch of blood."

Ah, we were back to the more distancing "guy" rather than Brandon.

"After that," Andy went on, "the bleed in his leg quit pumping. I considered CPR, but I knew he was beyond my help. His belly had been exposed and ripped open, and when I tried pushing on his chest his insides bulged out." He paused, swallowing hard. "I needed to call 911, but I didn't have cell service where I was. I knew reception was better by the open areas along the river but I was also worried that whatever had attacked Brandon might also try to attack me. I saw a knife in the snow on the other side of his body and I went around to get it. I'd left mine back on my sled. When I walked around Brandon's feet, my boot snagged on something and I tripped and fell. Turned out it was one of the ski poles Brandon had been using. Somehow it had ended up beneath him but the bottom of it was sticking out just enough to grab me. I landed face-first in blood-drenched snow with my legs on top of his. With the arterial bleed in the one leg, there was blood everywhere."

"What happened with the knife?"

Andy looked even more troubled—if that was even possible.

The man emanated misery from every pore. He held up his right hand and I saw angry gashes across his palm and the insides of all four fingers, two of these deep enough to have been sutured.

"I'm right-handed," he said. "I fell by the river and my hand slid down over the blade. This was the result."

This didn't bode well. I knew from watching CSI shows that the injuries Andy had on his fingers were a type of classic offensive and defensive wound found in stabbings. They happen when a hand slides down over the blade while stabbing someone because blood and sweat make the handle slippery, or, in the case of a defensive wound, when a hand wraps around the blade to try to stop it from penetrating. It wasn't hard to see why Andy had been arrested and my concern must have shown on my face because Andy slumped even lower in his seat before continuing.

"When I reached the river, I heard crunching sounds behind me just before something burst out of some bushes. I whirled around, lost my footing, and that's why I fell. My hand slid down the knife handle and the blade sliced me. It hurt like hell, and it made me flinch and fling the knife sideways out onto the ice. It skittered a few feet and then dropped into a crevasse of open water. I got to my feet as fast as I could to face the creature, thinking I was a goner. But it just stood there, about twenty feet away, staring at me."

He paused a moment, and his eyes lost their focus as he conjured up the memory. Then, with a shudder, he went on. "Good thing it didn't charge at me," he said. "Otherwise, I would have ended up like Brandon."

"What *did* it do?" I asked.

"After a few seconds it simply turned and scrambled down the bank onto the river ice. There is an area there where the river bends, slowing the current, and it's heavily shaded. The ice in that spot was unbroken all the way across. Once the thing got to the other side, it disappeared into the woods. I think I was literally and figuratively frozen to the spot at that point, at least for a few seconds. Maybe a minute. Then I remembered dropping my phone when I fell. My hands were frozen because I hadn't had any gloves on since finding Brandon, but I dug around in the snow until I found my phone. Thankfully it was still working, and I called 911."

"You went back to Brandon after you called?"

Andy nodded. "The 911 operator told me to return to him and wait for the authorities, and like I said before, I went back along the trail the animal had taken. I think Brandon might have blazed the same trail initially because I did see the occasional hole in the snow off to the side like a ski pole makes. The 911 operator said the first responders might need to holler to me to find the exact spot and that I should return to it as soon as I could." His eyes grew big, and his color paled. "That's why I took the trampled path. I thought it would be quicker. As it was, it became a long, uncomfortable wait once I got back to . . . the spot."

I had no doubt of this and shifted topics slightly to get him off that particular image and memory. "You used an interesting word to describe how the animal descended the riverbank. You said it 'scrambled.'"

He nodded, looking thoughtful, and some of the color returned to his face. "Yeah, it was kind of awkward the way it moved, sort of a half trot, half tumble, and the bank there wasn't that steep."

"How did it look running across the river?"

Andy shrugged. "It was surprisingly agile once it hit the ice.

And while I didn't see it come busting out of the bushes behind me, I can tell you it did so with considerable strength and speed."

"How do you know?"

"Because it destroyed most of the branches in its wake. Honestly, the thing was terrifying. It was about as far from the friendly looking Hodags you'll see around town as it could get."

"I'm curious. I get why you followed the trampled animal trail back to Brandon from the river. Why didn't you follow it to get to the river?"

Andy appeared to think about this for a moment before answering. "I saw the path, but it wasn't clear to me at the time that it would take me to the river. It started off in the wrong direction, but it made a bit of an arc farther on. Plus, I didn't want to run into what I thought at the time was a bear."

His explanations all seemed reasonable and, more importantly, honest. I was thinking of my next question when he said, "What are the odds the victim would turn out to be Brandon of all people?" He looked like he was about to cry.

What, indeed? I assumed it was a rhetorical question and rather than try to answer him, I hit him with a question of my own. "When was the last time you saw Brandon or had any level of contact with him—email, phone, anything—prior to this?"

"It's been a year or better."

He studiously avoided looking at me after this and for the first time in the interview, my internal lie detector began clamoring. Why had I let Rita talk me into this? If it all went sideways, which I was beginning to believe would be the case, it was bound to have a negative effect on our relationship.

"Okay, Andy," I said, "I want to go back to the beginning, back when you first heard something, when you first saw the animal, when you first found Brandon, all of it. Do it in chronological order and give me times as best as you can."

He let out a weighty sigh and nodded, staring down at the tabletop. "It was early morning, about seven thirty. Normally I'd have gone out sooner, but the sun isn't up until around seven thirty these days and it's darker than a—" He stopped himself and smiled guiltily. "It's hard to navigate in those woods until the sun gets up. I was working my way through the trees from Dad's cabin to the river and the snow was deep—knee high or higher—so it was slow going. The fittings on my snowshoes broke last year and I was mad at myself for not replacing them. I was lugging my sled behind me with all my fishing gear on it. Then I heard someone yell."

"Yell what?"

He gave a quick shake of his head. "There were no words. It was just . . . a yell. The sound of pain or distress." He shrugged, giving me an apologetic look. "I wasn't even sure if it was human."

"How far from the river were you?"

"I don't know exactly. Fifty yards maybe?"

"Could you see the river from where you were?"

"No. The trees there are thick and they're mostly conifers—evergreens—making it hard to see through them. I could hear it, though."

"Hear it how?"

"There's a sound the ice makes when pieces move and bump together. It's a kind of creak and groan."

I was familiar with the sounds he described. The waters surrounding Door County often freeze in the winter and when the thaw comes I can sometimes hear the sounds of ice collisions from my store.

"When you first heard this distressed sound, what did you do?"

"I stopped and listened to see if I'd hear it again." His face flushed with guilt. "I wasn't terribly concerned yet because there are certain animals, like rabbits or birds of prey, that sound very humanlike when they scream." He paused, looking thoughtful. "Though maybe scream isn't the best description of what I heard. It was more . . . guttural," he concluded. "The second time I heard it, there was no doubt it was human, because I distinctly heard the word 'help.'"

"What did you do next?"

"I dropped the rope on my sled and took off in the direction the sound had come from, or at least where I thought it had come from. Sound does funny things out there with all those trees and the water. It was tough going because the snow was deep, heavy, and wet. I'd gone maybe twenty yards when movement caught my eye off to my right. I went toward it and found the . . ." He grimaced. "I found Brandon."

He teared up, his expression haunted. Then he squeezed his eyes closed. One tear rolled down each cheek. "I don't want to talk about this anymore," he said, his voice breaking. "I don't want to see it anymore, but I can't unsee it. I have nightmares every time I try to sleep. Not that anyone can sleep in this place."

He opened his eyes and fixed his gaze on me. "I've explained myself six ways from Sunday to a dozen people over the past few days and I just can't do it anymore. Each time it's like I'm reliving it all over again. So believe me or don't; I don't care. Because honestly, I'd rather spend the rest of my life behind bars than encounter that thing again."

CHAPTER 5

Our time was up, and our visit ended on Andy's sad, morbid note. I watched Roger hug his son, an awkward occurrence because the guard wasn't too keen on contact. I felt bad for Roger; you could practically smell his despair. And Andy looked like a man already standing at the gallows.

While I thought I might want to talk to Andy again at some point, I felt I had enough to get me started. Unfortunately, the case seemed straightforward in a way I thought wouldn't make either Roger or Rita happy. Still, my curiosity regarding the Hodag, its history, and its relevance to this city had me intrigued, and on the way back from the prison, I asked Roger if he'd drive me by the Rhinelander Chamber of Commerce, where perhaps the largest of the many Hodag statues welcomes folks with its friendly, albeit horned and toothy, grin. I wanted to see what type of propaganda the city had for its local monster and maybe chat with folks who knew the history of the legend.

Roger was happy to take me there but opted to wait outside in his car. "I'm well known around town. If you want people to open up to you, you'll have better luck if I'm not by your side, particularly lately."

Inside the chamber building I was greeted by a woman standing behind a counter and backed by all kinds of Hodag merchandise and trivia. A tag on her shirt told me her name was Cordelia. She looked to be in her forties or fifties with short gray hair and large brown eyes.

"Hello there," she said with a big smile. "Ooh, I love your gloves. Where did you get them?"

The gloves in question were hot-pink leather on the outside, warm fleece on the inside, and cuffed with a fluff of pink-and-white faux fur. They were not my usual fare but had been a Christmas gift from Devon, whose taste in apparel was questionable at best. Still, it was the thought that mattered, and they were amazingly warm, so much so I would have been willing to wear them even if they were covered in gold glitter.

"They were a gift from a friend," I said.

"They're lovely."

"Thank you."

"What can I help you with today?"

"I'm here to learn all I can about Hodags," I said, and her eyes lit up even brighter than they had over the gloves.

"Well, you've come to the right place," she said, handing me a map of the city with a legend at the bottom that detailed where many of the Hodags in town could be found. More than two dozen of them.

Cordelia made a circle above the map with her finger. "Visit all these spots, mark them off on your map, and then bring it back to win a prize," she said.

Oh, goody. A Hodag scavenger hunt. "What sort of prize?" I asked.

Cordelia waved a dramatic hand toward the promotional merch behind her, some on shelves, some hanging on the wall. It included stuffed Hodags and Hodag-themed items like Frisbees and pennants. "Whatever you want," she offered gleefully.

"How do you know folks haven't marked these spots off without visiting them just to get a prize?"

Cordelia looked appalled, as if the idea had never occurred to her. "It's on an honor system," she said. Her smile had tightened, as had her tone. She eyed me with suspicion and I'm certain what I said next didn't help my cause any.

After staring at the map for a few seconds, I said, "Have you heard about this fellow who claims a Hodag killed someone last week?"

She quickly dismissed my question with a *pshaw* followed by a nervous chuckle. "That story is ridiculous," she said. "The Hodag is a gentle creature. Businesses all around town use it as their mascot. So does the high school. Heck, it's featured in children's books."

"So are bears and wolves and all kinds of other wild animals known to kill humans," I countered. Cordelia made a face, clearly displeased with my analogy. "The statue you have outside looks friendly enough," I said, hoping to soften things a bit. "Have you ever seen a live one?"

I thought she'd scoff at the question, but instead she answered without hesitation. "Not me personally but I know several people who have."

"Really? I would love to talk to them. Would you be willing to give me names and put me in touch with them? Or I can give you my contact info and you could have them call me."

Cordelia frowned and eyed me with suspicion. "What's your interest in the Hodag exactly?" she asked.

"It's personal," I said.

She chewed on this for a moment before smiling dismissively. "Well, you know how it is with folks who claim such things," she said. "Often there's alcohol involved and then imaginations get carried away and juicy gossip gets created and repeated. Everyone in town embraces the legend, some with more enthusiasm than others. Do you know we've trademarked the Hodag?"

This last bit was an odd segue, one I suspected was meant to be diverting. Before I could answer, she hurried on.

"A few years back, this town in Michigan tried to claim the Hodag as their mascot and I can tell you, it caused quite the brouhaha in these parts. There were all manner of arguments on the matter. But Rhinelander remains the one and only official home of the Hodag." She puffed up with pride at this.

"That's all good and fine, but this story I heard about the man who was killed sounds legit," I said, deciding to be intentionally provocative. "Do you think there might be a homicidal Hodag on the loose?"

Cordelia's smile, which had been looking quite forced, disappeared completely. "You can't be serious," she said.

"As a heart attack," I quipped.

Cordelia wasn't amused. "If you start spreading rumors like that around here, it will get you laughed out of town," she said. "We're quite protective of our Hodag heritage because the livelihoods of lots of folks in the area depend on it. Take for example our Hodag country music festival. It brings in tons of people, between thirty and fifty thousand every year. We've had big names come to perform, like Tim McGraw, Reba McEntire, Kellie Pickler, and Garth Brooks, just to name a few. People come from hundreds, even thousands of miles away just to be a part of our Hodag heritage. And they bring their disposable income with them. The festival generates a lot of money for folks in these parts."

"I'm sure it does, though I think it might be the big-name musicians you have that draw the crowds, not the Hodag."

Cordelia looked offended. "Will you be staying in Rhinelander long?" she asked, her brittle smile back in place.

While her tone was pleasant enough, I detected a not-so-subtle underlying edge to her body language, suggesting she hoped I'd tell her I was leaving immediately. Unfortunately for Cordelia, not only was I not leaving town anytime soon, but I also wasn't done pushing her buttons yet. I wanted . . . needed to grease the wheels of the rumor mill in town with regard to Hodag sightings and figured this was as good a place as any to start. It seemed like a smart plan at the time. Little did I know.

"I'm going to stay as long as it takes for me to determine if a Hodag killed that man last week. And if I find it to be the case, I'll be sure to warn the public." I helped myself to a handful of the informational brochures she had out on the counter and held them up along with my map. "These are great," I said. "Hopefully they'll make my job easier."

That earned me a flinty scowl and, as I walked out of the building, a prickling sensation coursed down my spine.

How did it go?" Roger asked when I got back into his car.

"Interesting. When I suggested the Hodag might not only be real but also bent on killing folks, you would have thought I'd told the woman her child was ugly."

Roger chuckled. "In a way, you did. I warned you people here might get defensive when it comes to our beloved town mascot. You have to understand, there are dozens, maybe more than a hundred businesses and events here in town centered around the Hodag. I doubt any of them will take kindly to you suggesting it's a bloodthirsty killing machine."

"And yet, that's exactly what you need me to do in order to exonerate Andy."

Roger's smile faded and he sighed wearily. "Yeah. I didn't say it would be easy."

It was a little after three thirty and already it was growing dark. With the overcast, leaden sky and the dwindling daylight, the Hodag statue in front of the chamber building didn't look quite so friendly anymore.

When we got back to my motel room, Newt greeted me with great enthusiasm. Did I mention my relationship with my dog leans toward the codependent end of the spectrum?

"How did he do?" I asked Rita.

"He whined a lot."

"Sorry. He doesn't like being apart from me."

"Do tell," Rita said, her voice laced with sarcasm.

Rita was eager to hear how our visit with Andy had gone, but Roger suggested we get an early dinner and tell her about it then. I wanted time to unpack and do a bit of research on the Hodag and the area geography, and Roger said he had a quick errand to run. So after some discussion (and a bit of pouting on Rita's part), we settled on a five o'clock dinnertime at a Mexican restaurant located nearby. Though, as Roger pointed out, everything in Rhinelander proper was nearby. It wasn't a big city.

Come dinnertime, I didn't want to leave Newt alone in the motel room, but I also didn't want to risk messing up the interior of Roger's car, which I'd noticed on the way to the jail was pristine leather and unlikely to benefit from a layer of dog hair and drool. I decided to follow Roger in my car and Rita opted to ride with me and Newt. When we arrived at the restaurant, I cracked a window for Newt and told him to stay in the car. He sighed and promptly flopped down onto the seat with all the drama of a sullen teenager.

The place wasn't busy, and we were seated immediately. A waitress took our orders soon after our arrival and left us sipping margaritas, munching on nachos with spicy salsa, and filling Rita in on the highlights of our visit to Andy, of which, sadly, there were few. Moments later, a woman with shoulder-length dark, wavy hair streaked with gray walked up to our table. She had on fur-rimmed boots and wore a colorful caftan in rich jewel colors beneath a puffy beige winter coat.

"Hello, Sonja," Roger said.

"Roger," she acknowledged with a little nod before shifting her gaze to Rita. "I'm Sonja Mueller," she said as she began removing her gloves. "And you are?"

"Rita Bosworth."

Sonja's eyebrows raised. "A relative?" she said, looking at Roger.

Roger nodded. "My sister-in-law."

Rita smiled briefly and looked like she was about to say something more, but Sonja's attention had already moved on to me. She grinned, her deep brown eyes crinkling with mischievous humor.

"I'm Morgan Carter," I offered. "Nice to meet you."

"Oh, I know who you are," Sonja said, wagging a chastising finger at me. "You're the woman who's been blaspheming our Hodag."

I saw Roger and Rita exchange worried looks and then Roger immediately began fiddling with his watch. Rita leaned back in her chair, folded her arms over her chest, and arched her eyebrows at me.

"'Blaspheming' seems a bit harsh," I said.

Sonja let out a full-throated, from-the-belly laugh, making me smile. "You're right," she said. "Trust me, it could have been worse. Folks around here get mighty defensive about our Hodag. Welcome to Rhinelander."

"Thanks?" I said hesitantly. "I have to say, I'm impressed with the speed and efficiency of your gossip mill."

Sonja chuckled. "It can be quite effective, but in this case it was simply a matter of timing. I happened to stop in at the chamber office moments after you'd left, and I found Cordelia in quite a state." She looked over at Roger, who was studying his watch with such intensity, you would have thought it was a bomb he was trying to disarm. "I take it you're trying to prove Andrew is innocent?" Sonja said.

Roger didn't answer and Rita jumped in with something of a non sequitur. "Morgan is a cryptozoologist."

Sonja beamed her smile at me again. "What a fun field to work in," she said.

While it wouldn't have surprised me to learn she was mocking me—it tends to go with the territory—the comment felt sincere.

"Why don't you join us?" I said, gesturing toward an empty chair at our table. I was inclined to like this woman with her colorful dress, straightforward approach, and no-holds-barred laugh. I found her joie de vivre contagious and thought her presence at our table would make the dinner livelier if not more interesting. She accepted my invitation and not only settled in but immediately shucked her coat and helped herself to the nachos and salsa. Roger and Rita both shifted uncomfortably in their seats.

"Be prepared," Sonja said, pointing an about-to-be-dipped nacho in my direction. "You must have struck a nerve with Cordelia. She was on the phone to the mayor when I left, and she'd already called Howard over at the historical society. Lord knows who else she called to warn them about you."

"Warn them?"

Before Sonja could elaborate, the waitress arrived with our meals. Sonja ordered a margarita, declined a meal, and instead opted for a sampler platter from the appetizer menu.

"Sonja is a local artist," Roger explained once the waitress had left. "She specializes in Hodags and has sculpted several of the ones you'll see located around town."

"You must come by my studio," Sonja said to me. "It's not far, not that anything is in these parts. I have an assortment of Hodags you might find interesting. Each one is a little different because

I've incorporated minor physical variations reported by some of the locals who say they've seen one."

"They claim to have seen a living, breathing Hodag?" I said askance, thinking the bars in town must do a brisk business.

"Oh, yes," Sonja assured me with a laugh. "Living and breathing fire in one case, though that guy is a bit fond of his whisky." She winked conspiratorially. "I have a lot of history on the topic, not as much as Howard, of course, but a decent amount. I've even recorded video statements from a handful of folks who claim to have seen one."

"I'd love to see those," I said, not because I believed these people had had encounters with a Hodag, but because their descriptions might enable me to get a sense of what they had actually seen. Maybe there was a rogue bear or a mange-infested wolf roaming the woods around Rhinelander.

"Sure. Stop by anytime tomorrow. Or the next day. Or whenever. I'm there most of the time. Roger knows where I am."

"I'll do that."

Roger didn't look at all pleased by this turn of events. Sonja shifted her attention to Rita and pointed to the rhinestone-studded string attached to her eyeglasses. "I love this," she said, waving a finger around in a circle as if tracing the necklace. "The way those stones catch the light. Did you create it yourself?"

Rita, who had been eyeing our guest rather dubiously up until then, suddenly beamed. "Why, yes, I did," she said. "I took a jewelry-making class a while back."

"Nicely done," Sonja said. Rita blushed, making me wonder if I'd ever seen her do that before.

Our conversation shifted to the weather—plenty of snow was

threatened over the next couple of days—and Sonja teased me by suggesting I might want to hunt for a Yeti. She and Roger briefly touched on some local politics, and then, when I mentioned Newt, we talked doggies. Sonja told us she had a golden retriever that, like Newt, was visually impaired.

"His sight has been poor since birth," Sonja explained. "I named him Wally because as a pup he kept walking into walls until he managed to hone whatever inner radar it is he uses. Bring your doggy when you come. I'm sure he and Wally will get on famously."

I'd been dreading this trip from the moment I'd agreed to it because I feared Rita was expecting things from me I wouldn't be able to deliver. But by the time we left the restaurant, I thought things were shaping up into something interesting after all, thanks in large part to Sonja. I still had doubts about my ability to help Andy, but at least things wouldn't be boring.

Little did I know just how interesting things were about to get.

CHAPTER 6

W hen I got back to my motel room, I called Jon to fill him in on the events of the day. He'd tried to call me during our dinner, but I'd let the call go to voice mail.

"Never a dull moment with you," he said when I was done telling him about my visits to the jail, my encounter with Cordelia at the chamber office, and our surprise dinner guest.

"Apparently not. Have you had any luck getting more details about the case?"

"Some. I can tell you the evidence against the suspect is damning. I haven't seen an official report yet but got some thirdhand information from Zeke, my guy who used to work for the Rhinelander PD. He knows one of the city detectives pretty well, a guy named Hoffman, who's sharing investigative duties with the county detective since Hoffman is more familiar with the history between the two men and other incidents involving them. Zeke chatted with Hoffman about the case and Hoffman said the suspect had to have been holding a knife at some point because there were wounds on his hand of the type frequently seen in knife attacks."

"Yeah, Andy explained that. He said he picked up a knife he saw lying next to the victim so he could use it to protect himself. He carried it to the river and slipped on the snow along the river-bank. When he fell, his hand slid down over the knife blade."

"Oh, okay," Jon said, his comment laced with a healthy dose of skepticism. "Except the cops found the knife in the river, several feet from shore, like someone had intentionally tossed it out there."

"Yeah, Andy had an explanation for that, too." I told him what Andy had said about the knife skittering across the ice and into the water.

"Hoffman also told Zeke that Andy had a lot of blood on his clothing, including fine blood spatter. DNA isn't back yet, but the typing of the blood samples matches that of the victim, who happens to have the rare blood type AB negative. The suspect's type is O positive."

"Again, Andy had a reasonable explanation. From what he told me, the scene was extremely bloody, so some level of contami-nation would seem inevitable since he approached the victim and tried to contain the blood flow in an arterial wound while also checking for a pulse. He also said the victim gasped and blood sprayed out of his mouth. That would explain a spatter pattern, wouldn't it?"

"I suppose," Jon said.

"Andy also said that when he went around to the other side of the victim's body to get the knife, he got his foot snagged on part of a ski pole he didn't see. He fell into snow soaked with blood from the victim's arterial leg wound."

"Okay. This fellow seems to have an explanation for everything, though I imagine he's had some time to figure out a story to match the evidence his father has most likely shared with him."

"You're such a cynic," I teased.

"It tends to go with the job."

"Well, consider this. Maybe, just maybe, he's telling the truth. Innocent until proven guilty, right?"

"Yeah, but I have to tell you, it's not looking good, Morgan. The officers on the scene said there were a number of bloody footprints matching the boots the suspect was wearing and the snow around the victim was disturbed like one might see if there had been a scuffle. There was also a trail between the river and the victim's body marked heavily with blood drops and more of the bloody footprints matching the suspect's boots. This trail was well trampled, making them think Andy met the victim by the river, followed him to the tree where he then killed him, and then used this same pathway to return to the body after disposing of the knife."

"Andy said the second trail you mentioned, the one that was all trampled, was the one the Hodag used to get to the river and that he saw some holes like a ski pole might make in the snow alongside the trail. The victim, Brandon"—I was tired of referring to him as a victim—"was wearing snowshoes and using ski poles. Seems more likely, or at least equally as likely, that the trail was so well trampled because Brandon had snowshoed over it, whatever attacked him followed the same trail right to him and then used it to leave, and Andy followed it back from the river because it was easier to navigate than the knee-deep snow."

"Well, there's some evidence to support your theory," Jon admitted. "The investigators did find snowshoe prints on that trail leading to the tree where the body was found. But their theory is that Andy followed the victim—"

"Brandon."

"Sorry. Andy followed *Brandon* to the tree where the two men scuffled until Andy killed Brandon."

"The skepticism is strong in this one," I said, paraphrasing a line from a *Star Wars* movie, one of Jon's favorites.

"I'm just the messenger here. But I'm also a cop. It's how we roll."

"All the evidence you just mentioned is open to interpretation."

Jon hesitated. "I suppose so, but like I said, if his father shared the evidence with him, Andy has nothing better to do while sitting in his jail cell than to concoct a story fitting said evidence. You sound as if you've already decided this guy is innocent. Don't let your relationship with Rita, and hers to Andy, color your objectivity."

"I won't. I'm not. And don't let your naturally suspicious nature color your objectivity."

"Fair enough," Jon said with a chuckle. "I realize you're in a tough spot here because of Andy's connections to Rita."

"True, but believe me, I still have plenty of questions and doubts."

"Such as?"

I knew his challenging me this way was him making sure I didn't jump to emotional conclusions. I also knew he had my best interests at heart. Still, I felt myself growing annoyed by his challenges. Why, I wondered? Had he hit a nerve? Was I trying too hard to exonerate Andy before I had a chance to examine things with an objective and serious eye? Rita was dear to me, a family member for all intents and purposes. My only family, really. Just an hour or so ago I'd been convinced Andy was guilty. Now here I was defending him. Maybe I *had* lost my objectivity.

"One question I have is why Andy doesn't have more injuries. If the two men struggled and fought as much as this site supposedly indicates, you'd think the injuries would be more equal. From what I understand, they're both roughly the same size and build."

"Easy," Jon said. "Andy did a sneak attack from behind."

"Except it sounds like all Brandon's injuries were on his front."

"Maybe Brandon was incapacitated in some way, with a head injury or some such."

"Any reason to think that's the case? Did Zeke get any info about Brandon's autopsy?"

"Not that I know of, but I'll ask him."

"What about animal prints? Does Zeke know if they found any at the site?"

"They did not. Hoffman said they didn't find any identifiable animal tracks in the snow, though they were looking for something big, like a bear."

I had to admit, things weren't looking too good for Andy. Sure, most of the evidence was subject to interpretation, but people had been convicted on far less.

"There's something else you should know, Morgan."

"Whaaat?" I whined, not liking the ominous tone in his voice.

"I told you Zeke is from Rhinelander and worked for the police department there. Zeke's connection to Hoffman is how I was able to get the information I shared with you. But during their chat on the phone, Hoffman made it clear to Zeke how far-fetched he thinks the suspect's story is. He clearly believes the guy is guilty, particularly in light of the history between him and the victim."

"Andy," I said tiredly. "The suspect's name is Andy."

"Sorry. Occupational hazard."

I knew Jon's tendency to use the generic "suspect" term enabled him to distance himself. Normally it wouldn't have bothered me but in this case it did.

"I'll simply have to find enough evidence to convince this Hoffman fellow," I said. "I can be very persuasive when I want to be."

"Don't I know it," Jon said with a laugh. "But it's not going to be easy. No one will be rolling out the welcome mat for you, Morgan. In fact, they might be planning to shut you down already."

"What do you mean?"

"After Zeke's chat with Hoffman this afternoon, he got an email from him saying how Andy was pushing his ridiculous defense so hard he'd hired some charlatan who claims to be a cryptozoologist to come to Rhinelander and prove there's a killer Hodag on the loose. He closed the email by saying most folks in Rhinelander wouldn't take kindly to what you're trying to do."

"Good grief," I said, appalled. "I've been in town for only a few hours. The gossip mill here is scarily efficient."

"I think you'll understand why when I tell you the name of Hoffman's wife." I waited for his answer though I already had a growing suspicion. "It's Cordelia."

"Oh, hell," I said, and Jon laughed. "I've jumped right out of the proverbial frying pan into the fire, haven't I?"

"It would seem so. I'm sure Hoffman's email is mostly hyperbole, but you should watch your back just the same. I wish I could be there with you."

"I wish you could be here, too, but only because I'd enjoy your company. I can take care of myself, and I've got both Newt and Rita watching my back for me. They don't get any more formidable than that dynamic duo."

Jon laughed again and the sound of it heartened me. But it also made something inside me ache with longing.

"I look forward to our dinner together when you get done with this one and come home," Jon said.

"Me, too. Until then, good night, Jon."

"Good night, my crazy monster hunter."

This time it was my turn to laugh.

I ended the call and caved to Newt's pleading eyes and the hopeful wag of his tail by donning my coat and boots and leashing him up for our last walk of the day.

The motel's neighboring businesses were mostly shut down for the night, or in some cases, for the season. Newt pulled me across the parking lot to a slope leading down to a culvert bordered by a field at the bottom and then another parking lot for a long, dark building. I had no desire to try to navigate the hillside, but Newt seemed determined to go down, so I unhooked his leash and let him go. I waited, huddled inside my winter coat, watching him sniff his way to the culvert and finally do his business. As he slowly meandered his way back up, stopping every few feet to smell something, I danced in place to try to keep warm, though my hands were positively toasty inside my new pink gloves.

The gloves made me think of Cordelia, and that made me think of Jon's warning to watch my back. I turned and scanned the area around and behind the motel and saw something that made my heart skip a beat.

Amid a row of trees running behind the motel, I saw a shadowy figure that then ducked behind a trunk. I might not have seen him at all—something about the general shape made me jump to my gender assumption—if not for the lights on the buildings behind those trees. Even so, I thought my eyes might have been playing tricks on me until Newt came up alongside me and a deep growl rumbled in his throat as he stared at the same spot. Still unwilling to let my imagination get the better of me, I thought Newt's reaction might have been because he sensed my own anxiety. Except then I saw the shadowy figure again, and this time he was on the move. I got a vague impression of a long coat and a knit cap before he disappeared into the night.

The hour wasn't overly late, but the area was largely deserted with little in the way of car or foot traffic. Even so, another person out walking wouldn't have concerned me had it not been for his furtive behavior.

Maybe it was a kid.

But I dismissed this idea almost as soon as I had it. The figure had been too big.

I leashed Newt and made my way back across the parking lot toward the motel, but rather than use the door we'd come out of, which was close to the back of the building and therefore close to my room, I headed for the main entrance, which was well lit, reassuringly welcoming, and far from where I'd seen the figure. The clerk behind the front desk smiled at me as I led Newt down a long hallway past meeting rooms and the indoor swimming pool to the hall that ran along the back of the motel, where my room was located.

I couldn't deny a feeling of relief as I keyed in and locked the door behind me, but I was also aware of how close one wall of my room, with its nice wide window, was to that line of trees behind the motel. The drapes were closed but I wanted to check to make sure the window was securely locked. I stood in front of it, hesitant, half convinced I'd see some horrible face leering at me as soon as the drapes parted. But when I finally flung them aside with all the drama of a b-grade horror movie, all I saw was a swath of pristine white snow extending out about ten feet to the tree line. On the other side of those trees, lights from the buildings beyond glowed warmly. I checked the lock and closed the drapes tightly. Then I crossed the room and rechecked all the locks on the door.

I was tired from the day's excitement and thought I'd doze off quickly, but sleep eluded me. After tossing and turning for the better part of two hours, I got up in the dark and went back to the window, parting the drapes. With no light behind me I was able to see outside easily thanks in part to a gibbous moon shining down on all that white snow. Warm air blew up from the heater beneath my window, but it wasn't enough to stop the chill that shook me when I looked more closely at the snowy expanse outside.

There was one clear set of footprints that led from the far end of the building right up to my window before then disappearing into the line of trees.

CHAPTER 7

My elusive shadow made sleep nearly impossible. I tossed and turned most of the night and even the reassurance of Newt's warm body next to me didn't help. The combination of those footprints outside my motel window and the secret I was hiding about the anonymous letter had my nerves firing all night.

Could it have been David out there watching me? Were those his footprints in the snow leading up to my window?

It had been a little over two years since David Johnson, or at least the man I knew by that name, murdered my parents and then disappeared. It turned out he was an impostor who had stolen the identity of the real David Johnson, who had died. After establishing the fake identity, my David . . . no, fake David—thinking of him as *my* David in any form made my stomach turn—had then constructed a detailed and elaborate plan to meet, date, and marry me, most likely with a goal of getting rich quick. I didn't have any money of my own to speak of at the time, so the only way for him to get access was to marry me and then murder my parents so I'd inherit. Would he have then killed me, as well? I'll never know for sure because his plans fell apart when my father discovered his subterfuge before any marriage could take place.

David hadn't killed me then because I hadn't been present when he murdered my parents. And he must have had a good laugh over it all when I became the main suspect. Did he want to kill me now? Murdering my parents had been an act of desperation, an in-the-moment thing, unplanned. I don't think their deaths where and when they happened were part of David's original plan. He gained nothing from the act other than avoiding exposure and arrest by the police. And arrest was unlikely given that David's very existence was hard to prove.

The New Jersey detective in charge of the case, who ironically is Jon Flanders's uncle (because my relationship with Jon isn't under enough strain already), has always regarded me as a prime suspect. I inherited my parents' wealth. I was the only person anyone had seen with them right before their deaths. I was the only living person other than Rita and Devon who claimed to have seen David, and they had seen him only briefly. And since they were clearly biased in my favor, it was easy for the New Jersey police to dismiss their statements and believe I'd simply made David up. And miraculously, David had left virtually no trace of his existence, though with the enhanced powers of hindsight it was easy for me to see how his supposed introvertive shyness, OCD level of cleanliness, and frequent wearing of gloves because he supposedly had Raynaud's disease—a disorder where the fingers turn white and bloodless when exposed to cool temperatures—had been part of the ruse all along. The police couldn't find even one fingerprint for the guy.

Had last night's shadowy figure been David? Were those his footprints outside my window? If so, what did he want?

As the first rays of morning light eked their way around the curtain on my window, I shoved thoughts of David aside. I considered opening the drapes and looking for more footprints but quickly dismissed the idea, content to live in the shadows for now. It was time to play ostrich and bury my head in the sand, or in this case, the snow. I dressed while making a cup of coffee in the little machine in my room and focused instead on the plan to visit the scene of Brandon's death and the river where Andy claimed to have seen a Hodag. Once I was dressed and had coffee in hand, Newt and I headed outside for a walk.

The morning air was crisp and cold, and the sunlight reflecting off the snow made it sparkle as if covered in sequins. Newt wasn't as impressed with the visual beauty, and he made short work of his business. Once I was back in my room, I settled in with my laptop and typed up some thoughts I'd gleaned from my Hodag research while waiting for Rita to come knocking. She texted me half an hour later and we met at my car.

It took us nearly twenty minutes to reach Roger's cabin, though calling the structure a cabin was an understatement. It was a large log home nestled in a heavily wooded parcel of mostly evergreen trees, though the occasional oak, maple, hemlock, and hickory were peppered throughout. Roger's house was at the end of a road, and while we passed other homes on the way to it, the lots were large, and the trees provided a screen of privacy. Despite knowing there were neighbors, when we arrived at Roger's place I had a sense of isolation.

Inside, a huge stone fireplace on one wall was bordered on two sides by large windows that looked out into the woods. In keeping with the log exterior, the décor was very north woods: log beams overhead, knotty pine paneling on the walls, wood floors, and lots of throw pillows and woolen blankets decorated with evergreens, black bears, and wolves. It wasn't quite rustic, however, as the furniture was soft, buttery leather; the kitchen appliances were all state-of-the-art; and the rugs were expensive woven wool.

"We've got a bit of a hike to get to the area where Brandon died," Roger told us. He glanced at my feet, which were clad in warm, faux-fur-lined boots. "The snow is about two feet deep still, much the same as it was on the day in question, though the trail we're going to follow has since been well trampled by rescue folks, police, and such. Yesterday's snowfall was minimal and brief, so we should get a good sense for what Andy experienced."

Our trek through the woods was a pleasant one. Pine resin scented the air, a nearby woodpecker's rat-a-tat-tat echoed through the trees, and dappled sunlight painted shadows and sparked glimmers on the surrounding snow. As Roger had promised, there was a well-packed trail, though deviating from it in places gave me a better sense of what it had been like for Andy. Trudging through two feet of snow was a definite workout. Newt loved it, of course, and he plowed into the snow with his head, leapt about like a frolicking deer, and flopped and rolled until his fur was packed with the stuff. Eventually we reached a spot where the snow had been trampled in a wide circular area.

"This is where Andy was when he first heard the call for help," Roger said. "He dropped his sled here and hurried on ahead."

We continued to follow the trail, which meandered in and out between trees, and when Roger stopped for a second time, I knew where we were without him having to tell us. For one thing, the area was closed off by police tape that had been wrapped around trees. The other clue was a dark stain covering a wide area of flattened and disturbed snow near the base of a large oak tree. Even this many days later the smell of blood lingered and there were signs of animal activity, holes dug into some of the darkest snow. To the left, in the nine o'clock position, was another trail tamped down by footprints and marked by dark splotches of blood.

"That's the path Brandon and the creature took," Roger said, pointing. "It's also the one Andy said he followed back here from the river."

I couldn't discern any specific prints in the packed-down snow—animal or human—but on one side of this trail two less defined ones veered off, sets of footprints where someone—presumably Andy and/or the police—had navigated the deep snow one plunging footstep at a time.

I recalled Andy saying he didn't have cell service here and I took out my phone and checked—sure enough, not a single bar.

I handed Rita Newt's leash. "You guys stay here," I said. "I want to explore on my own before we trample it more."

I half expected an objection from Rita or Roger—or both—but when none came I took off, following beside the footsteps angling away from the purported Hodag trail. A few minutes later I reached the river just below the shaded bend Andy had mentioned and I took a minute to catch my breath and survey my surroundings.

I saw an area of heavily disturbed snow close to the bank about ten feet ahead and wondered if this was where Andy had lost his footing and fallen, cutting his hand and losing his grip on the knife. An area of bloodstained snow seemed to support this theory, plus, about five or six feet from shore, the ice gave way to a narrow strip of open water. It was easy to imagine a knife sliding across the ice and dropping off the edge into the river. Farther upstream where the trees were thickest, the ice appeared solid, lacking the fissures and openings I could see near me.

I stared into the woods on the opposite shore and tried to imagine a creature like the ones I'd seen in the statues around town peering back at me. It was a stretch. I checked my phone and saw I had a single bar of service. So far, everything fit Andy's version of events. I had to wonder why Andy would have bothered coming here to the river to call for help if he'd known the victim was Brandon. Wouldn't it have made more sense to simply walk away and let someone else find the body? Maybe he thought the proximity to his father's cabin and his footprints in the snow would be enough to lead the authorities to him once they identified the victim.

Then a bigger question came to me. Why had Brandon been out here in these woods? No one had mentioned the existence of any fishing equipment on or near his body and if he also owned property in the area, wouldn't the police have mentioned it? Since I had a bar of service, I pulled off my hot-pink gloves, shoved them into my pockets, and typed out a message to Devon, asking him to check the property records for the area to see if Brandon owned anything close by.

As I put my gloves back on and waited to see if the message would go through, I realized that even if Brandon did own something nearby, it didn't explain what he was doing out here. If he had no hunting or fishing equipment with him other than a basic knife, what had made him go snowshoeing through the woods? Was he just out to enjoy the walk? Had Andy invited him out here and then challenged him to some kind of fight? If so, why had Andy dragged his sled full of fishing gear along? For the weapons, perhaps? But then why leave it some distance behind? Maybe Andy had invited Brandon out for some fishing in an attempt to mend their broken fences and it had gone horribly wrong. Except again, why leave the sled behind? And would Brandon have accepted such an invite given the history between the two men? My mind tried to make sense of things, to fit the evidence into a story, but no matter how I went at it, the scenario didn't jibe with the police version of events. Maybe it wasn't Andy who had attacked Brandon. Maybe a rogue bear had done it.

Or a Hodag.

I shook that idea off, feeling frustrated at having so many questions and not enough answers. I turned to head back to the others but hesitated when something caught my eye, a flicker of movement across the river. The sun reflected brightly off the ice and water, and I shaded my eyes with my hand to try to see better.

At first all I saw was the occasional sway of a tree branch in the wind and, just when I'd convinced myself my imagination was getting a little too creative, I heard crunching and grunting noises from across the river. A second later it sounded like it was coming from off to my left. I whirled around but then quickly turned back, hearing it from behind me this time. I realized the alley created by the tree-lined river made the sounds seem to come from every direction at once.

I caught a hint of movement on the opposite shore again and squinted at it, seeing little more than varying shades of white and green among the shadows. I was about to give up when it emerged from between two evergreens, the bright sunshine highlighting it clearly. A chill raced down my spine, giving birth to goose bumps from my head to my toes.

Standing on the other side of the river staring back at me was a freaking Hodag.

CHAPTER 8

⌐

Almost as soon as I saw the creature, it melted back into the shadows. I blinked hard, squinted, continued to stare, and briefly entertained the possibility I was losing my mind. After all, I was admittedly stressed over the not-so-anonymous letter from my stalker and the PTSD I'd been dealing with ever since the murder of my parents. Had I really seen a Hodag? Or had it simply been a trick of the light? I closed my eyes and mentally replayed the moment. In my mind I saw the animal as clear as day. It couldn't have been a figment of my imagination—it had been too real!

Some tiny voice in the back of my brain whispered, *But doesn't every crazy person convince themselves of the same?*

It occurred to me I could cross the icy river up where the ice was thicker and search for the creature, but I quickly discarded the idea as much too high on the extinction side of the Darwinian scale of natural selection. Instead, I hurried back to Roger and Rita as much as one can while goose-stepping through snow.

"Any great insights?" Roger asked when I returned. I took Newt's leash from Rita, and he leaned against my leg, just enough to let me know he'd missed me.

"Actually, yes," I said. Roger managed to look both pleasantly surprised and wary of my answer. "I saw something, an animal of some sort, across the river."

"Really?" There was a sprinkling of suspicion in Roger's voice, enough to make me think he hadn't been fully convinced of his son's story. He seemed to realize this, immediately cleared his throat, and uttered his next question with a high level of conviction. "It was a Hodag, wasn't it?"

"Um . . . I'm not sure. It was across the river, and I saw it for only a second or two before it disappeared back into the trees. I didn't get a good look, but . . ." I hesitated, not wanting to give Roger false hope but also determined to be honest. "It did bear some resemblance to a Hodag, with horns and tusks and spines down its back."

"It *was* a Hodag!" Roger said with obvious relief, slapping a hand against his thigh. "We need to tell the police." I shot him a cautionary look and his shoulders sagged. "Yeah, yeah, you're right," he said, punctuating the comment with a dejected sigh. "I don't suppose you got a picture of it?"

I shook my head. "It was there and gone in the blink of an eye."

Roger scowled. "They won't believe you any more than they believed Andy." Then his expression brightened, and he snapped his fingers. "What we need to do is catch it. Too bad you didn't have a gun on you."

I found his enthusiasm for shooting at the thing a bit unsettling.

Newt had been sitting and wagging his tail throughout Roger's growing excitement, and he'd created a fan-shaped depression in the snow. I noticed something dark in the tiny wafts of white his tail had flung to the sides and bent down to get a closer look. It was nearly an inch in length and curved and narrowed to a point on one end like a claw. I picked it up and stuck it into my pocket.

"What was that?" Rita asked, eyeing me suspiciously.

"Nothing important," I lied. "Let's go back to the motel and discuss this, come up with a plan of action. I don't want us going off all willy-nilly."

"Now isn't the time for discussion; it's the time for action," Roger insisted. "Let's go after it."

"I don't know, Roger," I said, cautioning him again. "I'm not sure what I saw and if it was any kind of animal, it could be highly dangerous. Going out in the woods half-cocked to try to find it is a suicide mission."

Roger frowned and emitted a frustrated sigh. "My son's life and freedom are at stake here," he said.

"Yes, and that's too important to risk messing it up. Let's go back to the motel and talk it through. Or better yet, how about a change of scenery? I'd like to take Sonja up on her invitation to visit. Maybe it will help if we listen to these interviews she's done. Let's grab some lunch and then head to her place."

Roger frowned and nodded, though with obvious reluctance. I suspected his agreement was only to buy time and placate me, something that was confirmed once we got back to his cabin. Rita and I got into my car and waited for Roger to get in his, but instead he walked over and tapped on Rita's window. I don't think his choice of windows was a random one. He'd been closer to my side of the car, but I think he knew I posed a greater threat of resistance. Rita lowered her window and Roger leaned in, managing to look at everything in the front area of the car except for me.

"Sonja's place is easy to get to," he said, rattling off some simple directions. "I'm going to hang here for a bit. There are some things I need to tend to. How about we meet at the motel this evening sometime? Say about six? We can do dinner and talk then."

I had no doubt this had been Roger's plan all along from the moment I'd suggested a visit to Sonja. I was equally as certain there was no point in trying to talk him out of it.

"Dinner sounds good," Rita said. I wasn't sure if she'd guessed what he was up to but just before she closed her window and we drove away, she added, "You be careful out there, Roger."

He was already walking away, and he acknowledged her admonition with a wave of his hand without looking back.

"I know a nice little sandwich place if you're interested in lunch," Rita said.

"Sounds good."

Once we were back on the main road, Rita said, "You know Roger is going to try to find the animal you saw, don't you? Turn right at the next light."

I nodded.

"What do you think the odds are of him being successful?"

"Is he an experienced hunter?"

Rita scoffed. "God, no. He'll go down to the river in the summer and cast a line into the water but only to spend time with Andy. As for actual hunting? He gets squeamish at the sight of blood. I watched him nearly pass out once trying to remove a hook on a fish he'd caught. He typically has Andy do it for him. Take a left up here."

"Then I'd say his odds are slim to none. Right now, his love for his son is overriding his common sense. But who knows? Maybe he'll surprise us."

"Yeah, and maybe pigs will fly." Rita shook her head in disgust. "It's a fool's errand, but then men often are fools, aren't they? Park anywhere along the street here. We'll need to walk."

We both fell into a comfortable silence while I parked but once I was in place, Rita leaned forward and stared me in the face.

"Do you really think it was a Hodag?" she asked.

I didn't know how to answer her, but she wasn't about to let me dodge the question.

"Come on, Morgan," she cajoled. "Tell me."

I sighed. "I honestly don't know, Rita," I said. "I'm inclined to think I might have experienced a form of . . . pareidolia."

Rita smiled but wagged a finger at me. "You're not getting out of it that easily," she said. "Besides, I'm not sure you used it properly, since it means seeing expected or familiar things in random shapes and lines, and who would expect to see a Hodag?"

"We *are* in Rhinelander," I reminded her.

"Good point," she conceded.

I thought that would be the end of it, but no. Rita studied me intently for the next few seconds while I shut down the engine and looked around, pretending not to notice. Then she said, "You've been uncharacteristically distracted ever since we got here, Morgan. Something's up. What aren't you telling me? Did something happen between you and Jon?"

"Nope. All good on the Jon front. It's status quo for us." I gave her a meager smile.

"See? That." She wagged a chastising finger at me. "That's the saddest excuse for a smile I've seen on you in a long time. What's going on? Is it this case? Did I force you into doing something you didn't want to do? If I did, I'm sorry, but Andy holds a special place in my heart. I hope you can understand that."

"Of course, I do, Rita. And I promise you I'll do my best to exonerate him if he's telling the truth." I expected her to come back with a quick affirmation of his innocence, but when she didn't, I opened my car door to get out. Rita stopped me with a hand on my arm.

"Talk to me, Morgan."

I looked over at her, prepared to deny that there was anything to discuss, but was momentarily struck dumb. She gazed affectionately at me, her white hair forming a sort of halo about her head. Her glasses were perched on her aristocratic nose and sunlight coming in through the windshield made the rhinestones sparkle. Her blue eyes stared piercingly at me over the tops of the frames. Somehow she managed to look loving and stern all at the same time. More than anything I wanted to unburden myself, to tell her about the mysterious letter I'd received, to voice my fears about David. But then, in addition to the white sparkly-ness of her, I also saw the dark circles under her eyes and the deep lines etched into her face, reminders of her age and the stress she was under. It wouldn't be fair to add my burdens to hers.

"I haven't slept well is all," I said. "Sometimes I have nightmares about my parents and their deaths and when I do, it makes for a restless night." This was essentially the truth, just not the whole truth. Rita narrowed her eyes at me, and I sensed her bullshit detector doing a random check.

I left Newt in the car, and we walked half a block to the café. Once inside, I half expected Rita to try digging into my psyche again, but instead she kept the conversation focused on Andy, reminiscing about her time with him when he was a boy.

"He was a sweet young man, quiet, shy, always polite, always saying please and thank you, never interrupting or throwing tantrums," she said with a wistful smile once we'd ordered. "I wish you could have known him back then, Morgan, because if you had you'd understand why I'm so convinced of his innocence. For him to have done what he's been accused of would be so out of character for him."

While I enjoyed listening to her talk about Andy, it pained me to see the raw belief on her face, to hear the naked hope in her voice, not because I doubted what she was saying or feeling, but because I was afraid I'd let her down and this young man she clearly loved so dearly would end up paying the price.

CHAPTER 9

 ⌒

When we were finished eating—Newt got his own roast beef sandwich to nosh on—I drove us to Sonja Mueller's place. It was a multiacre property a few miles outside town with a long, curving driveway bordered by woods on both sides. Several hundred feet in, the landscape opened up to reveal an old Victorian home sitting perpendicular to the drive and backdropped by a more modern-looking barn beyond. A black wrought iron fence encircled the front yard of the house and at the gate protecting the entrance like a couple of marble lion statues were two Hodags. One of the statues closely matched the cheerfully grinning Hodag sitting on the chamber of commerce property but the other one had a narrower face, upward-slanting eyes minus the red coloring, and a leering, mischievous grin. Both statues had spines along their backs and tusks and horns protruding from their heads.

I left Newt in the car for the time being and cracked a couple of windows for him. Rita and I walked through the front gate and onto a roofed porch that stretched across the full facade of the house. I knocked and rang the bell but when there was no answer, Rita and I both looked to our left, where a mechanical hum emanated from the barn.

"I think that must be her studio," I said, gesturing toward the building.

"She's probably busy. Maybe we should come back another time. And call first," Rita said with an admonishing look over the top of her glasses.

Rita didn't cotton to Sonja, though I wasn't sure why. I'd sensed it at the restaurant last night and picked up the same vibe now.

"Sonja invited us to drop by, remember?" I said.

"She invited *you*," Rita grumbled.

"You didn't have to come with me."

"Yes, I did. You get into too much trouble when you're on your own."

I rolled my eyes at her and did my best to act annoyed, but the truth was, her watching over me this way plucked at my heartstrings.

As suspected, we found Sonja's studio and workshop—and Sonja—inside the barn. A hefty golden retriever with a graying muzzle—presumably the near-blind Wally Sonja had mentioned the night before—greeted us at the door, raising his nose to the air and then letting out a neutral *woof* while wagging his tail. I held my hand out in front of his nose, and after a sniff, he apparently found me acceptable. Rita did the same, and when Wally then sat and stared in the general direction of Sonja, we ventured deeper inside.

Sonja's barn studio was a huge, open space housing a dedicated work area with a pottery wheel, a kiln, and a variety of projects in progress, while the other end had two large tables covered with stains and what appeared to be various molds for projects. An overhead exhaust system vented to the roof and hummed consistently, the source of the sound we'd heard out front. In the center of the barn, two rows of shelving units stood side by side facing each other, sentinels marching toward the back wall, creating a small hallway of sorts. The shelves were filled with what I assumed were Sonja's wares: vases, statues, statuettes, modernistic sculptures, and of course, an impressive array of Hodags. There were large Hodags and small ones, green, yellow, blue, and brown ones, and some that were plain alabaster-colored shapes waiting to be brought to life. Their personalities were as varied as their colors with teeth-baring grins that ranged from kid-lit friendly to my worst nightmare. Some of the Hodags stood erect like bears while others were depicted on all fours, often atop a cut log, no doubt an homage to the lumber industry that had spawned the creature's existence.

Sonja stood at one of the tables beneath the exhaust fan wearing goggles, a respirator, gloves, and an apron over her blue jeans and sweatshirt. She held up a hand as we approached, indicating we shouldn't come any closer. We halted and she held up one finger to indicate she'd be just a minute. We were about twenty feet away, but I could see what she was doing. Two halves of a mold lay on the table in front of her and she was brushing a thick liquid with a slight gold tint to it—some sort of resin, I guessed—onto the inside surfaces of one of the halves and then laying down pieces of an open mesh fabric on top of this, sealing it in place with a few more brushes of the resin. She had the half she was working on tipped up in order to coat one of the sides more easily, allowing us to see the mesh already lining the interior. She cut a few more small pieces of the material, carefully placed them, covered them with resin, and then put down her brush. After stripping off her gloves, she stepped away from the table, removed her respirator and goggles, and greeted us with a big smile.

"Welcome!" she said. "Sorry to make you wait but the resin has a short window of time before it hardens, so it's something you have to finish once you start."

"What are you making?" I asked. I'd tried to venture a guess from the interior shape of the mold she was working with but hadn't been able to make sense of it.

"It's a dinosaur, a velociraptor to be exact. The school commissioned me to help them with a large, outdoor diorama project they're constructing to highlight the late Cretaceous period."

"How fun," I said. "Do you work with fiberglass a lot?"

Sonja nodded. "I do clay sculptures, too, but fiberglass is quickly becoming my favorite, especially for outdoor stuff. It makes for a sturdy sculpture that takes paint well and stands up to our Rhinelander weather."

"Fascinating," I said, genuinely intrigued. "I might commission you to do some cryptids for me. I think they'd make a fun addition to my store back home."

"I'd love to," she said, smiling. "And as you can see, I've got a good start on it with the Hodags. Welcome to Hodag central."

I walked over and eyed her collection more closely while she undid her apron and took it off, hanging it on a wall hook.

"There's a surprising amount of variety in these," I said over my shoulder. "I believe you mentioned last night that you try to reflect some of the specifics from eyewitness reports you've heard."

"I do."

"And you said you had video interviews of some of these eyewitnesses?"

"I do. Why don't we go into the house and have some coffee? Or tea if you prefer. The recordings are on my computer, but I can play them on my TV to make it easier to watch." Without waiting for an answer, she headed for the door with a come-on wave of her hand, saying, "Follow me."

When Sonja saw Newt in the car, she paused and looked back at me. "You're welcome to bring him inside if you want. Wally gets on great with other dogs."

"If you're sure you don't mind."

"Not a bit," she said with a smile.

We spent a few minutes doing introductions between Newt and Wally and the two took to each other right away. Sonja became Newt's new best friend by bending down and scrubbing his neck ruff with her hands while murmuring something about what a good doggy he was. Newt expressed his gratitude with a sloppy lick on Sonja's cheek, making her laugh with delight.

With introductions out of the way, we followed Sonja into the house through a side door that led to a mudroom, where we removed our coats and boots. From there we entered a relatively modern kitchen bearing hints of its Victorian ancestry—an antique, cast-iron stove modernized with gas burners; a large, scarred wooden table in the center of the room; a wooden hutch against one wall with a display of delicate bone china; and a chandelier with candle lights above the table.

The most delightful feature of the room, however, was a working fireplace built into one wall. It bore ashes from an earlier fire, and it was easy to imagine what a cozy room this kitchen would be with the fireplace blazing.

Once we all agreed on coffee as our beverage of choice, Sonja made quick work of setting up a pot to brew. Then she steered us into the living room, a delightfully warm space with beige walls outlined with chestnut wainscoting and crown molding. The furnishings—a sofa and two chairs—were big, plush, and covered in a maroon-and-brown brocade material. Their heavy wooden frames featured what I thought were lion heads at the ends of the carved arms, but a closer look revealed they were actually Hodag heads.

"I told you," Sonja said with a smile when she saw me eyeing them. "Hodag central. Make yourselves comfy and I'll get my computer set up in here while the coffee is brewing."

A chandelier hung in the middle of this room, as well, but there were standing lamps with stained glass shades by each chair and at either end of the sofa. Sonja flipped them all on, casting the room in a warm, colorful light. At the far end of the room was another fireplace and hanging above the ornate wooden mantel was a very modern flat-screen TV, creating an anachronistic conflict in my mind. A fire had been laid already and, with the flick of a lighter, Sonja had it blazing. The house, at least what we'd seen of it so far, was a study in contrasting styles and eras. The only surprise for me was the lack of any artwork. The walls were bare save for the TV and a large, gilt-framed mirror hanging over the sofa.

Newt and Wally curled up beside each other in front of the fire on a braided rug, creating a scene straight out of a Rockwell painting. I felt relaxed and oddly content, as if I could stay here forever, though the feeling didn't last, because ten minutes later we were watching disturbing videos of Sonja's recorded interviews with people who claimed to have seen a living, breathing Hodag.

CHAPTER 10

Sonja gave a brief prelude to the show. "I've noticed a distinct upturn in the number of Hodag sightings over the past two years. It got me curious, and I started contacting some of the people making these claims and asking them if they were willing to be interviewed. I told them I wanted their stories for artistic purposes and several folks have even bought sculptures from me after their encounters."

"Was that the main reason for your inquiries, artistic purposes?" I asked.

"Primarily, yes. At least in the beginning. To be honest, I half expected the people who were willing to talk with me would be borderline nutjobs or attention seekers, but there's something about their stories, most of them anyway, that seems authentic. I'm the first to admit I'm not a talented profiler like some FBI agent, but I do get gut feelings about people, and I've learned to trust them."

"Are you saying you believe they really saw a Hodag?" Rita asked.

"I'm saying *they* believe they really saw a Hodag. I'll let you make your own judgments."

With that, Sonja started the show. She turned out to be a skilled interviewer, cajoling and teasing stories from people without too much leading or suggestion. There were five total interviews, though Sonja told us she had spoken to three others who had refused to have their stories recorded for fear of ridicule or retribution.

The first interview was with a bald man in his fifties who had been out fishing at the end of the summer not far from the area where the encounter between Andy and Brandon had occurred. His description was brief but chilling.

"I heard rustling behind me and the undergrowth there is thick. Lots of berry bushes and weedy vines. When I looked, I didn't see anything at first, but some branches were moving a little like they'd just been disturbed. Suddenly something burst out of a particularly thick patch of vines."

The man paused and his gaze shifted away from the camera, his eyes taking on a wild, frightened look.

"It came at me hard and fast. It was a blur. Hard to see. It just slammed into me. But not with its head. It turned at the last second, like it was as surprised to see me as I was to see it, but in that second, just before it turned, I saw the red of its eyes. It had a ridge of spines down its back and claws on the front feet." He paused again and shuddered before engaging again with Sonja and her camera.

"The force of the collision knocked me back and I fell on my ass. The animal made a horrible growling noise as it ran off into the brush."

Sonja's voice could be heard next. "How big was it, would you say?"

The man screwed his face up in thought. "I guess it stood about thigh high. Head was higher than that, but the thigh is where it hit me. And it was solid. Heavy."

"Did it frighten you?"

"Hell yeah." He looked at the camera, and presumably Sonja, like she was an imbecile for asking.

"Do you think it was afraid of you?"

This question threw him for a moment, and I was glad Sonja asked it.

"Maybe?" the man said tentatively, scratching behind one ear. Then he shook his head. "No, I take that back. It was aggressive. It didn't try to run from me or hide."

"Yet you said it turned to the side at the last minute."

"Yeah, except . . . I don't know. Maybe it was me who turned?" the man said.

I could tell from the wild look in his eyes and the tremor in his voice that he was getting worked up.

"I tried to kick at it, and I think I took a step back. I might have turned a little when I did. But it turned, too. I think. Yeah, it did."

I could practically see the wheels spinning inside this man's head as he recalled, interpreted, and reinterpreted the events.

"What color was it?" Sonja asked.

"Grayish green but the spines on its back were darker. The eyes were red. And the horns and tusks were whitish."

"It had horns *and* tusks?" Sonja asked.

The man looked away for a second, frowning and squinting as if envisioning the scene in his mind again. When he turned back to the camera, his answer was unequivocal. "Yep, both."

The interview continued for a few more minutes as Sonja had the man describe the legs of the animal—"short and kind of stubby"—and the tail, if there was one—also "short and stubby."

Sonja asked him again what sounds the animal made and his answer was, "Grunts and growls."

The second interviewee was a woman who claimed she saw a Hodag run across the road in front of her car in late September during a drive back from a cabin she owned in the Upper Peninsula, or as the locals generally referred to it, the U-P. Her description was a night sighting, but she said the animal was clearly defined in her headlights for a few seconds and her description matched that of the first fellow with one exception: she thought the animal was only about two feet tall.

The third interview was one I dismissed almost immediately. Everything about the man told me he was making things up as he went along. His eyes constantly darted up and to the left and he stammered as he described what he supposedly saw but not when he talked about other things. He fidgeted constantly and his voice would crescendo and drop, crescendo and drop. I might have been willing to overlook all these things if it hadn't been for him saying the Hodag breathed fire and flames, had wings and flew over him, was at least six feet tall, and had been friendly and approachable, allowing him to pet it. He also claimed it had tried to communicate with him through telepathy. I made a mental note to check out Sonja's Hodag sculptures to see if any of them had wings.

The final two interviews were both men. The first sighting occurred last spring while the fellow was fishing near the woods where Brandon had been found, though on the other side of the river. He admitted the animal had been some distance away when he saw it and claimed it screamed as it ran off. The second one happened in late July while a man was hiking through woods north of town. His description was of a creature with "horns and scales and eyes that glowed like the bowels of hell!" One thing all the interviews had in common was the unlikelihood that what any of them had seen had been a bear or wolf.

"That's it," Sonja said when the videos were finished. "I've made sculptures of each of those Hodags and given them to the people who saw them, even the six-foot-tall, fire-breathing one."

"I would have liked to have seen that," I said with a chuckle. "I noticed you have a couple of guard Hodags out front by your gate."

"Yeah, those were my dad's creations. He was obsessed with Hodags, and I guess he passed his enthusiasm on to me."

"Your father is an artist also?" I said.

"He was. He taught me everything he knew about sculpting with clay, and it used to be the only medium I worked in. After he died, I started experimenting with fiberglass and I haven't looked back since. Most of my work is in fiberglass sculptures these days, though I still dabble in clay now and again, my way of paying homage to my father and his talent. He's been gone twenty years now. My mother had died the year before and he just didn't want to go on without her."

"Sounds like they were close," Rita said.

"Oh, yes. It's quite the story," Sonja said with a sentimental smile. "They were star-crossed lovers who met by accident at the port where my father's ship docked when he and his parents arrived here from Germany at the end of the war."

"A war romance?" Rita said with a tone of wistfulness.

Sonja nodded. "My mother's relatives were Polish Jews, and they had both the forethought and the money to escape from Poland in the early days. They fled to America, settled in New York City, and started a business there. My grandfather Dziadek was a talented jeweler and watchmaker and his business thrived. My mother, Paulina, was their only child and Dziadek desperately wanted her to learn the jewelry-making business so she could one day take it over. My mother dutifully studied under his tutelage and, one day, when she was seventeen, she went with him to buy some gems from a dealer near the port.

"My father's family had just arrived in New York and Dad and Opa Mueller, my paternal grandfather, were crossing a street on their way to a ticket office intending to purchase rail passes to Wisconsin, where my grandmother's cousins had settled a few years earlier. At the same time, Mom and Dziadek were crossing in the opposite direction on their way back from the gem dealer. A delivery truck driver lost control of his vehicle—turned out he'd had a heart attack and died—and the truck came barreling straight for Mom. Dad saw it coming and grabbed Mom about the waist, hauling her out of the path of the truck at the last second, saving her life."

"How romantic!" Rita said with a clap of her hands. The woman is a sucker for a good love story, and I have to watch her to make sure she doesn't sneak too many romances onto the shelves at my store. I find them now and again tucked in between the mysteries.

"It was," Sonja agreed. "But that's not the end of the story. It gets better. As a way of expressing his gratitude, Dziadek offered to buy Dad and Opa lunch at a nearby restaurant. The two older men dickered for a bit, and meanwhile, Mom and Dad took notice of each other and introduced themselves. They started up their own conversation and both were delighted when lunch was finally agreed upon. According to Mom, she and Dad sat making goo-goo eyes across the table while the two older men talked. According to Dad, he knew right away he would marry the beautiful girl he'd saved from certain death and would have proposed right then and there if he thought he could have gotten away with it."

"How lovely," Rita said, looking delighted.

"Mom and Dad managed to exchange names—his was Ernst, by the way—and Dad explained they were heading out to Wisconsin to join family there, though he couldn't recall the name of the town. Mom gave him her address in New York City, and Dad promised he'd write to her once he got settled. Here's where things get ugly."

"What? How?" Rita snapped, her tone demanding. She scowled, leaned back, and gave Sonja a suspicious look as if she thought the woman was personally responsible for whatever calamity was about to unfold in the story despite not having been conceived yet, much less born.

"Well, my father and his family came to Wisconsin and joined other family members who had settled in Minocqua. Dad kept his promise to write to Mom, beginning as soon as they arrived in Wisconsin. Except Dziadek had picked up on the attraction between the two young people, and when Mom kept waxing about that handsome Mueller boy who'd saved her life, Dziadek knew it wasn't going to be a passing fling. And he wasn't keen on Paulina hooking up with the Mueller boy because of things he'd learned about the family during the gratitude luncheon. Sure, Ernst had saved Paulina's life but there was no way Dziadek would ever approve of his daughter's dalliance with a man who was the son of a mere art dealer and a house cleaner, particularly since some of the houses my grandmother had tended to in Germany had belonged to officers in Hitler's regime. Clearly the Muellers were not the sort of people Paulina should be associating with, much less marrying. So Dziadek kept an eye out for any letters from Ernst and when they came, he intercepted them."

Rita gasped, a hand to her chest. "He didn't," she said, both angry and appalled.

Sonja gave her a meek smile. "He did. But Mom wouldn't let it go and after about a year, she stole some money and a few gems from Dziadek's stash and ran away, taking a train to Milwaukee. Since she had no idea where my father had ended up, she traveled around the city asking for Ernst Mueller by name. After several months her cash was gone, and rather than sell the gems, she got a job. It would take her nearly two years to find my father and even then it was only due to a bit of serendipity."

I glanced over at Rita, who was slack-jawed and clearly enthralled. I had to give it to Sonja; she knew how to tell stories as well as elicit them from others.

"Mom got a job working as a bookkeeper for a wealthy Milwaukee businessman who was making a killing in the lumber trade. While working for her father, Mom had not only learned how to keep books but also how to cook them, and it turned out this was a skill this lumber tycoon desired. The job not only paid a decent wage but it also came with room and board in the lumber baron's expansive, newly built home. And as luck would have it, the lumber baron's wife was looking to acquire some art sculptures for the estate's grounds. After asking around, she heard about this artist in Rhinelander."

"It was your opa!" Rita said excitedly, apparently unable to stand the suspense any longer.

Sonja laughed heartily. "Yes. The family had moved to Rhinelander by then and when Opa went to Milwaukee to deliver the commissioned pieces to his new, wealthy patron, he brought Ernst along. I wasn't there, of course, but I've been told the reunion of Paulina and Ernst was something to behold. There were some awkward and icy glares followed by finger-pointing accusations, an all-out yelling match, and eventual enlightenment once Ernst found out Paulina hadn't been ignoring his letters and Paulina learned Ernst had, indeed, been sending them. After that, the heat came from a different source—my parents always did have a rather fiery relationship—and the end result is me."

"That is one hell of a story, Sonja," I said. "Have you considered turning it into a book, novelizing it?"

She shrugged. "I'm more of an oralist than a writer," she said. "I prefer to use my artistic talents to create sculptures. Speaking of which . . ." She glanced at her watch. "I really should get back to work. I have a couple of commissioned pieces coming due."

"Of course," I said, and Rita and I both got up from the couch. Wally stayed put but my being on the move was Newt's cue to rise, as well, and when he did, he stretched and wagged his tail excitedly, sweeping my not-quite-empty coffee cup right off the table and onto the rug. The cup didn't break, thankfully, but the remains of my coffee left a dreadful-looking stain on the rug.

"Oh, dang it, I'm sorry," I said. "Have you got a rag or something I can use to sop that up?"

"No worries; I got it," Sonja said with a dismissive wave of her hand. She disappeared into the kitchen.

"What a great story about her parents, eh?" Rita said to me in a whispered aside.

"Quite the love story," I agreed.

"Maybe I should write it. I've always wanted to try writing a romance. Think I should ask her if it's okay for me to hijack her parents' lives? I would fictionalize it, of course."

I shrugged, amused by Rita's enthusiasm. She hadn't been this excited about anything since Jon Flanders first appeared in my store.

Sonja returned with a wad of paper towels and a spray bottle. I insisted on helping, and together we made quick work of the coffee spill. Despite Sonja's dismissal of my apologies, I think she was glad to show us to the back door once we were done.

"Thanks for your time," I told her as I tugged my boots on. "I appreciate it and I really am interested in having you create some items for my store. Would you consider a consignment arrangement?"

"Sure. I could do something in a month or so if you're willing to wait."

"Of course."

We traded contact info and when we were done, Sonja said, "Let me know if there's anything else I can do for you while you're in town."

Rita started to say something, but I nudged her with a subtle elbow to the ribs to stop her. "We certainly will," I said to Sonja. Then I took Rita by the arm and escorted her back to the car.

"Why didn't you let me ask her about the story?" Rita grumbled as I let Newt into the back seat.

"I think you should wait a bit, give it some time," I said. "Let's get this business with Andy sorted first."

Rita made a face but offered no further objection. I turned the car around to go back down the drive, once again coming face to face with the guardian Hodags at Sonja's front gate. I paused for a second or two, studying them, feeling an itch in my brain that refused to be realized. With a shrug, I took off down the driveway, and as we hit the part surrounded by woods, I caught movement off to the left. I slowed, thinking it might be a deer. Then I hit the brakes hard.

"What the heck?" Rita said.

I heard a whine behind me and glanced into the back seat to make sure Newt was okay before looking toward the woods again. My eyes played tricks on me as tree boughs swayed in the wind and sunlight filtered down from above, creating dancing shadows below.

"I saw something," I said, still staring into the trees. "Or rather, someone. Out there in the woods."

Rita looked in the general direction I was and then said, "Are you sure? I don't see anything."

Was I sure? Not one hundred percent. But if I was a betting girl, I'd put a decent stake on it. After giving it another half a minute, I took my foot off the brake and continued slowly down the driveway, glancing over at the trees every few seconds. No more moving shadows caught my eye and when I reached the end of the driveway, I stopped and looked at Rita.

"I swear I saw someone out there in the woods," I told her.

"Probably just kids," she said with a shrug.

This seemed unlikely given how isolated Sonja's property was. Not to mention it was a school day and these were school hours. I heard the sound of a car engine starting up off to my left and looked just in time to see a nondescript black sedan pull onto the road from the shoulder and take off at a rapid speed.

I turned and raised a skeptical eyebrow at Rita. "Still think it was just kids?"

CHAPTER 11

I t came on me fast and furious: a feeling like I couldn't breathe, my heart racing like a thoroughbred in the Kentucky Derby, a loud pounding in my ears, tiny lights circling in the periphery of my vision. I pulled the car over to the shoulder and shifted it into park.

"Morgan? Are you okay?" Rita said.

Newt sensed what was going on and whined behind me, his head hanging over the rear of my seat and pressing against my shoulder.

"No," I said. I opened my door and stumbled out, making my way to the front of the car, where I bent forward over the hood. The cold air against my face helped to ground me.

"Morgan, what can I do?" Rita had climbed out of the car after me, and she began rubbing a hand up and down my back. "Do you want me to drive you to a hospital?"

I shook my head. "It's a panic attack. Give me a minute. It will pass."

Newt was going nuts, whining in the back seat, eyeing me worriedly through the windshield.

"Try to slow your breathing," Rita said, still rubbing my back. "Breathe in as deep as you can and then hold each breath for a few seconds. Then blow it out nice and slow. Look through the windshield at Newt. Lock eyes with him. You're going to be okay."

I'd been hiding my panic attacks from Rita—from everyone, for that matter, though Jon had found out about them recently by accident—and her calming voice and soothing touch had the intended effect. My anxiety slowly loosened and ebbed, leaving me drained and enervated.

"How long?" Rita said.

I didn't need her to clarify. I knew what she was asking me. "Ever since my parents," I said, still leaning over the car, bracing myself with my hands on the hood.

"Why didn't you tell me?"

"I thought it would pass . . . go away over time. And I'm . . . I don't know. Embarrassed, I guess."

"Whatever for, child? Do you think you're the only person in the world to have anxiety attacks? I was a complete mess after George died. Thought I was having a heart attack practically every day. And his death was far less traumatic than your parents' deaths."

I nodded, debating. Should I tell her the rest? She deserved to know. "There's more," I said, just above a whisper.

"Tell me, but let's get back into the car first. It's freezing out here and Newt is having a conniption."

I nodded and straightened, then started toward the driver's side door.

Rita grabbed me by the arm and pulled me back. "Oh no, you don't. I'm driving," she said.

I didn't have the energy or the will to fight her on the matter. Besides, it was clearly the smart choice. My body was shaking like California during an eight-point quake.

Newt climbed halfway over the seat once I was back inside, nuzzling his neck and head against my shoulder. "I'm okay, Newt," I told him, stroking his big head. I kissed his muzzle. "Get into the back before you hurt yourself."

He dutifully retracted, albeit awkwardly, and sat in the back seat watching me closely. I looked over at Rita, who had turned sideways to face me, her expression patiently expectant.

"I got a letter," I said. "An anonymous one. Except I'm pretty sure I know who it's from."

"David?" she asked with a pained expression.

I nodded.

"What did it say?"

"That he's watching me."

Rita muttered something under her breath. I couldn't make out the exact words, but I don't think they were kind. She followed it up with, "He was probably making a vague threat, trying to spook you. I doubt he's really watching you."

"He asked if I found my Bigfoot."

Rita gasped and then tried to cover it up by coughing. I wasn't fooled.

"It had a postmark from Minneapolis," I added.

"Good Lord. Did you tell Jon?"

I shook my head.

"Why the hell not?"

"I don't want to worry him. Besides, what can he do? It's not like he's close by most of the time, and whatever David is up to, assuming it even is him, it's not likely to be within Jon's jurisdiction. I don't want him feeling pressured or guilty because he can't do anything."

"Of course it's David," Rita said irritably. "Who else could it be? You need to tell Jon. At least let him advise you. He might surprise you and have resources or contacts that could help."

"Let me think about it."

Rita sighed, turned to face front, and after staring out the windshield for a moment, she started the car. "You think the figure you saw in the woods at Sonja's place might have been David, don't you?" she said as she pulled back onto the road.

"The thought crossed my mind," I admitted.

"Hm. It does put a new wrinkle on things. I think you should go back home, Morgan. At least there you're on familiar ground. Jon might not be close by all the time, but he would be a hell of a lot closer than he is with you here."

I shook my head. "I'm not going to let David dictate my actions or my life. I promised you I would look into this thing with Andy and I'm going to see it through."

I saw a smile twitch at the corners of Rita's mouth. "That's the Morgan I know," she said. "Maybe we should put a plan together for what to do if David does show up. Though to be honest, I think cowardly, vague, long-distance threats are more his style. Still, it doesn't hurt to be prepared."

A *whuff* came from the back seat.

"Sounds like Newt agrees," Rita said.

I smiled but something inside me twisted uncomfortably, a cold, slithery sensation I recognized as my instincts warning me. For the most part, I agreed with Rita's assessment of David. He was more about the infliction of terror than any sort of real physical threat. It was all a mental game for him at this point. Wasn't it?

The rest of our ride was silent and when we got back to the motel, I told Rita I was going to take Newt for a walk. I needed to settle my nerves and my walks with Newt were always an excellent way to do that. By the time I returned, I was feeling better, at least until I saw Rita waiting for me outside my motel room door.

"I called Jon," she said, looking sheepish despite a defiant jut to her chin.

I gave her the stink eye. "Why?" It came out sounding whiny and that angered me.

"He needs to know what's going on with David."

She started to say more but I cut her off. "We don't even know for sure it is David, Rita. And it wasn't your news to share."

She wagged a finger in my face and leaned in toward me, the loose white hairs about her face catching the light of a wall sconce, making her look ethereal. "You aren't thinking straight, Morgan. It's not fair to keep this information from Jon for a number of reasons, but one in particular. If it is David—and let's face it, who else could it be—Jon could be in danger, too. David might see him as competition or a threat."

Shame washed over me because I knew she was right. I'd been so caught up in my own stubborn determination to prove I could manage things on my own, I hadn't bothered to consider the risk to Jon.

"You're right," I admitted. All my anger drained out of me, leaving me utterly deflated. "Damn it! Am I ever going to get that murderous creep out of my life?"

Rita didn't answer me, in part because she recognized the question as rhetorical, but also because my cell phone rang. When I looked to see who it was, Jon's name was on the screen. I showed Rita the phone. She said nothing and didn't look the least bit contrite.

"He's going to be mad at me," I said.

"He's entitled," she countered. "I don't think it will last long. Let him have his say and all will be well." She flashed a smug little smile that should have made me mad, but I couldn't muster up the angst. Then she turned and trotted off down the hall to her room.

I carded into my room and answered with a cheery, "Hey, Jon!" hoping I might set the tone of things, but I was rapidly disabused of that idea. Jon started in immediately, and I put him on speaker while I unleashed Newt, shrugged out of my coat, and then flopped down onto the bed to bear the full brunt of my forty lashes.

"Why didn't you tell me about this letter from David, Morgan? What the hell were you thinking? Why am I hearing about this from Rita? And don't try to tell me the note might not be from him. Of course it is. Who else could it be? The guy's a sociopath, or a psychopath. Probably both, and it's dangerous to just dismiss this like it's no big deal. You're smarter than this, Morgan. I know you are. You can't afford to be cavalier about it. If he's watching you, following you, we need to get you some protection. You can't be running around out there while he might be tracking your every move, waiting to make one of his own."

"Are you done?" I asked when he paused for a breath.

"Sorry, Morgan, but damn it, I worry about you. It's bad enough you go around poking your nose into murder cases. Now I find out your homicidal ex is stalking you. Why didn't you tell me about it?" This last question came out in a wounded, hurtful tone that made me feel instant shame.

"I really can't be sure it's him," I said. "The letter was anonymous. No return address. No name. Just a postmark from Minneapolis." It was a feeble attempt on my part to appease my guilt and Jon was having none of it.

"Come on, Morgan. Don't insult my intelligence. Or yours."

Busted.

"What can you do about it, Jon?" I asked. "It's not like it's happening there on Washington Island. We have no idea where David is. Besides, I don't think he wants to hurt me, not physically anyway. Inflict psychological torture? Perhaps. Probably. But I honestly don't think he'll kill me. If he'd wanted me dead, he would have killed me when he killed my parents. And he's had ample opportunities over the past two years to do me in."

"That's quite a leap, Morgan. You can't possibly know what he's thinking or what he wants. He targeted you as an easy mark, someone he could use to get his hands on some money." Jon's voice was tight, controlled, but I detected an undercurrent rumbling beneath his words.

"I don't doubt that getting his hands on my money was his original plan, but during the six months we spent together we grew close. I think David grew to genuinely care for me, and still does."

A pause, and then, "He's a con man, Morgan. Faking emotions is what he does best. You're being delusional if you think any of it was real."

The raw anger in his voice rang through loud and clear and it gave me pause. Jon had always been so mellow and even-tempered with me. This was a side of him I hadn't yet experienced, and I wasn't sure I liked it. But I also knew I'd purposely triggered him. Why?

"I need to go, Jon," I said, my tone intentionally cold. "I've got things to do but I promise I'll be careful and let you know if anything else happens."

Before he had a chance to object, I ended the call. I stared at the phone for a moment, half expecting him to either call me back or send a text. He did neither. It seemed we had reached a standoff. Newt sat a few feet away, staring at me, and even his expression seemed disapproving.

I needed a distraction and went over to the table and fired up my laptop. Devon had sent me an email letting me know he couldn't find any property owned by Brandon in the county, but a cruise through the man's social media accounts suggested he was living with a woman in Rhinelander by the name of Judith Ingles who worked in pharmaceutical sales. The woman owned a house, but it wasn't anywhere near the area where Brandon had died. Devon's email included the address, phone number, and email for this woman.

I started to look up what I could find on Judith Ingles, but the phone in my room rang before I finished typing out her name. My heart skipped a beat, thinking it might be Jon, but he would have called on my cell. I was about to ignore it, but then wondered if it might be David. I walked over and stared at the phone as it rang.

I'm not afraid of you.

I answered the call.

CHAPTER 12

Hello?"

"You're looking into the guy accused of murder who claims it was a Hodag that attacked some fisherman last week, right?"

The voice was shrill, anxious, and unfamiliar. Not David.

"Yes, I am."

"Be careful. Certain folks don't want anyone digging too deep into the case."

"Why is that?"

"Resistance. Look for the resistance."

"What resistance?" The call had gone dead. I muttered a curse and dropped the handset back into its cradle.

Newt raised his head, ears pricked at attention. Except it wasn't me he was reacting to. He was staring at the door to my room. A low growl emanated from his throat, rapidly segueing into a full-throated, menacing bark, and a second later, someone pounded on my door. It might have made me jump if Newt hadn't clued me in seconds before it happened. Still, my heart set to racing, wondering what surprises were in store for me next. I walked over to peek through the peephole and saw a group of people standing in the hallway.

I quieted Newt and opened the door, leaving the chain on even though I knew one hard kick or a couple of good shoves would have broken the thing loose.

"Yes?" I said to the man standing at the forefront of the group, which included one other man and three women, one of whom I recognized. It was Cordelia, from the chamber office.

"Are you the woman who's here to hunt for a Hodag?" the front man asked. He looked to be in his forties or fifties and had a full head of blond hair combed straight back from his forehead and held in place with some kind of pomade like a fifties matinee idol.

"That's her," Cordelia said accusingly. She pointed a finger at me, as if there were a crowd of people for her to choose from.

"What can I do for you folks?" I asked, ignoring the front man's question since Cordelia had already answered it.

"Might we come in?" the front man asked. "We'd like to speak to you."

I debated his request, then decided why not. I had Newt there to protect me and, despite Cordelia's obvious dislike of me, I didn't get a harmful vibe from these people.

"One moment." I shut the door and undid the chain lock. Then I opened the door and waved an arm toward the interior, inviting them in.

"I apologize for the unannounced visit," the front man said as he entered my room. He was tall and strode with purpose but stopped at the foot of the first bed when he heard Newt let out a low growl, causing the people behind him to nearly collide with his backside.

"It's okay, Newt," I said. Newt wagged his tail and that was all it took for the front man to dismiss him and shift his attention to me. I got the sense this guy was someone used to being in charge and getting his way.

"We thought it best to nip this in the bud as quickly as possible," the front man said.

"Nip what, exactly?" I asked. "And who is this *we* you're referring to?"

"We want to stop any rumors that a Hodag killed someone," he said, ignoring my second question. *Rude.* "Not just killed," he went on, "but torn apart from what I've heard. Rumors such as this can't be circulating around town. Not here in Rhinelander. I'm sure you understand." He flashed a toothy, obsequious smile. "You need to understand how tightly our commerce and industry is tied to the Hodag. A friendly, gentle Hodag."

I decided two could play the ignore game and I eyed the group. "I've had the pleasure of meeting Cordelia already," I said, making the woman scowl. "Who are the rest of you?"

"Oh, sorry. I'm Corey Michaels, the mayor here in town," said the front man. "And this is Jerry Cheever, the principal of our high school. You do know our school mascot is a Hodag, don't you?"

"So I've heard," I said.

Jerry Cheever, who I gauged to be in his late thirties or early forties, had his jacket unbuttoned, revealing athletic gear underneath. On his head was a thick knit cap with—no surprise—a Hodag on it. Tall with a broad, muscular build, he looked more like a gym teacher than a principal. Maybe he was both.

"This is Sherry Madkins and Daisy Almay," the mayor went on, pointing in turn to the two women standing on either side of Cordelia. Both women were blond, and Madkins, who looked to be in her late forties, maybe early fifties, was what Rita would have described as "sturdily built." Almay looked younger and was tall with an otherwise average build. "They own businesses here in town that are part of the lifeblood of our economic survival, and they, too, use the Hodag as a mascot in their advertising."

Mayor Michaels turned back to me and sighed. "No doubt you've heard about our annual music festival?"

"I have. You attract some big names."

"We do, and as a result the Hodag Country Festival brings thirty to fifty thousand people to our community every year." He jutted his chin out proudly. "Do you have any idea what sort of revenue a crowd of that size generates for our local businesses? I'm sure you understand why we simply can't risk damaging anything so important to our survival on some silly rumors about a man-killing Hodag."

"Even if you have one?" I countered.

Cordelia tutted and folded her arms over her chest, shaking her head. I stared at her until she rolled her eyes and looked away.

"Let me see if I understand you correctly, Mr. Mayor. You don't care if a member of your community might have been killed, disemboweled even, or that another member of your community may go to prison for a crime he didn't commit if it means even one tiny black mark on the reputation of a creature pretty much everyone knows isn't real?"

The mayor stared at me, blinking hard and fast, unsure how to answer my question.

"We just don't want to see this thing sensationalized," Jerry Cheever said.

"You want to sweep it under the rug," I said.

"No, that's not what he said," Sherry Madkins said in a patently false tone of friendliness. "Perhaps you could keep your findings to yourself, or share them only with us and let us decide what is newsworthy."

"What sort of business do you own, Ms. Madkins?"

"My husband and I offer fishing charters on water and on ice. We operate year-round and also do guided hunting expeditions at certain times of the year."

I shifted my gaze to Daisy Almay. "And your business is?"

"I sell real estate and handle vacation rentals."

"I see," I said, running my gaze over the group before once again zeroing in on Daisy. "Do you think Hodags exist?"

Daisy hesitated, fiddling with a button on her coat and shooting wary glances at her companions before answering me. "I think they are a significant part of our history and culture and, as such, very much a part of our current times in some form or another."

I had to give her credit. It was a well-crafted nonanswer. "How about you?" I said, looking at Sherry Madkins.

"Same."

Coward.

I briefly looked at Cordelia. I had little doubt as to what she believed and felt certain she was behind this impromptu visit, which made me feel a teensy bit mean-spirited toward her. I thought she'd be angry if I left her out of things, so I let my gaze quickly slide past her and toward Jerry. I was rewarded with an irritated *humph* from Cordelia, a petty victory perhaps, but sometimes you have to take them where you can.

"How about you, Mr. Cheever?" I asked. "Do you think the Hodag is real?"

"Clearly the Hodag is an important part of our heritage, our current identities, and our culture. As such, it very much exists, even if only as an imagined part of the fabric comprising our whole."

Said like an educator and I wondered if he'd ever taught philosophy. Did they even teach philosophy in high school these days? I moved on to the man in charge. "How about you, Mr. Mayor? What are your beliefs regarding the existence of Hodags?"

"They are an integral part of our identity here in Rhinelander and, as such, whether or not such a creature exists is irrelevant."

Said like a politician and likely member of his high school debate team.

"Okay," I said. "While I commend all of you on your dedication and devotion to a creature whose existence reportedly rose out of a massive fraud perpetrated by a man determined to bilk innocent, gullible people out of their hard-earned money—"

"Gene Shepard was merely a prankster!" Cordelia objected.

I ignored her outburst and continued. "And given how the folklore surrounding the Hodag describes it as fearsome and a carnivore and a creature born out of the ashes of cremated oxen that had been abused by their masters, I'd say it already has a few black marks associated with it. Yet clearly those attributes haven't hurt things for all of you. Why would the idea of a rogue killer Hodag be any different?"

They all stared blankly at me for an uncomfortable amount of time, and then Mayor Michaels said, "We prefer to promote a kindly, friendly image of our Hodag. Fierce but not ferocious and definitely not that of a menacing, murderous monster."

While I had to give the mayor props for his alliterative abilities, clearly he and the others had a blind spot when it came to admitting they might have a killer animal roaming the woods around town. They wanted a Hodag that was more like Barney, the beloved purple dinosaur, not one that was an efficient killing machine.

I walked over, opened the door to my room, and once again waved an arm, this time toward the hallway. "While I do appreciate you dropping by, I need to get back to work. Thanks so much for the kind welcome to your lovely town."

They stood there staring at me for a few seconds and then, without another word, they filed out the door and into the hallway. It was kind of creepy how coordinated they were, like they shared some kind of hive mind. I closed the door hard behind them, set all the locks, and then watched through the peephole to make sure they were leaving. Once they disappeared down the hall, I quietly undid my locks, opened my door, and peered out into the hallway in time to see them leave out the side exit, the same exit and entrance I'd been using.

As soon as they were outside, I told Newt to stay and scooted down the hall to peek out the door's windowed top half. There they were, huddled in the parking lot, heads bowed together, talking and gesturing. Snow had begun to fall, and it drifted down in fat, lazy flakes, spotting the backs of their conniving heads. I felt certain I hadn't heard the last from this not-so-welcome wagon. Had I just encountered the resistance my mysterious caller had warned me about, a group of overly exuberant Hodag protectors determined to preserve the creature's reputation no matter what?

I waited until they all climbed into a van bearing a logo of—surprise!—a Hodag and watched as they drove away.

What was going on here? Was the town engaged in some kind of cover-up? What the hell had Rita gotten me into?

CHAPTER 13

Rita called a little before six to ask if I wanted to go out to dinner with her and Roger. I was relieved to hear Roger would be joining us as I'd been worried about him ever since we'd parted company earlier in the day. I was having trouble focusing my thoughts on my research at that point, so I was more than happy to put it aside and accept Rita's invitation. Besides, there was always the fun possibility that more folks from the town resistance squad might confront me while I was out in public.

Rita opted to ride with me and Newt, and we followed Roger to the Hardwick restaurant, a family-owned place serving old-fashioned home-cooked meals like fried chicken, pork chops, and meat loaf with sides of macaroni and cheese, coleslaw, and mashed potatoes. The building housing the restaurant was your basic rectangle with a covered portico across the front and parking on either side. The entrance was in the center of the porch and to the right of it stood a three-foot-high sculpture of a grinning blue Hodag atop a log. It truly was impossible to escape the things; they were everywhere.

The highlight for me came before the meal itself: thick slices of warm, homemade sourdough and rye breads served with two different whipped butters, one with herbs and garlic, the other plain. I ate so much of the bread, I had little room left over for my chicken. Nothing went to waste, however, as I cleaned the meat off the bones and stuffed it into a napkin as a treat for Newt later.

Roger remained somber throughout the meal, and I got a sense his earlier enthusiasm for the hunt had waned. Just as well, I thought, and wondered if the not-so-welcome wagon had also paid him a visit. As a local businessman himself, the pressure on him would have been even greater. Maybe he was simply starting to realize the odds and the facts—at least so far—were heavily stacked against Andy. Curious, I told them about my visit with the mayor and his gang of sidekicks.

"The people here seem overly worried about what I might find," I concluded. "Plus, I'm not sure I buy into the idea of my investigation affecting local businesses much. Heck, if I could find an actual, living Hodag, I would think the townsfolk would be delighted. It would be a gold mine for their tourist trade, even if I prove it killed someone. There are plenty of people out there who would be drawn to something like that."

Roger looked at me disapprovingly and said, "It sounds like you've already made up your mind. And before you dismiss the concerns of the local business owners as hyperbole, keep in mind this story hasn't spread much beyond the local area. What happens if it goes national? Mayor Michaels is right. The Hodag festival is a huge source of income for many of these folks and anything posing a threat to it won't go over well."

"I haven't made up my mind yet, Roger," I assured him. "But you have to admit, things do look rather grim for Andy. I'm not sure finding proof of the existence of a Hodag would even help him much unless I can also prove the creature was responsible for killing Brandon. With every day that goes by, the likelihood of that happening grows slimmer."

Rita shot me a look of betrayal. "Morgan, Andy didn't kill Brandon. I'd stake my life on it. I know the boy."

Rita was like a stuck record on this topic. "He's not a boy anymore, Rita; he's a man who had a contentious and violent history with Brandon. You need to consider you might not know him as well as you think you do."

Apparently, I burned my last bridge with Rita with this comment because she dropped her fork onto her plate with a clatter and then slapped her napkin down on top of it.

"Roger, would you be so kind as to drive me back to the motel?" she said.

"Of course." Roger reached into his pocket, took out his wallet, and tossed a pile of cash into the middle of the table. "That should be enough to cover my meal and Rita's plus provide for a generous tip," he said. Then he and Rita both got up, put on their coats, and left without another word.

Talk about a not-so-subtle snub. Their rude dismissal left me feeling irritated, and I sat for another ten minutes or so to finish my coffee and chew over the evening's events. Once again I cursed my stupidity in accepting this case. My relationship with Rita was on the line and I was walking a tightrope of possibilities and truth.

When I was done, I added enough cash to cover my part of the meal, gathered up my napkin of chicken, and headed for the parking lot. The snowfall that had started earlier was much heavier now. I saw a big empty field out behind the restaurant and, knowing how much Newt loved the snow, I leashed him up and took him back there. The field ran at a gentle downhill slope, and I let Newt off his leash a few feet into it and watched, smiling, as he took off running, slipping, and sliding in the inch or so of new snow topping what was already on the ground. I hadn't felt that cold when I first left the restaurant, but a bitter wind blew unobstructed up through the field, and it occurred to me, belatedly, to use the remote-start feature for my car so it would be warm by the time Newt was done with his romp.

I'd parked in one of the two side lots for the restaurant, and I could see the back end of my car from where I stood. I pulled off a glove and tucked it under my arm so I could more easily fish my fob out of my coat pocket. Then I raised my arm, aimed the fob, and hit the appropriate button twice. It took a couple of tries and some re-positioning of my aim, but I finally saw my rear lights flash and a plume of exhaust rise in the air. I'd slipped the fob back into my pocket and started to turn back to Newt when a hint of movement by the other rear corner of the building caught my eye. A shadowy shape stood there, backlit by dregs of light from the restaurant windows. I blinked and the figure disappeared. It startled me so much I took a step backward and lost my footing. I windmilled my arms to try to remain standing and just managed to regain my balance.

My heart pounded in my chest and tiny lights began to float around the periphery of my vision. I told myself the figure was probably nothing, just another customer checking out the backside of the building.

I hollered for Newt, wanting, needing the protection of him at my side. He was there in an instant, nudging my free hand with his snowy nose. I kept my eyes on the far corner of the building, watching, waiting, and cursing David Johnson. This was all his fault.

My whole body began to quake, tiny temblors in my limbs and torso. I thought I might end up losing my dinner but managed to keep it down. I didn't bother to leash Newt again; I simply told him to stay with me, took off my remaining glove, and shoved it into my pocket. Then I kept one hand down at my side so Newt could touch my fingers with his nose every other step. My heart pounded so hard I saw a tiny flashing light in the corner of my eye with each beat.

When I reached the car, I unlocked the back door and had Newt jump in. Then I quickly climbed into the front driver's seat and locked all the doors. I jabbed at the start button to get the car out of remote mode and then carefully backed out, scanning the parking lot, what I could see of the empty field, and the outside perimeter of the restaurant. As I drove toward the front of the restaurant, I glanced in my rearview mirror and again saw a shadowy figure by the back corner. And once again, before I could make out any details, whoever it was slipped behind the building and out of sight. I began doubting myself. Had I imagined it? Had my overstimulated, overwrought imagination manufactured a mysterious figure out of normal light and shadow? I considered driving around the entire perimeter of the restaurant to look for my watcher but opted to get the hell out of Dodge instead.

Unable to shake my paranoia, I drove aimlessly for several minutes, circling around a series of blocks, checking my rearview mirror for headlights. If anyone was following me, I couldn't tell. I finally drove back to the motel and was lucky enough to secure a parking spot close to the side back door. I didn't see anyone lurking in the trees or anywhere else, so I shut the car down, let Newt out, and hurried to let myself into the building.

My room was the fourth one from the entrance, just past an intersecting hallway that led to the front of the motel. I was still shaking and when I went to stick my card in the slot, I dropped it instead. Cursing, I picked it up and managed to slide it home on the second try. I pushed down the handle to open the door just as a hand clamped down on my shoulder.

CHAPTER 14

I bit back a scream and whirled around to confront my accoster. The only reason the scream wasn't realized was because some rational part of my mind registered the lack of reaction from Newt. When I saw who was standing behind me, I understood why.

"Jon!" I said, both shocked and pleasantly surprised. "What the hell are you doing here?"

"I think you know."

"I hope this isn't because of the anonymous letter," I said, mentally cursing myself for uttering something so stupid. The answer was blatantly obvious.

"Of course, it is, Morgan." The look he gave me was part irritation, part impatience, part concern. "I can't believe you didn't tell me about it," he went on, now managing to look hurt, as well. "David could be here in Rhinelander watching you and waiting for an opportunity to ... to ..." He let out an exasperated sigh and ran a palm down the back of his head.

"I think maybe he is here," I said quietly.

Jon was instantly at attention. "What? Why? Have you seen him?"

"I've seen someone," I said, giving him a meek smile. I sighed, carded the lock on my door again, and pushed it open. "You might as well come in," I said, stepping in myself and holding the door wide as Newt pushed past me.

Jon followed, saying, "Tell me."

"There's someone, a figure always conveniently obscured by trees, shadows, darkness...." I shrugged. "I can't say for sure who it is." I looked away from him then, embarrassed by what I had to say next. "I'm not even sure what I've seen is real." I shrugged out of my coat, tossing it on the far bed.

Jon plopped down onto the closest bed and patted the space next to him. I took it and stared at the floor.

"The panic attacks?" Jon said softly.

I nodded.

"Are they getting worse? More frequent?"

"I don't know. Maybe. It's hard for me to tell the difference between a panic attack and my reaction to legitimate threats."

"Have you been outwardly threatened by someone here?"

I shook my head, unable to get even the simple syllable of "no" past the sudden stranglehold on my throat. Tears burned behind my eyes, and I struggled to hold them back, determined not to break down despite a powerful urge to do so. Something inside me wanted to let it all out, to sob, to swear, to stomp my feet, punch my fists, maybe even throw something. But I held it in, feeling the emotions expand inside me like air pumped into a balloon, unable to escape past the narrowing constriction in my throat. When would I explode from the pressure?

Jon draped an arm over my shoulders, and at the same time, Newt put his head on my thigh. Out of habit, my hand came up and stroked my dog's big furry head and, as always, it had an instant calming effect. Some of the air eased out of my balloon.

Jon said, "I rearranged some things back home, called in a couple of favors, and freed up my schedule for a day or so. I'm sorry if I scared you out there in the hall. I just got here and checked with the desk to see what room you were in. I was coming down an intersecting hallway when I saw you and Newt cross by up ahead."

"You should have hollered."

"I didn't want to disturb any other guests," he said with a shrug.

I leaned into him. It must have surprised him because he stiffened for a second before relaxing and pulling me close. He wrapped his other arm around me. It felt good, safe and secure, and yet alarm bells clanged in my brain. Giving in too easily was what had given David his edge with me. I didn't want to make the same mistake again. I shrugged my way loose but stayed seated beside him.

Jon sighed and stood. "I need to go up to the front desk and get a room."

"You can stay with me," I blurted out, readily throwing the caution I'd clung to seconds ago to the proverbial wind. Worried he might misinterpret my invitation, I hastily added, "I have two beds. No reason you can't have one of them."

Jon looked at me long and hard for an uncomfortable amount of time. Then he turned away and said, "I'm going to get my own room. I'll be back as soon as I'm checked in."

He left, leaving me to ponder what had just happened. Had I scared him off with my invitation? Had I insulted him? Were his feelings toward me cooling? Was I moving too fast? Or too slow? It was all so overwhelming, and I shook my head like I was shaking dice in preparation for rolling them out, hoping for a different result.

In the end, Jon was able to get the room next to mine, one with an adjoining door. Seconds after we opened the shared door, a sheepish-looking Rita came knocking.

"Are you mad at me?" she asked. "I really thought Jon needed to know."

"I probably should be," I told her. "But no. I understand why you called him. Are you still mad at me?"

She looked at me like I was crazy. "I never was."

I raised a skeptical eyebrow.

"Okay, maybe I was a tiny bit annoyed," she conceded, holding her thumb and forefinger up so they were just shy of touching. She strode into the room and headed for the table in the corner, nodding approvingly when she saw the partially opened door to Jon's room. "I'm sorry if I seem too biased about all of this," she said, dropping into a chair and palming back a few errant white hairs floating about her face. "It's just that I know Andy, both the boy and the man. I believe in my heart, my gut, and my brain he's innocent."

"I get it," I said, annoyed. How could I not? Rita had been beating that particular mantra into my brain from minute one. She and Roger both. They were as unwilling to face possible painful truths as those yahoos from the town who had visited me. "We'll keep putting our collective heads together and somehow we'll get to the bottom of this," I said. "Maybe with Jon here, we can get more information out of the police regarding the evidence they've collected."

As if on cue, Jon entered through the adjoining door, raising his eyebrows at Rita.

"It's fine," she said with a dismissive wave. "She's not mad. I told you she wouldn't be."

"Well, just for the record, *I'm* a little mad," Jon said, giving me a scolding look. "You're far too eager to try to do everything by yourself, Morgan. Utilize those of us who are here to help you. You shouldn't be going anywhere alone until we figure this out. Have someone with you at all times."

I tried to look properly reprimanded while wondering if Newt counted as someone, but knew I hadn't quite pulled it off.

"I'm serious, Morgan," Jon insisted.

"I know, I know. I promise to be more careful." This wasn't quite what he'd stipulated but I thought it a good compromise, particularly since he didn't seem to realize I was parsing words. Rita wasn't fooled, however. I saw her start to say something and jumped in to quickly forestall her. "It's been quite an eventful trip," I said to Jon. "Let me summarize what I know so far for you."

We spent the next hour discussing my visit to Andy at the jail, our trek into the woods where Brandon had been killed, my glimpse of something across the river, and the visit to Sonja with her videos of the Hodag sighters. When I mentioned the figure in the woods outside Sonja's house, Jon stopped me.

"Was it David?" he asked.

"I don't know," I said, feeling tired and sounding whiny. "I never saw him clearly."

"Are you sure there was someone there? Maybe the trees and the light played tricks on you."

"I wondered that myself at first but then we saw a car pull out from the shoulder of the road in front of those same woods and take off at a fast clip."

"I don't suppose you got a plate number?" Jon said.

I didn't answer him. I just gave him a look.

"Right," he said with a sigh.

"How are we going to find David, assuming it even is him?" Rita asked.

"I have some ideas," Jon said. He looked at me. "Do you have the letter with you?"

I nodded and dug it out of my computer bag. He studied the envelope for a few seconds, then delicately removed the folded letter and flattened it out on the corner table. He laid the envelope next to it and took a picture of both with his phone. "I can take these back with me and have them checked for prints," he said when he was done.

"You won't find any other than mine," I told him. "Even after David lived with me for a time, the police couldn't find any of his prints in the house we shared. He was meticulous when it came to ensuring he left no trace behind, always wiping things down and wearing gloves."

Jon said, "That very meticulousness makes me think his prints would tell us something. I'll bet he's in the system."

"Go ahead and try to get prints," I said with a shrug. "But my money's on them not being there."

Jon nodded, carefully refolded the letter, and slid it back inside the envelope. "This isn't the only angle I'm working on," he said.

"I've had Devon and one of my officers back home digging around, trying to track David's movements going all the way back to the incident with your parents. I even managed to talk Uncle Karl into helping."

Since Jon's uncle Karl happened to be Karl Swenson, the New Jersey detective who had been convinced that I'd killed my parents, and might still be, for all I knew, his involvement on any level wasn't something I welcomed. My facial expression must have conveyed this because Jon quickly added, "Uncle Karl has a lead already."

This surprised me. "Really? I didn't think he was looking at anyone other than me."

Jon gave me a look of patient tolerance. "Surely you can understand why he considered you as a suspect. You had opportunity and millions of dollars' worth of motive."

"Yeah, never mind about actual evidence, right? What about the fact that David disappeared right after the murders, after my father confronted him and told him he was going to expose him as the charlatan he was?"

"There's no proof the confrontation happened, Morgan. Just your word."

"And clearly my word isn't nearly enough. Your uncle Karl ignored the facts because he was so convinced I was the culprit. He wasted valuable time trying to make the evidence fit me, giving David more time to disappear. And now, here we are." I heard my voice rising, the desperation, exasperation, and fear I'd felt back then returning in a heartbeat. I sucked in a deep breath and blew it out slowly, forcing myself to calm.

"Hey, I'm on your side, Morgan," Jon said. "We've talked about this before. David was a ghost both before and after the murders of your parents. It was impossible to prove he'd ever existed. Anyone would have looked at you first under those circumstances. Uncle Karl has come around and he's open to the idea of David, or whoever he really is, as the killer."

"He's open to it? Wow, that's big of him."

Another look from Jon, like I was a petulant child he had to deal with. Maybe I was.

"Why the change of heart?" I asked. "What's different now from two years ago?"

"Similar cases but this time the swindles were successful. The women's descriptions all fit the one you, Rita, and Devon gave of David, and like in your case, the culprit claimed he had OCD and Raynaud's and wiped everything he touched and wore gloves all the time. He left behind no trace of his existence. The names and identities he's used are different, but the basic physical descriptions and the MO are all the same."

"Do they know where he is?" I asked.

"They did, as of two months ago," Jon said. "A wealthy heiress up in Ontario filed a complaint with the Canadian police about a man she met and dated for several weeks who managed to gain access to one of her investment accounts and then disappeared after wiping it out."

"Wait," I said, feeling my ire rise. "You had all these leads on David, and you didn't think to tell me?"

"How much did he get?" Rita asked quickly. No doubt she was hoping to distract me. Her question didn't, but Jon's answer did.

"Nearly half a million, and that's after he took another woman for nearly twice that," he said.

Rita let out a low whistle.

"Damn," I muttered. "With that kind of funding, he'll have had all kinds of freedom to travel about and stalk me. He's not using the David Johnson ID anymore?"

Jon shook his head. "No, that identity was flagged right after the murder of your parents. He used the names and identities of two other dead men with these last two women he scammed, going by Mark Talbot with one and James Wright with the other. We think he might be using the name of a live person now, a man named Adrian Dunlevy, which is a change in his MO. The real Adrian Dunlevy discovered someone had been going around using his name although so far there's no indication of any funny business with his financial accounts."

"What does the real Adrian Dunlevy do?" Rita asked.

"He's a high-priced lawyer out of Chicago," Jon said.

"What makes you think the Adrian impersonator is David?" Rita asked.

"A woman who had been approached by him said the man had an odd habit of wearing gloves both times they were together. He said it was because he has Raynaud's."

"Are they watching this woman?" I asked. "Maybe they can catch him next time he approaches her."

Jon shook his head, making a face. "Unfortunately, she confronted him about his odd behavior and she's certain she scared him off."

"Damn," Rita muttered.

"How does he manage to steal these identities so easily?" I asked.

"It's not as hard as you might think," Jon said. "Aside from Dunlevy, all the names he's used have been those of deceased men. It makes me think the use of Adrian Dunlevy's identity is about something else. If we can figure out what that is, it might lead us to him."

The idea of finding David both excited and frightened me. "Wouldn't it be more helpful to figure out his real identity?"

Jon scoffed. "I've been trying to determine that ever since I met you, Morgan. Every time I think I'm onto something, I hit a dead end. I think he's been using false names and identities most of his life. The man is a chameleon. He knows what he's doing."

"Of course, he does," I said with a frustrated sigh. "You should have told me about all of this before now, Jon."

"And you should have told me about the letter."

Point taken. "There's something else I should mention." I was about to tell him about the mysterious phone call I'd received warning me to watch out for the resistance when someone started pounding on the door to my room.

"Rhinelander police! Open up."

CHAPTER 15

⌐⟶

All three of us froze and exchanged worried looks, our eyes the only things moving at first. Then a second pounding came—not a friendly knock.

I went to the door and opened it. On the other side stood a man in a parka holding out a badge.

"I'm looking for a Morgan Carter?" he said.

"That would be me. What can I do for you?"

"May I come in?" he asked, and then he did so without waiting for my answer.

I shot Jon a look, but he ignored me and instead said, "What's this about?"

Our uninvited guest returned the favor by ignoring Jon and settling his gaze on me. "Yep, you fit the description."

Description? That sent a chill through me. Shades of New

Jersey and Detective Uncle Karl all over again. "And you are?" I let the question hang there after asking it with just enough tone to let him know I found him rude. It made me sound braver and more in control than I felt.

"I'm Detective Hoffman with the Rhinelander Police Department." He put his badge into his coat pocket and took out a cell phone. After a couple of swipes at the screen, he held the device out. On it was a picture of a glove, a hot-pink glove trimmed in faux fur. Except parts of the glove weren't pink anymore. They were a rusty brown color that made my stomach clench.

"Do you recognize this glove?" Hoffman asked.

"Maybe," I said. I mean, there could have been lots of other hot-pink, faux-fur-trimmed gloves in the area, right? I went over to the bed where I'd dropped my coat and fished around in the pockets. When I felt the first glove, a wave of relief washed over me, but when I couldn't find the second one, my relief swiftly turned to fear.

"It would seem you found my missing glove," I said, showing him the one I had. A tiny warning voice in my head told me something was off here. Why wasn't he showing me my actual glove instead of a picture? I waited, hoping he might produce said glove like a magician pulling a rabbit out of his hat.

"You ate dinner at the Hardwick restaurant tonight, Ms. Carter?" Hoffman said.

"I did. I ate with my friend Rita here"—I gestured toward her—"and her brother-in-law, Roger Bosworth. He's a lawyer here in town. Perhaps you know him?"

I don't know why I felt compelled to mention Roger was a lawyer. Surely in a town this small, the two men would know each other at least by reputation, though with Roger being a defense attorney, there might be no love lost between them. Still, dropping Roger's name might set Detective Hoffman back a step or two. Instead, it plopped me smack in the middle of a pool of quicksand.

"Did you have occasion to walk in the field behind the restaurant tonight?" Hoffman asked.

"I did. I'd left my dog in my car while we ate, so I let him out for a potty break and a bit of exercise once we were done. Why? Has someone complained about us being in the field?"

Detective Hoffman ignored my question just like he'd ignored Jon's moments before. Instead, he asked a few more of his own.

"You said you ate dinner with Roger Bosworth?"

"Yes."

"Did he leave the restaurant with you?"

"No, he and Rita left before I did. I stayed a bit longer to finish my coffee." I didn't mention the disagreement behind our parting ways.

Hoffman narrowed his eyes, tilted his head, and said, "Rita . . . ?" He gave me an expectant look.

"Bosworth," Rita said, waving a hand at him from the table. Hoffman shifted his attention and I sagged with relief as soon as his piercing gaze left me. It was as if his eyes had somehow held me upright and imprisoned. "That's me," Rita said. "I mean, I'm her. Rita Bosworth. I'm Roger's sister-in-law. By marriage."

Rita was obviously nervous. My mind whirled with discombobulated thoughts as I tried to figure out what was going on. Why was this detective here? I felt certain it wasn't to return my missing glove. And how had anyone found it and connected it to me anyway?

A voice in my head answered this question as a sense of dread washed over me.

They would have found it because they were out in the field for another reason . . . an official police reason.

Jon stepped in between me and the detective, his badge in hand. "Perhaps we could discuss this out in the hall?" he said.

Hoffman gave the badge a cursory once-over. "You're Chief Jon Flanders?" he said wearily, his bluster suddenly lessened. Jon nodded. "Zeke Walters had a lot of nice things to say about you, Chief Flanders, and I value his opinion. He's a good cop."

"Yes, he is," Jon agreed.

"You're outside your jurisdiction," Hoffman said. Jon simply nodded. Hoffman stood silent for a moment, eyeing all three of us before settling his focus on Rita. "Let me cover some basics. You and Mr. Bosworth left the restaurant together?" he said, apparently ignoring Jon's invitation to chat in the hallway.

"We did. I asked Roger to drive me back here to the motel. He dropped me off out front."

"And was that the last time you saw Mr. Bosworth?"

Rita paled a bit. "It was."

"Had Mr. Bosworth driven you to the restaurant?"

"No, I rode there with Morgan."

"Why didn't you come back with her?"

Rita glanced nervously at me, and I decided to let her off the hook.

"We had a bit of a disagreement over dinner," I admitted.

"About what?"

"About the investigation into her nephew's case," I said irritably. This Hoffman fellow was plucking my nerves. "I know you're familiar with it."

A hint of a smile curled Hoffman's lips. It didn't look particularly friendly and when he didn't respond, I went on.

"And I'm fairly sure you know who I am and why I'm here. So why don't we just cut to the chase, and you tell us what it is you're after."

Hoffman sighed and turned to Jon. "Tell you what. I'm willing to extend a degree of professional courtesy here but with limits. I need to take both of these ladies down to the station so we can chat with them."

"I'd like to be a part of that," Jon said.

Hoffman's lips rolled inward, and I sensed a no coming. But to his credit, he met us—or at least Jon—halfway. "You can observe, but only from outside the room. I'll let you drive them to the station if you want."

He'll *let* him? My irritation flashed into anger. "And what if I don't want to be questioned or talked to by you?" I spat out. "What right do you have to barge in here and . . ."

Newt, sensing my rising ire, nudged my thigh and pushed his muzzle into my hand. At the same time, Jon said, "Can you tell us more of what this is about?"

Hoffman appeared to consider this. Then, with a shrug and a what-the-hell sigh, he said, "We found Ms. Carter's glove next to a dead body."

Whoa, that was a sucker punch to the gut. A dead body? Where? And who was it? This last question sprang to the top of my list, though I had a sudden horrifying inkling of what the answer was going to be based on Hoffman's earlier questions. My dinner churned sickeningly in my gut, and for a moment, I feared I'd have to shove

Hoffman out of the way so I could get to the bathroom. Hopefully he wouldn't shoot me if I did.

"Who?" I managed to ask. It came out breathless, barely above a whisper. The walls of the room began closing in on me. Even Jon was momentarily stunned into silence.

"Oh my God, it's Roger, isn't it?" Rita said. Her complexion had gone as white as her hair. She looked like a ghost.

Hoffman didn't answer but the consternation on his face said a lot. "We have a male person who is deceased. We have not made a definitive identification as of yet."

Rita took out her cell phone and tapped at the device. Seconds later we heard a ring on the other end. I saw Jon and Hoffman exchange looks I couldn't quite interpret. Or maybe I just didn't want to. Denial comes easy at times. After several rings we heard Roger's voice mail message. Rita ended the call and stared at me with tears blossoming in her eyes.

"You need us to identify the body?" I asked.

"No," Hoffman said without hesitation.

"You don't think—" I started, but Jon cut me off.

"Morgan, I don't think you should be saying anything more."

Rita buried her face in her hands, and I heard her sob.

"We found your glove in the field behind the restaurant," Hoffman said. "That's also where we found the victim. And we have witnesses who can place you at the restaurant, though you've just admitted you were there, so that's a moot point. We also have witnesses who saw you wearing those gloves. But again, you've said as much already."

I was willing to bet the glove witness was Cordelia. She'd not only commented on but coveted my gloves when I was in the chamber office. And they were distinctive. Damn! Jon was right to shut me up. I'd said too much already.

"Roger is dead?" Rita said through her hands, her tone one of disbelief. The words were barely audible, and she was rocking back and forth in her seat. "No," she said feebly, shaking her head. "It can't be."

"Again, we don't have a positive ID yet," Hoffman cautioned.

His comment brought to mind a couple of new, and potentially horrifying, questions. Why was it they didn't know who the victim was? If it was a matter of visual ID, why wouldn't they want Rita to do it? Was the victim disfigured?

"What about security cameras?" Jon asked. I was impressed with the level of control in his voice because his face had been growing redder by the minute, and I could tell he wanted to get all up in Hoffman's business.

Hoffman sighed and shook his head. "There aren't any that cover the field," he said. "There's one behind the restaurant but it's there mostly to monitor the back entrance. It's aimed toward the ground and there's a small shed on one side of it and a trailer parked on the other side, limiting the view. Its range cuts out long before the field. There's also a camera at the front entrance to the building but the side parking areas aren't covered. We'll be reviewing the footage, but all it's likely to show is who came and went from the restaurant." Hoffman shot an impatient glance at his watch. "Time's a ticking," he said.

"You can go," Jon said to Hoffman. "I'll drive them to your station, and I promise we'll be there within the hour."

"Make it half an hour," Hoffman said, and then he turned to leave.

"What about Newt?" I asked. My dog's ears perked up at the mention of his name. Hoffman looked back at me, puzzled. "My dog," I explained. "I can't leave him here in the motel room. He has anxiety issues."

Hoffman rolled his eyes.

"Morgan meant to say *she* has anxiety issues," Jon said quickly. "Newt is her service dog."

It didn't take me more than a nanosecond to see what Jon was doing and I could have kissed him for it. Instead, I looked confused and said, "What did I say?"

"You said *he* has anxiety issues," Jon said.

I clapped a hand to my chest and jumped into my role, a little too eagerly as it turned out. "I must be more upset than I realized," I muttered. "Jon is right, Detective. I get panic attacks, bad ones. I have severe PTSD because of what happened to my parents."

Belatedly, I saw Jon wince and look away, subtly shaking his head. I realized I'd said too much and had likely just made my situation worse, but I couldn't take the words back. Maybe Hoffman won't notice, I thought. But the detective's next words dashed that hope.

"Why? What happened to your parents?" he asked.

CHAPTER 16

I don't suppose there's a chance Hoffman won't dig into my background?" I asked from the back seat as Jon drove us to the Rhinelander police station.

The question was largely rhetorical, confirmed when Jon didn't answer. He just stared at me in the rearview mirror. Next to him, Rita sat quietly. Too quietly for my taste.

I'd managed to partially deflect when Hoffman asked me what had happened to my parents by saying they had died in a horrific accident. The horrific part was true enough. If Hoffman learned the New Jersey police thought I might have slit open my own parents' throats, it wouldn't take much of a leap for him to believe I'd killed someone else.

Was it Roger? And if so, why? And when? He and Rita had left the restaurant several minutes before me. I'd watched from a restaurant window as he drove away. He had to have been on the road when I walked Newt in that field, meaning he had come back at some point. I remembered the shadowy figure I'd seen lurking by the back corner of the restaurant. Had he or she been the killer? Had it been David? The thought sent a shiver down my spine, making Newt, who sat on the seat next to me, nuzzle my neck.

"It's unfortunate you mentioned your parents," Jon said. "Maybe Hoffman won't look into it."

Yeah, and maybe pigs will fly.

"I'm certainly not going to offer up any information on the topic, though if Hoffman is any good at his job, he's bound to run a background check on you," Jon added. "I'm sure Rita won't mention it either."

Rita didn't respond. I leaned forward and put a hand on her shoulder, giving it a little squeeze. "Are you okay?"

She reached up and patted my hand. "I'll be fine. Don't worry about me."

Classic Rita. All tough on the outside, though I had my doubts about what might be happening on the inside. I knew she was being strong for me, or at least putting on a front to let me think she was okay, but I also knew the possibility of Roger's death had to be shaking her to her core. She'd tried several more times after Hoffman's departure to call Roger, with each attempt ending in voice mail. I thought I should try to get her to focus, to stop her mind from wandering, but before I could figure out how, Jon did it for me.

"Rita, what happened when you and Roger left the restaurant earlier tonight? Tell me step by step. What you talked about. What you did."

"There isn't much to tell. We left the restaurant and got into

Roger's car. He didn't say anything on the way out and I could tell he was upset. We both were. Once he got the car started, I asked him if he was okay. He said he was, but then he added that he didn't like the way things were going with Andy's case. He questioned whether Morgan could be fair and objective about things and I assured him she could."

Rita glanced back at me and smiled. "I was right, wasn't I?"

"Of course."

"That was pretty much it," Rita went on. "There wasn't any more discussion until we reached the motel. Roger pulled up under the front portico to drop me off. I think I said something to try to reassure him, but he seemed . . . I don't know . . . distracted."

She slumped in her seat for a few seconds but then said, "Oh!" and straightened up. "There *was* something. He got a call just as we arrived at the motel. When he took out his phone, I saw on the screen that it was a blocked number. I thought he'd ignore it, assuming it was spam, but he answered."

"Could you hear the discussion?" Jon asked.

Rita scoffed. "What discussion? After he said hello, Roger didn't utter another word. He just listened for a minute. Then the call ended. Roger said it was one of those vacation sales pitches but his whole demeanor changed. He was suddenly edgy, wired."

We had reached the police station and Detective Hoffman was waiting by the main entrance for us.

"You should have a lawyer with you, Morgan," Jon said.

"I'll be fine. I've got nothing to hide." This was inane bravado on my part, and I don't know why I felt compelled to say it. Clearly my innocence hadn't done me any favors when my parents were murdered, though I did consider myself a savvier interviewee because of that experience. "I'll be careful," I added, primarily to appease Jon, though this caveat didn't make him look any less concerned.

We all got out and followed Detective Hoffman inside, where we were buzzed through a foyer door and into the heart of the station. Rita was directed by a uniformed officer down a hallway to the left while Newt, Jon, and I were led to the right and into a small room containing a table, a couple of chairs, and at least two cameras. After Jon was escorted off to some unknown location by another officer, Hoffman joined me and Newt.

"Am I under arrest?" I asked.

Hoffman shook his head. "Not at this time, but this interview is being recorded."

"Understood." I almost added that I knew the drill because I'd been down this road before but managed to stop myself.

"Walk me through the timeline of your evening," Hoffman said. "Beginning with your dinner with Roger and Rita and the disagreement you had."

"Well, I'm here in Rhinelander at Roger's request because I'm a cryptozoologist. Do you know what that is?"

Hoffman nodded and said, "I do."

"Andy Bosworth claims a Hodag attacked Brandon Kluver. Says he saw the creature."

"Yes, I know. An unfortunate defense."

"Maybe, maybe not," I said. "I'm here to try to prove the Hodag exists." I expected skepticism or surprise from Hoffman at this revelation but was disappointed. No doubt Cordelia had already filled him in.

"Anyway, our dinner discussion was over the unlikelihood of any success on my part in exonerating Andy. I tried to gently suggest to them that perhaps they don't know Andy as well as they think they do. It made them mad, and they left. Rita rode to the restaurant with me but opted to go back with Roger. She said Roger got a phone call just as they arrived at the motel, and whatever it was about, it seemed to excite him. You'll probably want to ask her about that."

"We're talking to Mrs. Bosworth," Hoffman said. "Did you leave the restaurant right after the Bosworths?"

"Not right away. I sat for maybe ten minutes to finish my coffee. Then I went out to my car and took Newt for a walk in that field behind the restaurant. He loves the cold and the snow. Me, not so much, and once I got out there I thought to use my remote start on my car to warm it up. That's why I took off my glove. I must have tried to put it into my pocket and dropped it—I don't honestly remember, because when I went to use my fob I saw a figure lurking about near the back corner of the restaurant."

"Hold on," Hoffman said, raising a hand to stop me. He leaned forward in his chair and pinned his steely-eyed stare on me. "Why didn't you mention this person back at the motel? Did the three of you cook up this story during your drive here?"

"No! I didn't mention it earlier, because I didn't know it was relevant. Once you told us Roger had been killed and found in the field behind the restaurant—"

"We haven't confirmed the identity of the victim," Hoffman interrupted.

"And why is that?" I challenged. "Either it is or it isn't Roger. Rita tried calling him several times and he's not answering. And clearly you must have reason to believe it's Roger. Otherwise, why all the questions about him? And if you're not sure the victim is

Roger, why wouldn't you want Rita to ID him? Why are you torturing her with all this vague innuendo?"

Hoffman leaned back in his chair and laced his fingers together, resting his hands on his belly. "I'm the one asking the questions here, Ms. Carter."

"Sorry, but while Rita is a tough old bird, she isn't a young one and this thing with her nephew has really stressed her out. I'm worried about her. And the way you're treating this . . . treating us, seems unnecessarily cruel."

I caught the tiniest hint of a flinch from him with those words. It seemed I'd hit a nerve.

Hoffman shook his head, looked up at the ceiling, sighed wearily, and then looked back at me. "The victim we found matches some of the physical characteristics of Mr. Bosworth, such as height, weight, and hair color, and we found Mr. Bosworth's ID on the body." Hoffman stopped there, no doubt hoping the silence would prompt me.

"But?" I said after waiting nearly half a minute. I was willing to play along for now but not about to give him full satisfaction. "What aren't you telling us? How did he die?"

Hoffman didn't answer. Was he hoping I'd answer my own question and implicate myself? I sat back in my chair and folded my arms over my chest, determined not to give in to the silent treatment this time. It worked in my favor. Sort of.

"It appears someone caved his head in with a rock. And we found your bloody glove beneath what was left of his head."

"Oh my God." If he was going for shock and awe, he succeeded. My arms went limp, my hands dropping into my lap.

Newt, sensing the change in me, rose from where he was lying on the floor and put his head in my lap. Seeing this, Hoffman's expression softened a smidge.

"What about Roger's phone?" I asked. "You can see who the call was from, can't you? Even if it was blocked?"

Hoffman narrowed his eyes at me. "Depends, but it's a moot point for now. We didn't find a phone on him or anywhere nearby."

This was puzzling. And concerning. "Can't you check his phone records?"

"We can but that takes time. I don't suppose you have an idea about where his phone might be?"

"Me? Of course not. You're welcome to search my car, my motel room, anything of mine you want."

Hoffman broke into a big grin. "I have evidence techs waiting at the motel right now," he said, glancing up at the camera and nodding.

Crap!

"And speaking of phones, how about yours? Mind if we take a look at it?"

I'd walked right into that one. I hesitated, trying to think if there might be anything worrisome on my phone, but then said, "Don't you need a warrant to do that?"

"Not if you're willing to offer it up voluntarily. Assuming, of course, you have nothing to hide."

"I don't have anything to hide, but I'm not comfortable handing over my phone if I don't have to." I was stroking Newt's head like crazy, trying to calm myself. This hot seat was a place I'd been before, and I wasn't liking it any more now than I did back then.

As if he'd somehow read my mind, Hoffman said, "Tell me about what happened to your parents."

My body went cold. A weird sensation of impending doom

unraveled in my gut and spread, growing as it went, firing off nerves all over my body. Newt sensed something wrong immediately and whined, pushing his head into my tummy. My breathing quickened because it felt as if all the air was slowly being sucked out of the room. Hoffman said something to me, but it was as if he spoke from far, far away. His voice sounded muffled, his words garbled. Little lights appeared along the periphery of my vision and the already too-small room began to shrink. Then blackness.

"Morgan? Morgan, talk to me."

I felt a heaviness in my lap and against my chest. Something squeezed my head like a vise. Slowly I realized the vise was hands—Jon's hands—and the voice in my ear was also his. The weight pushing me down, grounding me to the chair, was my sweet boy Newt, the majority of his hundred-plus pounds now on me as he somehow managed to climb and curl most of his massive body into my lap.

Gradually, my breathing slowed, and Jon took his hands away. "Are you okay?" he whispered, one of those hands now gently massaging the base of my neck.

The room slowly came into focus. I saw Hoffman staring at me with a mix of suspicion and fascination. The door to the room was open and just beyond it I saw a female uniformed officer watching me intently. Apparently I was now the station entertainment.

Hoffman stood abruptly, shoving his chair backward. It made a teeth-chilling screech like nails on a blackboard as it scraped across the floor.

"Take her back to the motel," he said irritably. "But she needs to stay here in town, and I'll want to talk to her again." With that, he strode out of the room in a huff, wafting citrusy aftershave and bitter disappointment behind him. The female officer stepped aside to let him pass but then resumed her position of observation. Hoffman might have given up on me for now, but apparently she was hanging in until the bitter end.

The weight of my dog, so comforting moments before, was quickly becoming onerous. I gently pushed against his shoulders. "It's okay, Newt. You can get down now."

He did so awkwardly but stayed close to my side, watching me, his nostrils working overtime as he tried to sniff out my mood and situation.

"Are you okay?" Jon asked again.

I nodded. "I didn't do anything, Jon. It's like New Jersey all over—"

"Let's get going," he said loudly, talking over me. He reached down and tugged my arms. It hit me then that even though Hoffman had left the room, we were still being watched and probably recorded, as well.

I stood, Newt practically glued to my side and Jon offering a steadying arm, and made my way out of the room on wobbly legs. In the hallway, I wasn't sure which way to go but the female officer directed us to our right.

"Rita," I said, stopping when we reached the front foyer.

"She's already in the car," Jon said, nudging me along with a hand at the small of my back. He held the door open for me, a totally chivalrous move and something I might have balked at on a different day, but for now I didn't mind it. In fact, it made me feel less exposed, more protected, less alone in the world. And right then, it was exactly what I needed.

CHAPTER 17

When I awoke the following morning, I didn't open my eyes right away. I had little recollection of returning to my motel room or going to bed other than seeing the mess my room was after the police had finished searching it. My clothes had been strewn about and my toiletries had been tossed willy-nilly all over the bathroom counter. I still had my laptop thanks to Jon. He'd had the fore-thought to put it in his room and lock the adjoining door before we went to the police station.

My mind was crystal clear upon waking and I didn't want to hear, do, or see anything before I could sort through my thoughts. I started recounting all the strange things that had happened since I'd arrived in Rhinelander: mysterious people spying on me at least twice, an anonymous phone call warning me to look out for the resistance (though it seemed the resistance had found me anyway),

Roger's death—murder, call it what it was—and my bloodied glove being found beneath Roger's battered body.

There was Andy Bosworth and his Hodag. It would have been easy to dismiss Andy's claims as nonsense born out of desperation, but I'd seen something, too. And Brandon Kluver was dead, with plenty of means, opportunity, and motive pointing a finger at Andy. Then again, it had appeared as if I'd had all those things when it came to my parents' murders, and here again with Roger's. Yet I knew I was innocent. Was it fair of me to think otherwise of Andy at this point?

But still . . . a Hodag?

Damn this case! Why had I let Rita talk me into it? If only Andy hadn't gone out fishing that morning, assuming he actually had. If only Brandon—

It hit me then and I bolted up, eyes wide open. Newt was stretched out on the floor next to me and he jumped up and half climbed onto the bed. I saw Jon seated at the table over in the corner and he also jumped, spilling coffee out of the mug he was holding.

"Ah, damn!" he muttered, shaking the hot liquid off his hand. "Are you okay, Morgan?"

"I'm fine," I said, stroking Newt's head. "Sorry if I startled you but I had a sudden brainstorm. Are you okay?" As Jon nodded, I registered the fact that his presence wasn't part of my usual morning diorama and glanced over at the other bed. The sheets and blankets were disturbed and the depression of someone's head was clearly visible on the pillow.

"Do tell," Jon said, wiping off his hand with a napkin. I saw remnants of a muffin on a plate beside his coffee cup. He was dressed in sweatpants and a T-shirt, and his pale blond hair stood straight up on the crown of his head, making him look like Dennis the Menace. It was adorable.

"I will," I said, "but first I need to pee, and somebody needs a w-a-l-k." This was a pointless attempt to quell Newt's enthusiasm. He knew both the word and its spelling, something that became obvious when he excitedly ran over, got his leash from where it was hanging on the doorknob, and brought it to me, tail wagging so fast and hard his whole back end was doing the Macarena.

"I'll come with, if that's okay," Jon said. "I'll fix you a cup of coffee to take along."

"Sounds perfect."

Ten minutes later we were walking across the frozen parking lot in crisp morning air carrying steaming cups of coffee in Styrofoam cups, our breath making tiny clouds of mist with each exhalation. I'd found an old pair of gloves in my car and the sight of them was a constant reminder of the Damoclean sword hanging over my head. Still, I was excited over my morning revelation.

"Do I have to drag it out of you?" Jon asked as I unhooked Newt's leash at the edge of the parking lot.

Newt took off in a serpentine pattern, tail curved up and wagging happily, working his way toward the culvert below. He kept his nose to the ground and would occasionally blow white tufts of powdery snow into the air like a demented coke addict.

"It hit me when I woke up this morning," I said. "I've been so focused on Andy and what he did at the scene where Brandon's body was found that I completely forgot the other piece."

Jon pondered my statement for a moment before asking, "And what exactly is that?"

"Why was Brandon out there? Does the police report address how he got there, or mention any trails he might have walked, or a vehicle he might have driven? Or how about equipment he might have had with him? Andy said Brandon had ski poles and I saw holes from them alongside the path the animal supposedly took, but that path ended at the tree. Where did it begin? Brandon wasn't plopped down in the middle of the woods by the river. He had to have gotten there somehow, though how doesn't matter as much as why."

Jon looked thoughtful and I awaited the *Brilliant deduction!* comment I was sure was coming. Instead, he said, "Hoffman told Zeke they think Andy invited Brandon out to Roger's cabin and the two of them walked to the scene together before Andy attacked him."

"Was Brandon's car at Andy's cabin?"

Jon's brow furrowed. "Brandon doesn't own a car. Maybe Andy picked him up somewhere and drove him out there."

I shook my head. "Doesn't make sense given the history of animosity between the two men. Would Brandon have gotten into Andy's car to go anywhere?"

"Maybe Andy told him he wanted to talk things out and make peace." Jon's face broke into a wicked smile. "You know, to bury the hatchet."

I winced.

"Too soon?"

"A bit. Moving on. What about the trail from Andy's cabin to where he left his sled? Wouldn't there have been more than one set of footprints or tracks there if Brandon had been with him?"

"When snow is that deep, the person behind the lead might take advantage of whatever trail has been blazed, using the same footprints to minimize their own efforts. Brandon could have gone first, and maybe Andy stepped in the same holes Brandon created, not leaving any footprints of his own."

"Except Brandon's body was found wearing snowshoes, so he wouldn't have made any footprints to speak of other than snowshoe tracks. And if we can see holes from his ski poles on the one path to the river, why don't we see them between the cabin and where he died? If Andy was luring Brandon out there, why did Andy abandon his sled some distance from where the body was found? Wouldn't he have wanted all his tools along with him?"

"All he needed was the knife."

"Yeah, about the knife. You said you were able to view a police report. Did the police examine Andy's sled and find his knife on it? And did they try to determine if the knife in the river was Brandon's as Andy claims?"

Jon nodded. "The report I saw was a preliminary one, but it did say that Brandon's live-in girlfriend identified the knife as one Brandon had purchased a few weeks earlier."

"So Andy abandoned his sled, which had his knife on it, and followed Brandon some distance farther into the woods so he could kill him using Brandon's own knife? Does that make sense?"

Jon sighed, cocked his head to the side, and smiled at me. "It does not," he admitted. "But maybe Andy dragged the sled out later, or maybe he simply had two knives, one he carried with him and one he left on the sled. Most of this evidence is open to interpretation."

"Therein lies the problem," I said. "I need to talk to Brandon's girlfriend to see if she knows what he was doing out there that day. If Andy did invite him, odds are Brandon would have told her."

I saw Newt doing his business halfway up the hill and handed my coffee to Jon. "Gotta do a pickup," I said, removing a poop bag from the roll on the leash. I had to trudge through deep snow for a good thirty feet to get to the spot and nearly fell twice. After finally retrieving the goods, I was tying the bag closed when something whacked me in the back of the head. Cold chunks of icy snow slid down my hair and beneath my collar. It took me a moment to figure out what had happened, but once I turned around to look behind me, I knew.

"Wasn't sure my arm was good enough to score from here," Jon said, a devilish grin on his face. Our coffee mugs were on the ground at his feet, where he had dug out a small depression in the snow. He stepped away from them, already packing a second snowball between his gloves.

"You're asking for it now, mister," I muttered, digging up a handful of the older, wetter snow and packing it between my hands. Jon was already flinging his second missile my way, but I had a secret weapon he hadn't anticipated. As his snowball came at me, Newt leapt up and snatched it out of the air with his mouth, jaws snapping. This was a game Newt and I had played before. I took aim and fired.

Over the next two minutes, the air was filled with snowballs flying, snowballs getting eaten, and snowballs finding their targets. Fortunately, all of the latter group were ones I threw. Jon finally flung up his arms in a classic sign of surrender.

"Not fair," he laughed, panting slightly. "It's two against one."

"Hey, be thankful he only knows how to intercept them and not throw them."

Despite Jon's efforts to protect them, our coffees had gotten knocked over in the melee, staining a small area of snow a pale brown. I stared at the spot. "I suppose I could try for a coffee snow cone," I said.

"As long as it's not yellow snow," Jon said with a grimace. "There's a coffee shop not too far from here. I'll drive there and get you whatever you want."

"Seems fair. After all, you abandoned your duties as keeper of the coffees."

Jon reached over and flicked some clinging bits of snow from a strand of my hair. "Why don't you take a nice hot shower and I'll have a latte waiting for you when you get out."

"Done. Make mine vanilla. And get one for Rita, too. I'm going to check in on her before I get in the shower."

As Jon went to his car, I gathered up our disposable coffee cups and tossed them into the trash can beside the side exit. I swiped my key card through the outside lock and heard it click. Before yanking the door open, I glanced back to wave at Jon's car as it pulled out, but my hand froze in midair when I saw the nondescript black car at the far edge of the lot, a plume of mist coming from the tailpipe. Distance, the angle of the car, and tinting on the side windows made it impossible for me to clearly see the face of the driver. All I could make out was a head topped by a knit cap. Whoever it was, they appeared to be watching Jon rather than me. At least at first.

As I heard the motel door lock click again to indicate my swipe had expired, the driver's head turned my way. The face was little more than a flesh-colored blob, yet I felt eyes boring into me.

Newt, standing by my side, whined. I glanced down at him and saw his questioning look, the tentative wag of his tail. He wasn't sure if he should be worried or not and, frankly, neither was I. By the time I looked toward the car again, it had quietly pulled out of the lot and onto the road, heading in the opposite direction Jon had gone.

A classic overreaction, Morgan. Your nerves are still on edge from last night.

After my mental scolding, I swiped my key card a second time, telling myself the person in the car was probably just someone who had pulled into the lot to make a phone call, or check directions, or answer a text message. There was no reason to think the driver had been watching me or Jon.

I hurried to the door of my room and couldn't resist a cautious glance down the hallway in both directions as I swiped my card to get inside. Even after throwing all the locks and checking to make sure the connecting door to Jon's room was also secured, I couldn't bring myself to climb into the shower. I'd seen *Psycho* too many times.

CHAPTER 18

Instead of showering, I called Rita. When she answered with an obviously groggy, "Hello?" I realized I'd awakened her. It hadn't occurred to me she might still be sleeping, because I knew she was typically an early riser. I'd forgotten how late it had been by the time we got back from the police station. Plus, all the emotion and trauma of last night had undoubtedly taken a toll on her.

"Rita, sorry, I didn't think you'd be sleeping. I'll hang up."

"No. No need. I'm more muzzy than sleepy. What time is it?"

"Nearly eight thirty. Are you okay?"

"What?" A pause. "Oh. Right." She sighed and I realized she was recalling what had happened last night.

"Jon went to get us some lattes. He should be back shortly. Want me to come to your room? I could run down to the lobby and grab something to eat. The motel offers breakfast."

"Not hungry," she said. "Let me wash up and brush my teeth and then I'll come to your room. Okay?"

"Sure. Whatever you want."

"Don't coddle me, Morgan," she said with a hint of irritability. "I'm not some fragile old woman. What I am is mad as hell. What happened to Roger is wrong on so many levels and whoever did it is not going to get away with it. I'm not walking away from his murder and I'm not abandoning Andy either. I'll be there in a few and we'll put our heads together to figure this thing out."

With that, she ended the call. I stared at my phone for a few seconds, unsure of what to make of this version of Rita. I shrugged it off and called Devon instead.

He answered with, "Hey, boss, how's it going in Hodag land?"

"Not great." I filled him in on the events of the past twenty-four hours. "I think I might need a good criminal defense lawyer. The one I used when my parents died has retired. Can you do some research and find me the best one you can?"

"Gads, is it really that serious?"

"It might be," I said, a familiar feeling of dread washing over me. "Have you found anything else on Brandon Kluver?"

"Some. Seems he had a bit of a drinking problem. Got a DUI two years ago and lost his license as a result, though he just got it back. He's also been through a few jobs. He was fired from the paper mill back when he and Andy Bosworth got into it on the job over a decade ago, and after that he kind of bounced around with some low-level service jobs. Worked at a couple of Kwik Trips in the area and did a stint at a grocery store for a year. Most years he's been doing seasonal farmwork during the warmer months and then taking odd jobs during the winter."

"No wonder he doesn't own any property. Sounds like he's been living paycheck to paycheck."

"Well, I think the girlfriend eases things some. She works for a pharmaceutical company and from what I can tell, she makes good money. I think there's family money there, too."

"What exactly does she do?"

"She provides samples of new drugs and educates health-care providers on their uses. She travels a lot, and since Brandon doesn't seem to own a car, I'm guessing he used hers to get around."

"How long had they been together?"

"Couple of years, judging from their social media."

"Okay. Good work, Dev. How are things with the store?"

"All under control. You doing okay? You sound more stressed than usual."

"I'll be fine. It's just this case. I'm really regretting letting Rita talk me into it."

"Could you have said no?"

I sighed. "Probably not."

"No probably about it. How's she doing?"

"Not great, but she sounded feisty on the phone a bit ago, so that's encouraging." There was a knock on my door. "That's probably her now. Gotta go, Dev."

"Tell her hi for me. And that I'm sorry about Roger."

"Will do."

I disconnected the call and looked through the peephole to see Rita on the other side. I undid all the locks to let her in and then did them back up again. By the time I turned around, Rita was sitting on one of the chairs at the corner table. She looked as haggard as she'd sounded, with dark circles beneath her eyes, a slight stoop to her usually rigid posture, and a frightening pallor to her skin. But there was also a spark in those eyes, and I was glad to see it.

"Jon should be here with our lattes any moment," I said.

She stared, unfocused, at a spot somewhere between the two beds. "Do you think Andy knows?" she said, her voice low. "This is going to kill him. He and his father were so close. How am I going to tell him?"

"We don't know for sure there's anything to tell yet, do we?" I said.

Rita gave me a *get real* look. "Roger hasn't answered any of my calls and I bet I've tried a dozen or more times. I couldn't sleep last night, so I drove out to his cabin, but it's all marked off with police tape."

Yikes. "Was his car there?"

Rita shook her head. "Wasn't at the restaurant either. I went by there, as well."

No wonder she looked so worn this morning. She was out driving around half the night. "You should have let me go with you," I said.

"Right," Rita said with a humorless chuckle. "Because you're not in enough trouble already. Why not let the cops see you poking around the scene of the crime?"

She had a point.

There was an odd-sounding knock at the door, which, as it turned out, was actually a couple of soft kicks because Jon was in the hallway with his hands full. I wondered how he'd gotten into the building, but then realized he'd probably come in through the automatic doors at the motel's entrance.

"I come bearing gifts," he said as he entered. "I have vanilla lattes for all and some maple-and-bacon muffins with a brown-sugar crumble." He licked his lips as he hoisted the bag in the air. "Still warm from the oven."

The aroma rapidly filling my room was mouthwatering. Despite thinking I wasn't hungry and Rita's claims of the same, we attacked those muffins like we hadn't eaten in days. They were incredible and the combination of food and coffee was energizing.

"What's on your agenda for today?" Jon asked me as we ate.

"I need to shower and then I want to pay a visit to Brandon Kluver's girlfriend. That is assuming, of course, the police don't arrest me beforehand."

"Yes, on that note," Jon said, stifling a burp, "I'm going to visit the Rhinelander police station and chat with Detective Hoffman to see what I can glean and perhaps get some of the information you want, like an inventory of what Brandon had with him out there in the woods when he was killed."

"Do you really think Hoffman will share anything with you?"

Jon shrugged. "Won't know if I don't try. I'm hoping he'll extend a little more of his professional courtesy. But before we do any of that, you were about to tell me something last night when Hoffman showed up."

"Oh yeah, I almost forgot. It was two things, actually. One, I was paid a visit yesterday by the city mayor, a couple of local businesswomen, the high school principal, and the one and only Cordelia."

"Really?" Jon said, looking puzzled. "And what did they want?"

"They want me to stop trying to prove that a Hodag might have killed Brandon. Short of that, they want me to sweep my findings under the rug. They claim the Hodag is too instrumental to many of their key economic factors, not the least of which is their annual

Hodag Country Festival, which draws thousands to the city every summer."

"Did they threaten you in any way?"

"You mean other than their display of strength in showing up as a group? No."

"What's the second thing?"

"I got a phone call yesterday from some man who warned me to be careful and look out for the resistance."

"Resistance?" Jon said, puzzled. "Do you think he meant the group that visited you?"

"Don't know."

"I don't suppose you got a number for the caller?" Jon asked.

I shook my head. "It came in on the motel phone."

Rita, who had so far been quiet—too much so for my tastes—said, "None of this explains why someone would want to kill Roger. I don't understand it."

"I don't either, Rita," I said. "Maybe Jon can get more information out of the police."

"I'll do the best I can, but I can't make any promises. I don't have any authority here, just my connection through Zeke and I have no idea how much weight that will carry. And after that, I'm afraid I'll have to head back home."

"So soon?" I said. "I was hoping you'd come with me to talk to Brandon's girlfriend."

"Sorry, Morgan. I have to go back."

"I'd like to go with you when you talk to the girlfriend," Rita said.

I wasn't sure this was wise, but I didn't really want to leave Rita alone in the motel for any great length of time either. The best thing she could do would be to go back home and distract herself with stuff at the store. Of course, I knew she wouldn't.

"Okay," I told her.

"Don't go until I get back from my chat with Hoffman," Jon said.

"I won't. I haven't even contacted the woman yet. For all I know, she may be out of town. Devon says she travels a lot for work."

"Best get to it, then," Jon said, slapping his thighs and standing. "I'm going to hop in the shower quick and then I'll be off to see Hoffman."

Rita stood, shuffled toward the door, and said, "Holler at me when you're ready to go see this girlfriend. I'm going to go lie down until then."

I watched her leave, casting a worried look at Jon. He answered my unspoken concern with a shrug.

Jon went to his room, closing the door between our suites to give me some privacy, though I didn't hear him lock it. I left my side unlocked and headed for the shower. I was about to climb in when my cell phone rang. Glancing at the screen, I didn't recognize the number and almost let it go to voice mail. But then curiosity got the better of me.

"Hello."

"Hi, are you Morgan?" A woman's voice. I turned off the shower so I could hear better.

"Yes," I said. "This is Morgan."

"Okay. Good. I know this will sound strange, but I've been told to tell you to be at the Shepard Dog Park here in town by ten o'clock this morning. It's just off Highway 17, or Boyce Drive. You're supposed to come alone and not tell anyone about it."

"Is this some kind of joke?"

"I honestly don't know," the woman said. "This guy gave me a hundred bucks to call you and give you this message and that's what I'm doing. Do what you want with it. He did say it was a matter of life and death."

"Uh-huh," I said, my skepticism clear.

"For what it's worth, the guy looked really shaken and scared. That's the only reason I agreed to do this. Good luck."

The call went dead. I stared at the phone, my mind whirling. Surely it was a joke or prank of some sort. But why would anyone do that? And how did they know I was in Rhinelander?

I pulled up a map on my phone and easily found the dog park the woman had referred to. It was only a mile away. A quick glance at my watch told me it was twenty before ten. I stood there, naked, trying to decide what to do. Then I dressed, pulled on coat and boots, leashed up Newt, and quietly slipped out of my motel room.

The dog park was a fenced-in area on a couple of tree-covered acres sandwiched between the river and the road. Parking was minimal but I was lucky enough to see someone close to the gate pull out and I slipped into the spot they'd vacated. There were plenty of people about, some in the park, some outside it, though no one appeared to be paying me any attention. It was broad daylight in an open and public place. Plus, I had Newt. After a minute of hesitation, I got out of the car.

My dog's protective abilities were immediately compromised once we passed through the double gates and entered the park proper. A large, rambunctious goldendoodle met us first thing, and before I knew it, Newt was romping around like he was a puppy. It made me smile and I figured if nothing else happened, Newt's utter glee at playing with the other dog would make the trip worth it.

Eventually, the goldendoodle's owner leashed it up and hauled it toward the gate, though the dog clearly didn't want to go. I called Newt over to get him out of the way and stood in place for a bit, watching the other dogs and their owners, trying to figure out why I was here. No one approached me or looked familiar, and according to my watch it was two minutes past ten. Unsure of what to do, I went to the left of the gates and started following the fence line. It ran along the top of an embankment overlooking the river, which had frozen over everywhere except the very middle, where a narrow swath of fast-moving water about three feet wide headed downstream. Dozens of trees, more than half of them evergreens, filled the middle portion of the park, scenting the air with the smells of cedar, balsam, and pine.

Minutes later, I'd reached the far end of the enclosed area and paused at the corner, looking down at the river and thinking about Andy's story. The opposite bank here was heavily wooded much like the spot where the Hodag had supposedly been, and as I stared into the darkness on the other side, it was easy to imagine the creature emerging from the shadows. A chill shook me, as much from the cold as from my thoughts, and I hugged myself in an effort to get warmer.

"Morgan?"

I whirled around. Newt, wagging his tail, stood next to a tall man who was bundled in a heavy parka, a fur-lined hood pulled over his head. I peered at the face buried inside that furry hood and gasped, afraid to believe my own eyes.

"Oh my God!"

CHAPTER 19

Roger! You're not dead?"

"Not yet," he said, just above a whisper.

Relief and joy washed over me, quickly followed by confusion as Roger put a gloved finger in front of his face.

"What the hell, Roger?" I said, lowering my voice and glancing around us. No one was within earshot. "The police took me down to the station last night because my glove was found next to a dead body behind the restaurant where we ate dinner. The police seem to think the body was yours and that I killed you."

Roger nodded and surveyed our surroundings with a worried expression. "They'll figure it out soon enough," he said. "They'll be coming for me next."

"They who? What are you talking about?" Newt, sensing how upset I was, nudged my hand with his nose. I patted him on the head to let him know I was okay. But was I? My thoughts were spinning, and I felt lightheaded. What the hell was going on here?

"'They' is whoever killed Rick," Roger said. "Or the police, because once they figure out the dead man isn't me, they'll think I'm the one who killed him."

"Who's Rick?" I said, struggling to make sense of what he was saying.

"He's the dead man in the field. I didn't kill him."

"Neither did I," I said. "But, Roger, I don't understand what's going on here. Rita thinks you're dead. Andy might have been informed for all we know and that means he thinks you're dead, too. Hell, we all did."

Roger nodded impatiently and patted the air between us to signal me to shut up. "Let me try to explain," he said. "Last night, after I left the restaurant, I got a call from a man who told me to just listen and not say anything. He said he wanted to meet me because he had information about what really happened to Brandon. He said he'd been following me for a couple of days, trying to decide if he could confide in me, but now things had escalated to the point where he had no choice." Roger paused, looking around again. The closest person or dog was about twenty yards away on the street side of the park, where a smidgen of sunlight had managed to eke its way through the trees.

"Rita mentioned you'd gotten a call just as you arrived at the motel."

Roger nodded and continued. "The guy was rambling, frantic, talking low like he feared someone would overhear him. He said things like *They're going to find me* and *It's only a matter of time* and then said he'd followed me to the restaurant but when I left, he couldn't get his car to start. Could I return to the restaurant to talk to him? He said he'd be out in the field behind the building away from the restaurant windows and cameras, waiting. And then the call just ended. Clearly the guy was paranoid."

"Yes, but you know the saying. Just because you're paranoid..."

"Right," Roger said with another impatient nod. "Anyway, I drove back to the restaurant, and sure enough, there was this guy out in the field behind the building. He was freezing cold, wearing nothing but a thin jacket and a pair of slacks. He said he'd been on the run for weeks and was out of money and living out of his car. He looked terrified and started pacing, maybe to keep warm. He had his eyes glued on the parking lot, and anytime someone arrived or left he looked like he was ready to run off."

Recalling the shadowy figure I'd seen lurking near the rear corner of the restaurant when I'd been behind it with Newt, I said, "I think I might have seen him hanging around when I walked Newt in that field."

"Yes, yes, he mentioned seeing you out there. He knew about you, and he considered approaching you, but you were still too much of an unknown, too new to the picture. He said your motives were suspect."

I looked at him askance. "*My* motives were suspect? How?"

"I don't know. Like I said, the guy was rambling, constantly changing subjects, and not making a lot of sense much of the time. Plus, he was so cold his teeth were literally rattling, making it hard for me to understand what he was saying at times. He did tell me his name was Rick but didn't give me a last name. I asked him if he had a warmer coat in his car and he shook his head and said he'd had to make a quick getaway and hadn't had time to grab a coat, his wallet, or much of anything else. Said he kept two fifty-dollar bills hidden in his car for emergencies and he'd been living off that. I tried to coax him to sit in my car with the heat on to warm up and I told him I'd loan him some money or drive him anywhere he wanted to go, but he kept saying it was too dangerous."

Roger swallowed hard and looked around anxiously. His edginess was making me uneasy.

"The guy kept repeating those two words," Roger continued. "Too dangerous, too dangerous, too dangerous. Then he said a bunch of things that sounded like crazy ramblings. He said he didn't want to be trapped in a car or be in the light coming from the restaurant windows because some of the customers inside looked sketchy. He kept ranting about a woman named Edna and how he couldn't trust her and how they were tracking him. But when I asked him for specifics, he went off on a different tangent and said I had to look for the resistance."

"Resistance?" I said. "I got an anonymous call from a man yesterday telling me essentially the same thing. But I have no idea who or what the resistance is."

"Neither do I. Honestly, at that point I figured Rick was mentally ill and had fixated on Andy's case for some reason. I wanted to get him some help and finally managed to talk him into putting on my coat while I went inside the restaurant to get him a cup of hot coffee. I thought if I could warm him up a little and also show him the restaurant was a safe place, it might help calm him."

"Geez, Roger. You realize the whole thing could have been a setup to rob you, don't you?"

"I considered that," he said, his expression troubled. "But this guy was legitimately scared. And as it turned out, his fear was justified. It took me longer than it should have to get the coffee because the waitress had just started a new pot brewing. I wasn't very nice to her, which means she'll remember me and tell the police I was angry or anxious. Frankly, I was impatient because I was afraid Rick was going to bolt on me, especially when I remembered my car keys and wallet were in the pocket of the coat I'd given him to wear. I had my cell phone, at least, because I use the pay app on it for stuff, though in the end I ditched it."

I started to ask him why he'd gotten rid of his phone, but he patted the air between us again, signaling for me to hush and be patient. He gave our surroundings a quick look before continuing.

"When I came out of the restaurant, I thought this Rick guy had taken off because I didn't see him at first. I panicked, thinking he had stolen my car, but then I saw it was still parked where I'd left it. As I walked toward the field, I saw a large heap on the ground and when I got closer I realized it was Rick. I thought maybe he'd collapsed from the cold or general weakness, so I used the flashlight on my phone to better see him. But as soon as I got a good look, I backed away because there was blood everywhere and half this guy's head was caved in." Roger shuddered and I didn't think it was due to the cold. "It was awful. His face was unrecognizable, Morgan."

Roger's color paled and I placed a steadying hand on his arm. "Are you okay?"

He took in a couple of deep breaths and blew them out slowly, creating clouds of mist between us. Then he nodded. "Sorry," he said. "The memory of it . . . it was horrible."

"I can only imagine. You must have been terrified."

He let out a humorless chuckle. "Oddly enough, my lawyer

brain—though some call it my lizard brain—kicked in and my thoughts at that point were practical and methodical. Maybe it was due to this whole business with Andy because I was instantly focused on how this was going to look to the police."

Roger swallowed hard before continuing. "I knew there was no point in calling for rescue for Rick. He had exposed brain matter. And I realized he was still wearing my coat with my wallet in an inside pocket that I couldn't get to without moving him. I didn't want to touch him, as you can imagine. I could explain away a stolen wallet and coat but not my DNA or some fibers all over the dead guy. Besides, I had no way of knowing for sure if my wallet was still in that pocket. Whoever had caved in Rick's skull might have taken it. Then I realized that made me a potential target, too. Whoever had done that to Rick might have my name, address, my ID. . . ." He trailed off, looking momentarily terrified, but pulled himself together again.

"Rick had a cell. He was clutching it in his hand when I first met him in the field, but I didn't see it anywhere when I came back with the coffee, meaning whoever killed him probably had it. They'd see my number as a recent call."

"Last night, I asked the police to check your phone records because Rita had told us about the call you got. But they said they didn't find any phones at the scene."

"They wouldn't have. Doesn't matter now. I tossed my phone in the river after jotting down your number. I didn't want to risk being tracked by GPS or cell towers. I could have just turned it off, but I wouldn't have been able to use it again. Better to just get rid of it."

"Did you happen to see my pink glove in that field? The police told me they found it covered in blood, and I'm sure they thought it was your blood, though I realize now it was Rick's."

Roger shook his head. "Sorry, no. It was so dark when I first got there, I don't think I would have seen it. I did use my phone to light things up when I went back and didn't see it then either, but it may have been under Rick's body. I found my car keys a few feet away, though, and once I had them I just wanted to get the hell out of there. I knew I should call the police but didn't want to use my own phone and risk getting embroiled in a murder investigation or make myself an easy target for whoever had killed Rick. I drove home but when I got there I saw moving lights inside through the front window and did a quick about-face. I realized then they were already on to me."

"They who?" I asked again.

Roger rolled his eyes heavenward. "I wish the hell I knew. All I know is the stakes must be huge or things wouldn't be this drastic. I mean, someone brutally murdered this guy, presumably to shut him up. I thought about going by my office but didn't dare. If they had my name and were in my house, they most likely would be at the office within minutes, if they weren't there already. So instead, I drove to an old client of mine who owns an auto repair shop. He owed me a favor and I cashed in last night and then some. He's letting me use an old truck of his and he gave me a handful of untraceable burner phones, one of which I used right away to anonymously call the police about a dead body behind the restaurant. The client and his wife were going to drive my car to the airport and leave it there in the lot."

"Wow, that's a lot of burner phones," I said.

Roger smiled. "They're part of his stash. Sometimes being a

defense lawyer and not asking too many questions of your clients comes in handy. Especially now because I need to lie low for a spell. I could use your help."

"Of course. What do you want me to do?"

"See if you can find anything at all about this Rick guy. I know it's a long shot, but Rita told me you have an employee who's a real whiz at digging stuff up."

"Yes. Devon, He's quite good, but you're not giving us much to go on here. Rick didn't give you a last name?"

Roger shook his head.

I thought for a moment and an idea came to me. "What about his car? You said he told you it wouldn't start after he got to the restaurant. Maybe it's still parked there. Do you know what it looks like? Or did you get a plate number off it by any chance?"

Roger shook his head, looking morose. "I didn't think to do any of that last night and didn't know what car was his anyway. I was so freaked out by the whole situation I just wanted to get away from there."

I racked my brain some more and another idea came to me. "Roger, when the cops came to see me last night, they told us there were security cameras at the front of the restaurant and by the back door. The one in the front should be able to see cars coming and going. Maybe we can identify this Rick guy on the footage and get a license number for his car. We might be able to see the car getting towed. And that could lead to an ID. What did Rick look like?"

As soon as I asked this question, I realized I already knew the answer. The police had said as much last night when they told me the victim had physical characteristics matching Roger. I let Roger give me a description anyway, thinking maybe he'd noticed a facial feature that might show up on the cameras, making it easier to identify which of the cars arriving at the restaurant had been Rick's.

"He was about my age, height, and build. I remember thinking how well my coat fit him once he put it on. His hair is similar to mine, too. You know, I can't give you too many other details because it was so dark out there in that field and I really couldn't see his face. And then when I came back with the coffee, well . . ."

"Right," I said grimacing.

"Assuming you could identify him, how could you get access to the security footage?" Roger asked.

"I have an idea or two. It might not work but what else have we got?"

"Okay, but please be careful. I watched to see if you were followed here and didn't see anyone but I'm no expert. I had you meet me here because I thought if anyone *was* watching you, it would seem perfectly normal for you to come to a dog park, and they wouldn't be likely to follow you in, because they'd look too obvious in here without a dog. You need to be careful, Morgan. If it was Rick who called you yesterday, your number will be in his phone same as mine."

"He called the motel, so I think I'll be okay. And I'll be careful," I told him. "What about you? Do you have a place to stay? Clearly you can't go home."

"The same fellow who loaned me the truck owns a fishing cabin about ten miles north of town. It's a bit dilapidated but it has a fireplace, plenty of wood, and the roof doesn't leak, so it will suffice for now. It's not ideal, but my face is too well known here in town. I took a risk meeting you today, but I figured a dog park was relatively safe and you'd feel comfortable coming here."

"Why did you decide to contact me instead of Rita?"

Roger cocked his head to one side and sighed. "Rita acts tough," he said, "but she's not a young woman and I worry about her. You seem to have your act together and I trust you to look after her and Andy. I may not like your approach to this business with the Hodag but you're the best bet I have for now. Plus, from what you told me it sounds like we're in this together now that you're also on the police department's radar."

"So it would seem. Can I tell Rita you're alive?"

"Sure."

"What about Andy?"

"No need. My lawyer friend has already taken over the case and he's up to speed on everything that's happened. He'll keep Andy apprised of what's going on, though I doubt the cops will tell Andy I'm dead. Eventually they'll figure out it's not me through prints or DNA, and with any luck they'll be able to ID this Rick guy."

"Not sure that will help us unless they're willing to share the info," I said. "Though my friend who happens to be the chief of police on Washington Island is helping me out and one of his employees has connections to the PD here."

Roger nodded. "I'm more or less useless at this point since I don't have access to much of anything, but I think I need to stay off the grid for now."

"Understood. How can I reach you if I need to?"

"You can't. The fishing cabin is too isolated for cell phones. I'll touch base with you again in a day or two. I'll come into town and call or text you but, of course, it will be from an unknown number. And I won't use the same burner phone twice."

"Why didn't you use one of them to call me?"

"I wasn't sure you'd come, and I didn't want you to say anything to Rita just yet. You know the building at the base of the hill alongside the motel, the one on the other side of the big culvert?" I nodded. "It houses the Department of Veterans Affairs. The woman who called you had just come out of that building. I wanted to be able to watch after the call to make sure you'd come and to make sure no one followed you. Plus, I didn't waste a burner doing it that way."

"Risky, but I guess it worked," I said with a shrug.

He glanced around us again. "We've been chatting together too long," he said. "I need to go. Walk over toward the street side with your dog. I'm going to follow this fence line back to the gate. Give me five minutes before you leave."

"Got it. Let's go, Newt." I skirted along the fence at the bottom end of the park toward the street side without a single look back. I'd almost reached the opposite fence when the paranoia hit me hard. By the time I finally walked back up to the gate and left the park, I was frantically studying every face around me, looking for any indication someone might be paying more attention to me than was warranted, and wondering if any of them might be a cold-blooded killer.

CHAPTER 20

⌒

My cell phone rang as I was loading Newt into my car and when I saw it was Jon calling, I knew I'd be in for a tongue-lashing. I debated not answering, but then decided it wouldn't be fair to Jon. I'd have to take it like a grown-up. I braced myself and answered.

"Hey, Jon."

"Where are you?"

"Minutes away." I tried to sound as cheerful—and innocent—as possible because I heard the undercurrents of worry and anger in Jon's voice.

"Where did you go? And why didn't you say something, or leave a note?"

"Sorry. Something came up. I'll explain when I get there."

This was met with a weighty silence I rushed to fill.

"Anyway, I'm pulling into the lot now and will be in my room in a minute." I ended the call, not giving him a chance to lecture me anymore. I suspected there would be plenty of that once I was inside, though I hoped my news about Roger would soften his anger.

Jon was waiting in my room, sitting on the bed he'd slept in, his body language suggesting he was more upset than I'd realized.

As I unleashed Newt and slipped out of my coat, I said, "Before you start chastising me again, sit tight until I can get Rita in here. There's more to my story, much more, but I didn't want to discuss it over the phone. I have some surprising news."

"So do I," he said.

"Hold that thought."

I called Rita, who tried to chastise me, as well, but I cut her off and told her to come to my room immediately. I then offered some preliminary explanations for Jon to keep him from questioning me before Rita's arrival.

"I really am sorry for ditching you the way I did, but I felt I didn't have a choice. I got a mysterious phone call from a woman asking me to come to this nearby dog park because someone there needed to talk to me. She said it was a matter of life and death."

Jon looked appalled. "Jesus, Morgan, it could have been *your* death. What were you thinking?"

"I wasn't," I admitted. "I acted on impulse and gut. But I thought a city dog park would be busy enough to make it a safe place to meet up. Plus, I had Newt."

"Who was this someone who needed to talk to you? Was it David?" There was a strong accusatory note to the question, and it took me off my guard for a second.

"What? No." A knock on the door saved me from further

explanations on that count and I went over to let Rita in. I made her sit on the bed next to Jon and stood in front of them.

"Roger is alive," I said.

Both of them stared at me, unblinking, for what seemed like an eternity.

I quickly summarized for Rita how I'd been led to the dog park and then finished with, "Never in my wildest dreams did I think the person I was going to meet might be Roger, but it was. He's alive. The dead man is someone Roger arranged to meet the night we all went to the restaurant, someone who said he had information about Andy's case. The dead man happened to bear a physical resemblance to Roger, and he was wearing Roger's coat at the time with Roger's wallet and ID in the pocket."

"Oh my God," Rita said. "Did Roger kill him?"

"No," I said quickly, but then I wondered how sure I was of my answer. And why Rita would go there.

"The police think he might have," Jon said. "That was my news, that the dead man they thought was Roger isn't. They ruled Roger out based on a scar and some hardware Roger apparently has in his left leg."

"Of course," Rita said. "He broke it in a car accident ten years ago. It was a really bad break, too. He had to have multiple surgeries on the leg."

Jon said, "The police got Roger's medical records and when they saw the dead man didn't have any injuries to the left leg, they knew it wasn't Roger. But they're very interested in knowing where Roger is."

"I honestly don't know. He told me he'd be staying off the grid for now other than some burner phones he said he'd use to contact me again at some later date. He made it clear he intends to lie low and hide, and not just from the police. Someone was inside his house looking around with flashlights last night right after he found Rick's body, so it seems the police aren't the only people eager to find him." I spent the next few minutes retelling Roger's version of the events of last night.

"The police haven't cleared you yet in this thing," Jon said when I was done. "Your glove is damning evidence, though circumstantial. The fact that they didn't see any blood spatter on your coat or clothes has them holding off for now, that and identifying the dead man. But they might question you again and they won't take kindly to finding out you know where Roger is and won't tell."

"I honestly don't know where he's hiding out." It occurred to me then to wonder why Roger hadn't trusted me with the information. Did he still have doubts about me? If so, why did he have me meet him at the dog park? Then another possibility occurred to me, one that made my mouth go dry. Had he not told me because he feared someone might try to force the information out of me by any means possible?

"The police don't have any idea who the dead man is?" I asked.

Jon shook his head. "Not that they're admitting to, though to be honest, I'm not sure they'd tell me if they did. I was able to glean some other information regarding Andy's case, though. They found a hair in Brandon's leg wound that isn't human. It's some kind of animal hair. I think they're assuming it's bear at this point, but they don't have a definitive answer yet. And if they get one, I don't think they'll share. Hoffman is pissed that Zeke basically used him to get information for me, so any professional courtesies they might have been inclined to extend have ended. They won't be sharing any more information with me or Zeke."

"That's unfortunate," I said.

"It is," Jon agreed. "Roger didn't get any more of a name from this guy?"

"No. All he got was a first name of Rick, assuming the guy wasn't lying. And some woman named Edna. He said Rick kept ranting about Edna."

"Roger didn't see anyone who might have killed this Rick guy? Maybe someone in the restaurant or parking lot?" Jon asked.

I shook my head. "He said he had to wait for the coffee because the waitress had to start a new pot and apparently she was slow. By the time he came out, the guy was already dead with his face bashed in. He didn't see anyone else out there, so whoever did it must have made a quick getaway."

"Lucky for Roger or he'd probably be dead now, too," Jon said. "That's some fast work and lucky timing, though it's only a temporary stay for Roger. Clearly someone knows about him if they were in his house. I wonder how they got onto him so fast? It couldn't have been from his ID because the cops found it on Rick's body, still in the coat pocket, though I suppose the killer could have found the ID, looked at it, and left it there. Otherwise, how would they know the two men met?"

"Rick's phone," I said. "Roger had his cell phone with him when he went for the coffee, but he said Rick had a phone in his hand when he first met him in the field and Roger couldn't find it after the fact. Hoffman told me last night that no phones were found on or around the dead man. Presumably whoever killed Rick took his phone and since Rick used it to call Roger, his contact info might have been in there."

Rita had remained quiet throughout this exchange, and I walked over and sat beside her, draping an arm over her shoulders. "Are you okay, Rita?"

She looked at me and smiled. "Roger isn't dead," she said, sounding scarily brittle. The smile disappeared. Her eyes had a lackluster appearance and her color remained exceedingly pale, making me worry that the shock of this might be too much for her.

"Yes, he's alive. This is good news, Rita," I said, rubbing her back.

But was it? Clearly this thing with Andy was much bigger than any of us had originally thought and it meant that not only was Roger still very much in danger, but also so were the rest of us.

"Maybe you should head for home and get away from all of this," I said to Rita.

When she didn't answer me right away, my worry for her ratcheted up a notch. But then she did that defiant jut of her chin and said, "I'm not running home with my tail between my legs. And I know you well enough to know you won't go home either, will you?"

"No. Not yet anyway, not that Detective Hoffman would let me even if I did want to." This earned us an exasperated sigh from Jon.

"I got you into this mess. I'm going to see you through it," Rita said to me.

"Seems to me you're at a standstill here," Jon said. "Until they identify Rick, there isn't much for you to do."

"Yeah, about that," I said. "The restaurant has security cameras monitoring the front entrance and from what the police told me last night, those cameras show vehicles coming and going onto the property. We know the approximate time Rick would have arrived because he told Roger he followed him to the restaurant. We know the guy looks like Roger. If the camera footage shows the faces of the drivers, we might be able to identify the car and get a plate number."

I saw a familiar spark in Jon's eyes and knew he was hooked. "The police will never share the video footage with me," he said. "But if there was a lone car left in the parking lot, the local guys probably figured it belonged to the victim and had it towed to their impound lot. You're not out of the woods yet, Morgan. They're probably biding their time to get all their ducks in a row before they come at you again."

"Crap," I said, thumping the mattress with my fist. "We need to figure out who Rick is."

Jon looked at his watch.

"How long before you have to leave?" I asked him.

"As long as I get back sometime tonight, it'll be fine. You can have me for a few more hours and I have an idea. If I can get the car's plate number, I can run it. And if the police here won't share it with me, maybe the restaurant owner will. Are you ladies up for some brunch?"

"Of course," I said.

"You betcha," Rita said, rising from the bed and straightening into her normal, rigid posture. "Let me go grab my coat and I'll meet you guys out in the parking lot."

"Sure."

Minutes later we were all loaded into my car. I handed my keys to Jon and asked him to drive so I could sit in the back seat with Newt. Rita rode shotgun and gave Jon directions. Eight minutes later we were pulling into the restaurant parking lot, only to discover a note on the door saying it was closed until tomorrow.

"The owner must have thought closing down for the day was the respectful thing to do," Jon said. He looked over at Rita. "I don't suppose you know who the owner is?"

She shook her head. "Sorry, I don't."

Jon looked back at me. "No clue," I said. "Let me see if I can find a name and contact number on the internet." I took out my phone and did a couple of quick Google searches, but all I came up with was the name W. G. Naughton—I was expecting a Hardwick—and a phone number for the restaurant. The restaurant phone got me a recording listing the hours of operation and a search for the name W. G. Naughton in Rhinelander gave me nothing.

I sat there for a moment, the car's engine idling, staring at the covered front porch of the restaurant. Then it hit me.

"I think I know a way for us to find out who the owner is," I said. I took out my phone and made a call but got no answer. "Plan B," I said. "Head for the north side of town."

CHAPTER 21

Less than fifteen minutes later, we were bumping along the drive to Sonja Mueller's house. I stared into the bordering woods but didn't see anyone lurking about. Of course, that didn't mean there wasn't someone there. Roger's and Rick's paranoia was proving to be contagious.

As soon as I got out of the car, I heard the hum of some type of tool running out in the barn. Its door was wide open and as soon as I let Newt out of the car, Wally came trotting out to greet us, nose to the air and tail wagging.

"What is this place?" Jon asked.

"Hodag central," I said with a smile. "You'll see."

Sonja was hard at work with a grinding tool, smoothing out the edges on a Hodag sculpture similar in size to the one on the front porch of the restaurant. She saw us enter and immediately turned off her grinder, though the exhaust fans continued to run.

"Well, well, I wasn't expecting you ladies back so soon. And with a handsome escort, I see." She smiled flirtatiously at Jon.

"I tried to call," I said.

"Yeah, I can't hear a thing with all the stuff I have running so I typically leave my phone in the house when I come out here to work."

I made the introductions, letting Sonja know Jon was a police officer, though I didn't say where.

"Would you all like to come inside for some coffee or tea?" Sonja asked. "I baked a fresh batch of oatmeal cookies this morning."

"That sounds wonderful," I said. "But we don't want to interrupt your work more than we have to and we're hoping you can help us with something. It shouldn't take long."

"Happy to help if I can," Sonja said with a bemused look on her face. She was watching Jon, who had wandered down the central aisle between the barn's shelves. He was studying all the Hodag sculptures with a curious expression, his mouth hanging open.

"I'm guessing you made the Hodag sculpture sitting out in front of the Hardwick restaurant," I said. "It resembles many of your others."

"I did," she said. "Do you want one like it? I'll give you a great deal on it."

"No, thanks. Although I may get back to you on that," I said, imagining how well a Hodag or two would fit with my store. "What we need is contact information for the owner of the restaurant."

Sonja's smile slowly faded. "Mind if I ask why?"

"I just need to speak to him or her about a minor matter," I said. "An incident that happened while I was dining there last night."

"I'm sure you could find the information on your own," Sonja said. "Do a records search, or just check with the chamber." It didn't seem Sonja had heard about the murder yet, a lucky break for us.

"That takes time, and my relationship with Cordelia isn't great," I reminded her. I hoped she would buy this excuse since I didn't want to tell her the police suspected me of murder and since Cordelia was married to the detective in charge of the investigation, she wasn't likely to be forthcoming with the information, even if I was her best bud.

Sonja dismissed this with a *pshaw* and the flick of a hand, as if batting away a pesky fly. "Cordelia will tell you. She has to. It's her job."

"Maybe," I said. "But I was hoping you could save me the hassle of dealing with her."

Sonja tipped her head to one side and considered me for a moment. "Okay," she said finally. "The owner's name is Bill Naughton. I don't know his phone number off the top of my head, but I have it in his file."

She walked back to her worktable and beyond it to a large filing cabinet against the wall. It didn't take long for her to find what she wanted, write down the info, and come back to me with it. "Do me a favor," she said as she handed me the slip of paper. "Don't tell him you got his number from me. I don't want my customers thinking I give out their personal info."

I promised Sonja I wouldn't and thanked her profusely, and after she made a failed sales pitch to Jon, who was still ogling the many Hodags in her shop, we left. My delight at getting the information we wanted faded fast when I called the number and got a message saying it was no longer in service.

"No worries," Jon said. "Another idea came to me when Sonja said Cordelia would have to share the information with you because it's her job." He wouldn't elaborate further and when we got back to the motel, he disappeared into his room, closing the adjoining door. Rita and I looked at each other and shrugged.

"Do you think Sonja purposely gave us a bogus number?" Rita asked me. "She didn't seem eager to give out the information."

"I'd be lying if I said the same thought hadn't occurred to me," I told her. "Though I'm not sure why she would do something like that."

"Maybe she just wants to respect her clients' privacy."

"Maybe," I said, unconvinced. My stomach growled so loudly Newt's ears perked up and he cocked his head to one side, looking at me strangely.

Rita laughed. "Sounds like lunch should be next on the agenda," she said.

"I'm oddly hungry," I told her. "Something about these investigations makes my appetite go wild."

Jon tapped on the adjoining door to my suite and then opened it. Judging from the huge grin on his face, I gathered he'd had some luck. "I have the name of our dead man," he said.

"What? How?" I asked, genuinely impressed. I suppressed a weird impulse to fling myself at him and give him a big kiss.

"I should have thought of it sooner; I called Zeke and asked him what towing company the cops here use for their impounds. He knows the guys who work there from when he was on the force and when I told him what I needed, he offered to call and ask the towing company for the license plate on the car. They gave it to him, he ran it for me, and voilà! The towed car is registered to one Ulrich Liebhardt, though the registration expired eight years ago and hasn't been renewed."

"Wow," I said, taking a slip of paper he handed me with the man's name written on it along with a date of birth and an address in Michigan. "Thank you!"

"You're welcome."

"I assumed Rick was short for Richard," I said.

"Ulrich Liebhardt is a classic German name," Rita said. "And there were lots of German settlers in this area. It makes sense."

Jon said, "The address is a last known and I'm guessing it's not current since it's in Michigan and like the registration, the license is expired. But if you put Devon on it and let him work his magic, I'm betting he'll be able to find more for you. I need to get back to the island."

"Rita and I were just discussing getting some lunch. Can you stay long enough to eat with us? You have to eat, right?"

Jon smiled. "Sure, but we need to make it a quick one. Why don't you call Devon and get him working on this while I go check out of my room."

Jon disappeared back through the adjoining door, and I had a strange urge to run after him and beg him to find a way to stay longer. It seemed I never realized how much I enjoyed having him around until I didn't.

"You really like him," Rita said.

I turned and looked at her. "I do. But this long-distance, part-time relationship stuff is frustrating as hell."

"He really cares about you. You'll figure it out. Give it time."

Would we? Part of me doubted it but another part of me desperately hoped so.

"Go ahead and call Devon," Rita said. "I'm going back to my room to freshen up before we go to eat. I'll meet you back here in ten."

I made the call to Devon, who was delighted to have more sleuthing to do. "I'll let you know as soon as I have anything," he said. "In the meantime, I emailed you contact info for a good defense lawyer out of Milwaukee who can help if need be."

"I'm hoping he won't be necessary," I said. "But thanks for getting the info."

After he assured me all was under control at the store, I ended the call and got on my laptop to do my own search for Ulrich Liebhardt while waiting for Jon and Rita to return.

My first clue that this break in the investigation wasn't going to be as much help as I'd thought came when my online search turned up nothing for Ulrich Liebhardt. I had to hope Devon would have better luck.

For lunch, we drove into town and picked a bistro, where I enjoyed a delicious prime rib sandwich, half of which I set aside for Newt. Our lunchtime conversation centered on Hodags, Hodag sculptures, Hodag culture, and Hodag legend.

"Did you know the Hodag is supposed to be a spirit born from the ashes of cremated oxen who were used and abused by workers in the lumber industry?" I said. With this revelation, Jon swallowed his current bite of sandwich with some difficulty while shaking his head. Rita watched him, amused. "Yep, rumor has it Eugene Shepard used to tell tales about the creature in the logging camps, describing it as having a dragon's body, fangs, and a snarling grin. He also said it smelled like buzzard meat and skunk perfume."

If I had thoughts of putting Jon off the remainder of his sandwich, they quickly dissipated. After that one slow swallow, he inhaled the rest of his food.

We discussed the town's fascination and adoration of this mythical creature with some amusement, doing so with lowered voices so we wouldn't offend anyone who might be listening in. Underlying it all but unspoken were three things: Andy's predicament and the murder of Ulrich Liebhardt, the creature Andy claimed to have seen and that I might have also seen, and the ever-present threat of David Johnson looming over my head. Jon didn't mention David again until we were done eating and had driven back to the motel. Rita went inside, leaving Jon and me alone in the parking lot while his car warmed up.

"I know I'd be wasting my breath if I asked you to go home and forget all this," he said.

"You know I can't."

He puffed his cheeks and exhaled through pursed lips. "Damn it, I don't like this, Morgan."

"I'll be fine. I'm in no more danger here than if I was at home. Please don't worry."

"Of course I'm going to worry," he said irritably. Then he immediately looked remorseful. "Sorry."

"No need to apologize. I like having someone worry about me."

He shook his head, and I couldn't tell if he was affronted or amused. "You are the most intriguing, infuriating, and exasperating woman I have ever known, Morgan Carter."

I grinned at him, and he rolled his eyes. Then he kissed me. It was a very nice kiss, one that made me moan a bit when it ended, both with desire and regret that it was over. Newt, standing beside me and staring up at us, whined. I couldn't tell if he was jealous or simply wanted a kiss of his own.

"A little something to remember me by once I leave," Jon said with a devilish grin.

"Not likely to forget *that* anytime soon," I said.

His expression turned serious. "Be careful and be smart, Morgan. Don't take foolish risks."

"I won't."

Jon looked down at Newt. "And keep this guy with you at all times."

"Of course. Like he'd let me do otherwise."

Jon bent down and cupped Newt's head between his hands. "You watch out for her, buddy, you hear?"

Newt let out another whine and Jon rewarded him by giving him a hearty scrub on his shoulders. "Good boy."

Jon looked at me one more time and, without another word, climbed into his car and drove away. I watched him leave until I couldn't see him anymore, fighting an urge the entire time to run after him and beg him to take me along.

As I turned to go inside the motel, I caught sight of a black car parked in the lot of another, smaller motel across the road. It looked like the same car I'd seen idling in our lot early this morning. And once again, as soon as I spotted it, it sped off. It was too far away to see the driver and it was a common enough vehicle in a common enough color to have been anyone. I couldn't be absolutely sure it was the same car I'd seen before, but in my gut I felt it was.

What the hell had I gotten myself into?

CHAPTER 22

I should have known when I didn't hear back from Devon until late in the evening that his search efforts weren't going well. Rita and I had just finished eating the salads we'd picked up for dinner from the Culver's across the road and Rita had retired to her room with a promise of hooking up with me again in the morning. She seemed out of sorts, and knowing she liked to stay busy and feel useful, I gave her an assignment, asking her to use her tablet to see what she could dig up on local Hodag history. I didn't really need the information but there was no harm in having her look.

Since my efforts at searching for something, anything, on Ulrich Liebhardt had been maddeningly unfruitful, I shut my laptop in frustration and was about to call Devon when he beat me to it.

"How's it going?" I asked.

"Mixed bag. This Ulrich Liebhardt guy is a ghost."

"Tell me about it," I said, my voice rich with sarcasm. "I take it you're getting stumped, too?"

"Pretty much. No marriage records, no property ownership, no businesses, no death certificate, nothing. Needless to say, there are no social media accounts either. The address on his car registration and driver's license is in Michigan. It's a house currently owned and occupied by a woman named Gretchen Walker, a forty-something hairstylist who bought it a little over ten years ago. There was never anyone by the name of Ulrich Liebhardt at the address, at least not on any official records. I suppose he could have been a renter, but I have a feeling he simply used the address because he needed one, and it has some significance or meaning to him. Maybe he knew someone who lived there, or he lived there as a child, or lived nearby . . . something. I find it hard to believe the choice was an arbitrary one."

"Can we call this Gretchen Walker and ask her?"

"Already tried," Devon said. "Found her on LinkedIn and got her number but she didn't answer. I sent her a text, too, but so far all I've gotten is crickets."

"Pass the information on to me and I'll try. Maybe she'll respond better to a woman."

"That's kind of sexist, isn't it?" Devon said. I could hear the tease in his voice.

"Nope, just reality. If I had a nickel for every guy who messaged me with a picture ripped off of some male model's profile, typically with them on a sailboat or in a military uniform or standing next to a fancy car, I'd be rich."

"You're already rich."

"You get my point."

"I do. I did turn up one interesting fact about Ulrich. He was enrolled in the medical school at the U-Dub but left during his final year."

"Left?"

"Yeah, it looks like he dropped out."

"That's odd. Why quit when you're so close to graduation?"

"My thoughts exactly. And it's the last thing I can find on the guy other than the driver's license, which was obtained right before he dropped out of school and has since expired. The car registration is long expired, too, and the car itself is one he bought in med school. It's more than twenty years old."

"Keep digging and let me know if you find anything."

"Will do. And, boss?"

"Yeah?"

"Thanks for this."

"For assigning you extra work on top of running the store?"

"Well, you *are* going to pay me extra, aren't you?" He didn't wait for me to answer, most likely because he knew I would. "Besides, things with the store are slow right now and this Ulrich guy is exactly the kind of challenge I like."

"Happy to please," I said. "And while I appreciate your dedication, don't let the lure of the puzzle interfere with your personal life."

"What personal life?"

Uh-oh. There was a definite downturn in his tone, telling me something was wrong. "What about Anne?" I asked.

"She's moved on to someone else," he said, trying and failing to sound indifferent. "One of those superathletic, bulked-up guys on the fire department."

Ouch. This was the physical opposite of Devon, who was tall, slender, and more wiry than muscular. "Oh, Dev, I'm so sorry. I know you really liked her."

"Not meant to be, I guess." Then with his typical, blunt, don't-make-me-feel-anything style, he rapidly shut down the topic with a definitive, "Night, boss."

I went to say good night back to him but realized he'd already ended the call. Poor guy. My heart ached for him.

Newt was signaling his need to go out, so I leashed him up and headed for the parking lot. Outside, I was delighted to see a lazy but steady snowfall, fat, fluffy flakes drifting down from the sky. There was already another inch of new snow on the ground, and I headed for the open field bordering the parking lot and released Newt to do his thing.

Much warier now after everything that had happened, I scanned my surroundings, searching for mysterious cars or skulking people hanging around, but saw nothing worrisome. The muffling effects of the snow made for a nearly complete silence, broken only by the faint jingle of Newt's tags as he explored, an occasional passing car out on the road, and the sounds generated by the mechanicals from nearby buildings. The new covering of snow made everything look fresh and clean, and the lights from the motel and other nearby businesses gave much of it a warm, cozy glow. It was a gorgeous winter night.

Once Newt was done frolicking and returned to me, I leashed him up and made for the motel's rear entrance. But before going inside, I worked my way around the back corner of the building and examined the strip of open land between the row of trees and the rear wall of the motel. It was about twelve feet wide, and I could see through to the parking lot on the other side of the building. With the new snow, the footprints from the night before last were nearly gone, little more than faint indentations leading from where I stood to the base of my room's window and then back toward the row of trees. Curious, I squeezed in between two of the trees to follow the trail of indentations on that side, but quickly saw they arced around and entered the motel parking lot on the opposite side of the building.

Who had been standing outside my window? Had it been David? The thought sickened me, and I spun around and practically dragged Newt back to the motel door. I should have noticed Newt's odd behavior as I carded the lock on my room's door, but thoughts of David, what he might want from me and where he might be, had me distracted. By the time I registered Newt's warning growl as he pushed past me and dashed into the room, it was too late. I caught movement coming out of the darkened bathroom just as the door closed behind me and a hand clamped over my mouth.

CHAPTER 23

I tried to scream but the hand over my mouth effectively muffled my efforts. Newt, however, had no such restraints and he went bonkers, barking so hard and loud that spittle flew from his mouth.

"Call off the dog or I'll shoot it," an unfamiliar male voice hissed into my ear. He snaked an arm around my waist and used me as a shield to keep Newt from getting to him. The hand over my mouth disappeared but I felt him jab what I assumed was a gun into my back. Fear for Newt outstripped concern for myself.

"Newt, it's okay. It's okay! Stop!" I said in my best commanding voice.

Newt backed up a step and stopped barking but eyed my captor menacingly while emitting a low, rumbling growl.

"I can't promise you I can control him if you don't let me go," I said.

The arm about my waist eased ever so slightly and then it released me. I hurried over to Newt, put a reassuring hand on his head, and gave my assailant my best stink eye.

I half expected to see David standing there even though I knew the voice hadn't been his. Instead, I found myself staring at a total stranger. He was of average height and build, and he had red hair grown a bit longer than a military cut and a face full of freckles. His feet were encased in a pair of sensible black boots, his pants were also black, and while his shirt was white, he wore a black winter jacket over it, currently unzipped and hanging open. What looked like a knit cap—once again in black—protruded from one of the pockets and I caught a glimpse of a shoulder holster beneath the jacket. This guy was either a cop of some sort or a professional hit man. I leaned toward the former, figuring if he was a hit man he would have done me in already. Maybe a PI? Either way, I didn't get a strong feeling of danger from him despite his unwelcome presence in my room.

What's more, I noticed his hands were empty. He saw me looking puzzled, shrugged, and formed one hand into a gun shape. "That was my finger in your back," he said, thrusting the hand forward to demonstrate. "Though I would have pulled my weapon if necessary." He lifted one side of his jacket to show me the real gun holstered there. "We need to talk."

Anger washed over me. "Fat chance, asshole. First, tell me who the hell you are and what you're doing in my room. How did you even get in here?"

He cast a nervous eye at Newt as he reached into his pocket and pulled out a small brown wallet. He flipped it open, revealing what appeared to be an FBI ID. "Can we sit, please?"

I let out a *pfft* of exasperation to make sure he knew how annoyed I was. "Newt, go lie down," I said, pointing to the space between the two beds. Newt did as he was told but didn't take his eyes off the stranger. I stood at the base of that space, slipped my coat off, and tossed it onto the bed closest to the door. Then I waved an arm toward the table with an impatient look at my visitor. Giving me and Newt as wide a berth as he could, he crossed the room, pulled out a chair, and sat. As I took the seat across from him, I noticed my laptop was open even though I distinctly remembered slapping it closed out of frustration before taking Newt outside. It currently displayed my desktop, but I couldn't be sure my visitor hadn't accessed other items. I closed the laptop slowly, staring at him the whole time, just to make a point.

"I'd like to see that ID of yours again, please," I said.

He dutifully set it onto the table. I picked it up and examined it more closely, comparing the freckled image on the ID with the one sitting across from me. It listed his name as Ian Forrester and the whole thing looked official enough, though I knew those things could be faked. The guy certainly dressed like an FBI agent, but I remained skeptical. Why would the FBI be nosing around in my room?

I decided to give my surprise visitor the benefit of the doubt and tossed his ID back across the table at him. Newt whined but stayed where he was.

"How about we start off with you answering my question by telling me what you're doing in my motel room?" I said.

"I'm wondering what you're doing here in Rhinelander," he countered.

I raised my eyebrows at him. "I asked first."

He wasn't easily intimidated. After leaning back in his chair and crossing one leg over the other, he stared right back at me. Calmly. He didn't say a word.

"I'm here on vacation," I said, figuring I'd throw him a bone to get things going. But rather than answer my question, he got an odd little grin on his face. The man was insufferable!

"Fine," I said, getting up from my seat. "I guess I'll just have to call the local police." It was a bluff of sorts; I didn't intend to really call the police, though I would if I had to. And given recent events, a call to the police was just as likely to end up with me being arrested as anything happening to this guy. But I'd realized my phone was in the pocket of my coat, which was currently lying on the bed farthest away, and I wanted it in hand. Just in case. He called my bluff by sitting in his chair looking as cool as the proverbial cucumber while I retrieved my phone. The thought of making a run for it crossed my mind, but I knew I'd never get the room door open fast enough. Besides, he had that gun, and I didn't want to leave him here with Newt.

"Sit down," he said, nodding toward the chair I'd vacated. He didn't say it in a commanding way, yet the tone was such that I knew he'd brook no resistance. Feeling a little better now that I had my phone, I returned to my seat.

"Your name is Morgan Carter, and you are not here on vacation," he said. "I've been watching you and you haven't gone anywhere or done any of the things a tourist would do. So, tell me, why are you really here in Rhinelander?"

I sighed and leaned forward, arms on the table. He might be an FBI agent but that didn't mean he was the only one who could use body language to his advantage. "I'm looking for a living Hodag," I said.

He scoffed. "Fine, play games, but a straight answer will get me out of here a lot faster."

"That *was* a straight answer," I insisted. "I'm here looking for a living, breathing Hodag. I'm a cryptozoologist. Do you know what that is, or didn't they cover that in FBI school?"

A flood of red washed over his face, starting at his neck and racing toward his hairline. "I'll tell you what you are," he said, his tone annoyingly smug. "You're the owner of a store in Door County that sells oddities and takes special orders from folks who are looking for one-of-a-kind items."

The fact he knew about Odds and Ends alarmed me a little, though I tried not to show it. I was about to explain what cryptozo-ology was, but he went on before I could.

"What were you doing at Sonja Mueller's place?"

I leaned back in my chair, unable to hide my surprise. "How do you know I went there?"

"I saw you. You stayed quite a while the first time."

A light bulb clicked on in my brain. I remembered the figure I'd seen lurking in the woods alongside Sonja's driveway when Rita and I had left after that first visit, and the black car parked along the shoulder of the road. I realized it had likely been this guy in the woods, not David as I'd initially feared. The relief flooding through me was so intense, I burst out laughing, an action that clearly un-settled Ian Forrester. He fidgeted in his seat, frowning, and I admit I felt the tiniest bit of satisfaction knowing I'd made him squirm.

"Why on earth are you hiding out in Sonja's woods, staking out her house?" I asked. "Shouldn't you be looking into these murders instead?"

"Murders? Plural?"

I gaped at him. "What kind of FBI agent are you anyway?"

"The kind investigating the theft of art and antiquities."

"Oh." I wasn't expecting this answer and it momentarily set me back on my heels. As did the question he asked next.

"Do you sell much fine art at your store?"

I stared at him, blinking several times, as I tried to parse this sudden change of subject. "Do I sometimes try to find artwork for my customers?" I asked rhetorically. "Yes. But if you're talking about classic forms of art by the masters, then no. I'm out of my depth on that one. To be honest, unless it's about cryptids or representative of something dark and twisted, I'm not interested, and neither are most of my customers." I recalled something then, and I raised a finger to let him know I was about to elaborate.

"However, I did have a customer once who asked me if I knew of any existing replicas, or someone who might be able to render a copy of a sixteenth-century painting by a guy named Balding or something like that. It depicted a naked girl being embraced by a skeletal figure presumed to be Death. I never found a replica and while I do know an artist who could probably paint a decent copy, I didn't pass on the name. That painting is a creepy little thing and one of them in the world is enough."

"The artist's name was Hans Baldung. And the work is called *Death and the Maiden*."

"And that more or less exhausts my knowledge of fine art," I said with a smile. "Besides, I've always believed the true worth of art can be determined only by those who admire it. Not everyone agrees on what's valuable."

Ian shrugged and then inexplicably changed subjects again. "Why are you hunting for a Hodag? And why didn't you buy one of Sonja's many sculptures if that's what you're after?"

"I just might buy one or more of Sonja's Hodag sculptures because I have customers I think would be interested in owning one. But it's not my primary reason for being in Rhinelander. I'm here to try to prove Hodags really exist." This earned me a skeptical arch of his brow. Can't say I blamed him.

"Why?" he asked, looking incredulous.

"Haven't you heard about the man who was killed last week in the woods north of here? It was a nasty, brutal death and now another man has been accused of murdering him even though he swears a Hodag did the deed."

Ian's face screwed up in thought. "I remember hearing about the death," he said. "Though I'm not familiar with the particulars."

"Well, if you've been watching me, then you've seen the white-haired woman who is often with me." Ian nodded. "She's one of my employees and the aunt of the man accused of the murder. She's convinced he's innocent and she asked me to come and try to prove his claim that a Hodag did it."

"Seems like a waste of time," he said.

"I thought so, too, at first. But then I saw something myself in those woods."

His brow furrowed, he shifted in his seat, and he eyed me with no small amount of suspicion. "A trick of light and imagination," he said with a flippant backhand.

I saw little to be gained in continuing down that road, so I changed gears. "You still haven't told me why you were snooping in my room," I said. And then, like a bolt of lightning, it came to me. "Wait. I get it. You think Sonja Mueller has stolen artworks." I laughed until the other shoe dropped. "And you think I'm somehow involved?" I said, aghast.

Ian rubbed his hands together almost as if he was wringing them. "We've had an eye on Ms. Mueller for a long time now, but I've been watching her very closely for the past week or so," he said. "You're the first and only visitor she's had, and you've been there twice. You also had dinner with her."

"You really think she's some sort of art smuggler?" I struggled to wrap my head around the idea given my interactions with Sonja. "She doesn't even have any art hanging in her house. The walls are bare."

Ian shrugged. "That means nothing."

As soon as he said this, I realized he had a point. "I suppose you're right. But it doesn't make her an art smuggler either."

With the tiniest flick of one eyebrow, he continued defending his cause. "Rumors swirled around her grandparents for decades. They immigrated to this country after the war and Sonja's grandmother worked in the household of someone high up in Hitler's regime before coming here. Some think she left Germany with artworks that had been stolen from Jewish families. Sonja's grandfather was a talented painter and sculptor who would recognize fine works of art. Plus, they seemed to live beyond their means, triggering a lot of speculation and the occasional investigation over the years, though no one ever found any proof."

"Maybe because the rumors were just that, only rumors," I suggested.

"Maybe," Ian said, clearly unconvinced. "But some of those rumors came from reliable sources. As for modern day, we've been paying closer attention to Ms. Mueller of late because we recently intercepted chatter about a stolen artwork about to be smuggled out of the country for a wealthy, anonymous buyer somewhere in the Middle East. That chatter led us here."

I must have looked skeptical because Ian shrugged and added, "It's the perfect setup. Think how easy it would be to hide a valuable canvas inside one of her sculptures and smuggle it out of the country. She regularly ships her artwork to places all around the world, especially those Hodag things, though honestly, I can't for the life of me figure out the attraction."

"I'm with you there," I said with a laugh. "Of all the creatures I've hunted for over the years, the Hodag ranks right up there as one of the ugliest. Though maybe it's their ugliness that makes them attractive to some. A bit of advice, though. Whatever you do, don't tell the locals you think Hodags are ugly. They don't take it well."

Ian laughed. It was genuine and transformative, making me instantly change my opinion of him. The air in the room suddenly felt more relaxed. Apparently, even Newt sensed it as he quit giving Ian his death stare and flopped down onto the floor between the two beds.

"The voice of experience, I take it," Ian said.

"Indeed. I gather you didn't find any missing artworks during your little impromptu—and may I add, illegal—search of my room."

"I did not," he said with a sly smile.

"Or any incriminating emails on my computer?"

The smile remained but he didn't answer.

"How did you get in here anyway?"

He fished in his shirt pocket and produced a key card. "The clerk working the front desk tonight was quite helpful once I threatened him with jail time for the pot he was selling in the parking lot. Good thing Wisconsin has been slow to legalize the stuff."

"You know, you could have just asked me," I said. "You've had plenty of opportunities. I'm glad to know it was you stalking me. All those times I saw you I was afraid you were someone else."

He looked confused. "Really? Who?"

"An old boyfriend who . . . it doesn't matter." I waved the topic away.

"Well, I hate to burst your relief bubble, but I haven't been stalking you," Ian said. "I've been watching the Mueller place and Sonja. When I said I'd been watching you and you hadn't done any-thing interesting, it was more or less a bluff. I ran your plate the first time you visited Ms. Mueller and then did a basic background check on you."

"But you were lurking in that row of trees behind the motel the other night and then trying to peek in my window here. And you were in your car out in the parking lot and in the lot of the motel across the road this afternoon."

Ian slowly shook his head. "I saw you and your white-haired companion on your first visit to the Mueller place. Today when you came to the Mueller place, you were also with some blond man. But that's it. Though I admit you piqued my curiosity initially, I more or less ruled you out early on. My search of your room was just to be sure I wasn't overlooking anything."

"For your information, the blond man's name is Jon Flanders, and he happens to be the chief of police on Washington Island in

Door County. Check him out." I couldn't hide the smugness in my voice.

"A cop? Really?" Ian said, eyebrows raised. He pondered this for a few seconds. Then he shrugged and said, "I'll check him out. As for who might be stalking you, it could be an investigator for an insurance company. Valuable stolen artworks are often insured for millions and the companies don't like to pay. If an investigator was privy to the same chatter we heard, they might have sent someone out to watch Ms. Mueller and check out any visitors she may have."

Forrester reached into a different pocket and came out with a business card, which he set on the table. "My cell number is on there," he said. "If you hear or know anything about Ms. Mueller that you think might help me, give me a call."

By the time Ian left, I was mentally and physically drained. I wanted desperately to crawl in between my sheets and drop off into a deep slumber, but my thoughts were racing like a greyhound at the track, round and round pursuing an ever-elusive bait. Damn David anyway! The man haunted me relentlessly.

I decided to call Jon despite the late hour because I was eager to have someone help me dissect my situation. Plus, I just really wanted to talk to him. I had no idea if he would answer and was so relieved when he did that I didn't feel a twinge of guilt when I heard the sleepiness in his voice. His reaction when I told him about my nosy FBI agent was skepticism followed by concern, topped off by a hint of anger. He assured me he would look into Ian right away to find out if he really was an FBI agent and get back to me. That piece was easy, he said. The realization that my constant shadow hadn't been Ian was harder for him to deal with.

"I'll let you know as soon as I have verification on this For-rester guy. In the meantime, be careful."

"I will."

He called me back less than half an hour later to let me know Ian Forrester was, in fact, an FBI agent working in the theft division. I hoped this information would be reassuring enough to allow me to fall asleep.

It wasn't.

CHAPTER 24

I managed to doze in fits and starts through the night but any little sound—someone giggling out in the hall, the heater in my room kicking on, a clink when Newt rolled over and his collar tags hit a leg on the table—made me start awake and then it would take forever for me to drift off again.

I got up a little before seven, and after a quick walk for Newt and a stop for coffee at the free breakfast station in the motel lobby, I hopped on my laptop, where I saw that Devon had sent me the contact info for Gretchen Walker. I punched in the woman's number on my phone and got her voice mail. I left a message telling her I was trying to get information on a man named Ulrich Liebhardt and, after a moment's hesitation, I added that Ulrich had recently been murdered and the reason for my inquiry was that I was trying to figure out who might have killed him. I knew the message was a gamble. Would the woman be curious enough to want to call me back or would my revelation frighten her into blocking me from future contact?

I didn't have to wait long for my answer. My phone rang a moment later and Gretchen Walker's number showed on my screen.

I answered the call with, "Is this Gretchen Walker?"

A second or two of hesitation, and then, "It is. Was Rick really murdered?"

She knew him. And her use of his nickname suggested she knew him well. My heart rate quickened.

"Yes, it appears so," I said, realizing as I spoke that, as far as I knew, his ID hadn't been confirmed.

"Are you a cop?"

"No, I'm an investigator looking into the death of someone else and I think Rick's murder might be connected. How do you know him?"

"We kind of grew up together. My mom did childcare in our home and Rick was one of three kids she looked after. She had him from when he was two until he was twelve, though it was only an after-school thing during those last six years. He was a latchkey kid after that. We went to the same school, and we were in some of the same classes, but our social circles didn't cross much."

"This was in Michigan?"

"Oh no. Sorry. We lived in Rhinelander, Wisconsin, back then. I moved to Michigan after my mom died. Followed someone I was dating at the time. The relationship didn't work out, but I found a great house and I like it here, so I decided to stay. Been here a little over ten years now."

"What can you tell me about Rick?"

She chuckled. "He was a weird kid, always dissecting bugs, snakes, and lizards with a magnifying glass, tiny tweezers, and razor blades he kept in a shoebox. He'd cut 'em and gut 'em and then look at their parts under a microscope. He sometimes kept things in little jars . . . pieces, parts, bug juices. . . ." She paused, sucking a breath in through her teeth. "It was more than a little creepy if you ask me."

No argument here.

"Rick and I kind of kept in touch for a few years after high school and his mom came by for a visit once, right around the time Rick was accepted into medical school. She was bragging about him big-time, though it came as no surprise to us. Despite his weirdness, the guy was wicked smart. We figured he'd either be a doctor or a serial killer." She let out an awkward giggle before continuing.

"Rick was always curious about what made living things tick. A friend of mine from high school who went to the same U of Dub campus as Rick told me how some laboratory company latched on to him at a job fair. She said they were übereager to recruit him and then she made up stupid puns about how the company went buggy over him, and how they were squirming with excitement like they had ants in their pants . . . that kind of thing. It was silly, but inevitable, I suppose. Everybody in high school knew how Rick was with bugs."

"What was the name of the laboratory company?"

"The what? Oh, um . . . geez . . . I don't remember. I think it might have been named after a woman? But I'm not sure. Sorry. They were located in the industrial park outside Rhinelander, but that probably doesn't help since they went out of business some years back. Right before I moved here, in fact."

"So when was the last time you heard from Rick?"

"It's been years. I heard he'd dropped out of med school right after I moved here. I sent him a Christmas card but I never heard back from him. I don't even have an address for him anymore. I've often wondered what happened to him. You said he was murdered?"

"Yes."

"How awful. Was it a robbery or something?"

"I'm not sure. That's one of the things I'm trying to figure out. Do you know if Rick's mother is still alive?"

"No, I heard she died right before Rick dropped out of med school. It's just as well. She always bragged about how he was going to be a doctor and she died thinking he would be. It would have broken her heart to know he dropped out."

"What was her name?"

"Freda Liebhardt."

"What about his father? Or any siblings?"

"Nope. He was an only child. Freda said her husband died right after Rick was born. Some kind of cancer. Leukemia, maybe?"

"I assume Freda worked at a job of some sort?"

"She did, at a bank. It's gone now, like so many of the smaller community banks. It got eaten up by one of the big guys."

Damn. Nothing but dead ends, quite literally in this case. "Do you know why Rick dropped out of med school?"

"No idea, but the friend I mentioned earlier said she heard rumors the laboratory company wooing him was offering him a huge paycheck."

"Do you know why Rick would have had your Michigan address on his driver's license?"

"What? No. That can't be right."

"Is Walker your maiden name?"

"It is."

"Ever been married?"

"No."

"You live alone?"

A pause too long for comfort followed before she answered. "You're getting rather personal here, Miss . . . what is your name again?"

"It's Carter," I said. "Morgan Carter."

"I'm not sure what my living situation has to do with Rick's murder."

"Nothing, most likely. I'm just trying to figure out why he had your address on his license. It might be related to his murder." That solicited a gasp, and I knew I'd made a mistake.

"I think I've answered enough of your questions," Gretchen said, confirming my fear. "Good luck with your investigation."

With that, the call ended, and I cursed under my breath. Newt gave me a look.

"I'm an idiot, Newt," I said, and he wagged his tail as if in agreement.

Traitor.

Despite my stupidity, my phone call to Gretchen had resulted in a lead or two for Devon to follow. I called him and told him what Gretchen had said about a company named after a woman that had once been in the industrial park outside Rhinelander but had closed around ten years ago. I could hear Devon tapping away at his keys and in a matter of seconds he'd found something.

"How about EDDNA?" he said. "All caps and spelled with two Ds."

"Oh my God! That has to be it! Roger told me Rick warned him about a woman named Edna, or what he assumed was a woman."

Devon said, "This EDDNA was an LLC working on solutions for climate control using environmental DNA. I'll send you an article about them from twelve years ago. Hold on." He paused and I heard more keys tapping.

An email arrived in my inbox and, as I opened it, Devon continued, sharing more of what he'd found. "Um . . . looks like their name was an acronym for Environmentally Diverse DNA. Makes sense, I suppose, because a lowercase e in front of DNA is a common acronym for environmental DNA. And here's an interesting side bit; the name Eddna with two Ds in it as a woman's name means 'rejuvenation.'"

"Appropriate," I said.

"What, exactly, is environmental DNA?" Devon asked.

Not remembering quickly enough that any question Devon asked while on an internet-connected computer was basically rhetorical, I started to answer. I got out only, "Well, it's the study of—" when he interrupted me.

"Ah, I see. It's pretty much what it sounds like. Here's what it says on the US Geological Survey site: 'Environmental DNA (eDNA) is organismal DNA that can be found in the environment. Environmental DNA originates from cellular material shed by organisms (via skin, excrement, etc.) into aquatic or terrestrial environments that can be sampled and monitored using new molecular methods. Such methodology is important for the early detection of invasive species as well as the detection of rare and cryptic species.' How about that, boss? Right in your bailiwick."

"Bailiwick?" I said, amused. "Your vocabulary is expanding."

"Yeah, that's what happens when I spend too much time around you and Rita."

"Any details as to why the company went out of business?"

"Hold on," he said, keys clacking away. "Hunh. That's interesting. It looks like they just disappeared."

"What do you mean?"

"Just what I said. They simply ceased to exist. Moved out of their building and vanished ten years ago. I don't see any mention of bankruptcy or buyouts . . . weird."

"Got any names of the executives who worked there?"

"Just one, from the LLC filings and the article I sent you, but I'm not sure it's going to help much."

"Why?"

"The name is Margaret Smith. And in case you were wondering, Smith is the most common surname in the United States."

"Great," I groaned, following it with a chuckle. With a surname as ubiquitous and common as Smith, finding her might be difficult.

"Let me work at this a bit and see what I can do," Devon said. "Might take me a while but I'm sure I can find something."

"Thanks," I said. "And good luck."

"I don't need luck. I have superpowers," he said in a hypermasculine voice. "I'm data-man!"

I couldn't help but laugh. "Get to it, Boy Wonder," I teased. "Find me some answers."

CHAPTER 25

⌐

While Devon worked his magic, I had plans of my own. I went knocking on Rita's door a little before nine and invited her out to breakfast. We picked a small café downtown and settled in with muffins and lattes while Newt waited outside in the car.

I'd sensed Rita disliked Sonja Mueller, and after the revelations my unexpected visitor had made last night, I was eager to pick her brain as to why.

"Did you know Sonja before we met her this week?" I asked her.

"Not really, though Roger mentioned her a time or two in the past because they dated."

"Dated? Really?"

Rita shrugged. "Roger waxed on about her for a couple of weeks last year after they started dating. To be honest, I thought she was just after Roger for his money."

"Is Roger that well off?" I asked, mildly surprised. I knew lawyers made decent money but didn't think a small-town guy like Roger would be well enough off to attract gold diggers.

"He is," Rita said. "Roger had an uncle on his mother's side that died eight years ago and left him a boatload of money. I mean, Roger was doing fine before the uncle's demise, but he's quite wealthy now. I don't know why he continues to work. He certainly doesn't have to."

"I'm surprised he didn't offer to help you out with your book-store after George died," I said.

Rita and her husband had owned a used and antique bookstore for decades. But George's accounting skills were only mildly better than his business acumen and when he'd died six years ago, Rita had been horrified to discover they were not only broke but deep in debt. She'd been forced to sell the store and my parents had been among those who bought up her inventory. My father had been a patron of the store off and on over the years and knew Rita and George on a business level. Once he learned of Rita's situation, he bought what I suspect was much more of her inventory than he wanted or needed and then offered her a job in our store.

"To be honest, Roger has always been a bit tight with his money," Rita said. "George hit him up for a loan a year or so before he died, and Roger turned him down. I didn't know about it until George's funeral when Roger told me. I think he knew George wasn't very good at managing his money and that a loan would be a risky venture."

I was amazed Rita was willing to help Roger now after he treated her and George the way he had. But then I realized she was probably doing it for Andy.

"If it wasn't for Andy . . ." she said, as if reading my mind. She shrugged and didn't finish the thought. She didn't need to. "Anyway, I gather Roger was quite smitten with Sonja at first, though something must have happened to sour him on her. He broke things off after a little over a month and despite Sonja's best efforts to worm her way back in, he's steered clear of her ever since as far as I know."

At this point, I debated telling Rita about my visitor from last night but held off because I wasn't sure if I should, and also because I got a call from Jon.

"Good morning," I said when I answered. "Are you calling with good news, I hope?"

"I am. I've continued looking into Ian Forrester and he checks out every which way. He's got a sparklingly clean record and is apparently a top-notch investigator."

"Good to know, I guess," I said, holding the phone tight to my ear so Rita wouldn't overhear.

"I can't imagine he'll contact you again," Jon went on. "Also, Zeke was able to garner a few more details regarding Brandon's death before Hoffman got word out to everyone to cut him off and there are some curious findings there."

"Curious how?" I asked, easing up on the pressure of the phone against my ear. I didn't care if Rita heard this part.

"The items they found on him or with him were a bit odd," Jon explained. "He had a cell phone, and I don't know what the analysis of it yielded, but there were no obvious texts or phone calls between him and Andy prior to the death. Brandon also had a pair of binoculars on him. They ended up beneath him when he was attacked. The strap was partially embedded in his neck wound, which is why Andy might not have seen them. The medical examiner did rule out strangulation and listed exsanguination from a variety of wounds as the cause of death."

"Okay, so far so good. I don't hear anything odd yet."

"Because I'm not done," Jon went on. "They found a weapon on, or rather under, Brandon. It was a rifle, and like the binoculars, it was buried beneath his body, suggesting he might have dropped it and then fallen on it. Or perhaps he'd leaned it against the tree while using the binoculars and it got knocked over in whatever scuffle took place. Whatever happened, it was deep in the snow beneath him. And here's the curious part. It wasn't an ordinary rifle. It was one designed to fire tranquilizer darts."

"Ooh, that is interesting," I said. "I wonder why the police didn't share that information with Roger. Are they trying to connect it to Andy somehow?"

"They may try but Brandon had the darts in a container tucked into an inside pocket of his coat."

"They'll say Andy put them there."

"The darts were homemade. And they still haven't identified what type of tranquilizer was in them."

"Sounds like Brandon was out hunting but not in any typical way," I said. "This should help Andy's case."

Across the table I saw Rita perk up as I said this. She leaned in closer and turned an ear toward me, trying to better overhear my conversation. I considered putting Jon on speaker but didn't when he uttered his next words.

"Now for the bad news."

"Uh-oh."

"Remember how I told you Adrian Dunlevy was David's latest stolen identity?"

"I do."

"Well, Mr. Dunlevy has been somewhat reluctant to work with the authorities in their attempts to find David. He keeps citing client privilege and the need for privacy. But since the Dunlevy ID hasn't been flagged yet, David is still using it, enabling us to track his movements."

That all-too-familiar sense of dread washed over me as I anticipated what Jon would say next.

"David was apparently in contact with a client of Dunlevy's in Minocqua, which is only forty minutes north of Rhinelander. The real Dunlevy found out when the client called his office to say she'd changed her mind about whatever David was going to do for her. But neither Dunlevy nor the client will tell anyone what that was."

"You said Dunlevy is a lawyer, right?"

"Yes, a rather pricey, high-end lawyer who caters to some very wealthy clients."

"So David is most likely posing as Dunlevy to try to get access to some of his clients' funds," I said.

"That's the working theory," Jon said. "Though, I can't discount his proximity to you. I don't think it's a coincidence."

"But it makes no sense. I didn't even know I'd be in Rhinelander until just a few days ago and there's no way David could have known unless he was watching me practically every minute. It has to be a coincidence. I don't know why I didn't see that before."

"Let me ask you something, Morgan. Have you changed your cell phone number, or your email, or any of your passwords since the murder of your parents?"

"No. Why?"

"If you never changed them, consider that David might have

access to them. He might be able to read your text messages and access your voice mail and emails."

I gave myself a mental kick in the ass for not realizing this sooner. Still, I struggled to wrap my head around it. "I'll change things right away, but I still don't understand how impersonating some fancy-pants lawyer gets David any closer to me. Why wouldn't he just remain anonymous?"

"I don't know," Jon said. "I just don't like the fact he's obviously been watching you somehow based on the letter you got and now he's a short drive away from where you are. I don't believe in coincidences."

"Okay. What do you think I should do?"

"You know the answer to that. I think you should come home."

I wasn't ready to abandon Rita and Andy yet and couldn't think of a clever comeback to what Jon had said. Silence filled the air between our phones. It also answered the implied question.

"Okay," Jon finally conceded. "Just don't do anything stupid."

"When have I ever done anything stupid?" I shot back, feeling insulted. I should have kept my mouth shut.

"Ah, let's see. A visit to the dog park at the behest of some unknown stranger right after Roger was supposedly murdered? Or how about hiding a letter—"

"All right already," I said, scowling at Rita, who was smirking at me from across the table. "I promise not to do anything especially stupid."

"What are you planning on doing today?"

"I'm going to visit Brandon's girlfriend and see if she can shed any light on what he was doing out there in those woods the day he died."

"I suppose that's okay."

The implication that he had say over what I did kind of rankled me, but I let it slide.

Jon said, "By the way, I tried to dig up more info on Ulrich but hit a dead end."

"Pun intended?" I asked.

"Oh, geez. No."

I couldn't help but chuckle at his discomfort before giving him my update. "Devon found some tidbits and I talked with someone who knew Ulrich when he was younger." I gave him a brief summary of what I'd learned from Gretchen Walker. "It sounds like Ulrich wanted to go dark after he dropped out of med school."

"He succeeded," Jon said.

"I've got Devon digging some more on the company that hired him, this EDDNA place. Maybe he'll come up with something useful."

"Let's hope someone does," Jon said. "Be careful."

"I will," I promised him. I meant it, though as it would turn out, I wasn't nearly careful enough.

CHAPTER 26

I invited Rita to come along with me to visit Brandon's girlfriend. "I need to call her first," I explained. "And there's no guarantee she'll be willing to let us come, or that she's even home, so fingers crossed."

Judith Ingles didn't answer when I called and after a second or two of hesitation, I decided to leave a voice mail explaining that I was an investigator trying to get to the truth of what happened in the woods on the day Brandon died. I had no idea if she'd respond to such a message, but as luck would have it, she called me back just as we were leaving the café and said she was at home, and she'd be willing to talk to me.

Judith Ingles's home was a modern structure built on the edge of town. It was the very antithesis of Roger's house, and frankly, most of the other houses I'd seen in the area. It was a basic box of gray concrete and glass, with sleek lines and a color so close to the day's overcast skies that the building was almost invisible. The interior décor was much of the same: gray walls, white rugs and furniture, white cabinets in the kitchen with gray-and-white granite for the countertops, and glass tabletops. The artwork was black-and-white photographs, and the accent pillows on the couch were in shades of gray and white. There wasn't so much as a colorful vase or tchotchke that I could see to break up the monotony and it struck me as an oddly colorless existence.

Judith was as monochrome as her house. Her short-cropped hair was platinum, her skin alabaster, and she was dressed in an off-white sweater with matching leggings. Even her eyes were a pale gray.

"I'm colorblind," she explained after inviting us in and seeing me eye the décor. "A lot of people ask me why things in my house are so neutral and that's why. I look for intriguing lines and contrasts of light and dark rather than color. And comfort, of course."

"That makes total sense," I said, admiring the sleek lines of the white Scandinavian-style couch and two complementary chairs. I couldn't help but compare this stark landscape with the very colorful one in my own apartment, which was furnished with a mélange of esoteric furnishings my parents had accumulated over the years during their travels around the world. In contrast to Judith's home, my place was a bright burst of colors.

Judith didn't seem to have any pets and with the white décor I could understand why. Newt would have sullied the purity of all that whiteness in no time at all.

"Can I get you ladies anything to drink?" Judith offered. "Coffee, tea, water? I also have some lemonade."

Rita and I both declined, and after removing our coats and boots at the door, we settled onto the couch.

Judith took one of the chairs and leaned forward eagerly, arms propped on her knees. "You said you're looking into Brandon's death?"

"Yes, we are," I said. "First off, let me say we are so sorry for your loss. We really appreciate you agreeing to talk to us during such a trying time. And secondly, we need to be up front with you about who we are and why we're looking into this."

"Okay," Judith said. She cocked her head to one side and eyed us warily.

"I gave you my name on the phone," I said. "But I didn't tell you her name." I gestured toward Rita. "This is Rita Bosworth. She's actually an employee of mine and though we aren't related, I consider her a member of my family."

I paused, waiting for the name to sink in. Judith was quick on it.

"Bosworth? As in Andy Bosworth, the man arrested for Brandon's murder?" she said, narrowing her eyes at Rita and adopting a mildly hurt expression. She leaned back in her chair as if to distance herself from us.

"I'm his aunt by marriage," Rita explained. "I knew him quite well when he was a little boy growing up."

Judith's face hardened and I jumped in to try to ease the situation.

"I'm here because Rita asked me to try to prove Andy is innocent, that he didn't kill Brandon. We've been looking into the case and some, um, irregularities and questions have arisen. We're hoping you might be able to shed some light on those."

Judith chewed the inside of her cheek as she sat there assessing us and I half expected her to throw us out. Instead, she surprised me.

"I never thought Andy Bosworth had anything to do with Brandon's death despite what the police kept saying. I know there was animosity between the two of them in the past, but Brandon had moved on from that long ago."

"We were trying to figure out how Brandon even got to those woods. There's no record of him owning a car. Did he use yours?"

Judith shook her head. "No, lately he's been using one of the snowmobiles we own to get around. The police called yesterday and said they found it on the other side of the river from where Brandon died. It was covered with pine branches, so they didn't discover it right away. They think he left it there and crossed the river on foot because he didn't trust the ice to hold up his weight plus that of the snowmobile. I guess he camouflaged it to keep anyone else from messing with it."

That answered one of our burning questions. Brandon must have risked crossing the river over that patch of unbroken ice I'd seen, or one similar to it at least.

"Any idea why he was out there?" I asked.

"No, but there was something going on with Brandon in the weeks before he died. He's had trouble keeping jobs in the past and the jobs he's had have been unskilled work and labor for minimum wage. It bothered him that I was the primary breadwinner, but he always did his best to bring in as much income as he could. He was a hard worker. But then, about a month ago, he started talking about this new opportunity he had to make some serious money. Said it was very hush-hush and he couldn't talk about it yet, but there would be a big payout in the long run. And he did have some extra cash. Quite a bit, in fact."

"He didn't tell you what this opportunity was?"

Judith shook her head and let out a humorless chuckle. "To be honest, I thought he was gaslighting me and was having an affair with some new sugar mama he'd found. I even went so far as to hire a private investigator to follow him."

This bit of news excited me. It might be just the thing we needed to exonerate Andy. "Did this PI follow Brandon on the day he died?"

"He never got started with the investigation," Judith said, crushing my hopes. "I'd just hired him the day before."

"Did Brandon have a computer?"

"He had a laptop I bought him last year for Christmas, but the police took it."

Of course they did.

"Did Brandon say anything to you on the day he died before he went out to the woods?" I asked.

"I didn't see him before he left. I was out of town for several days for a work thing and didn't get back until really late the night before. I was still in bed when he took off."

"What is it you do?"

"I sell pharmaceuticals to clinics and doctor's offices in a five-state region," she said, verifying what Devon had found out about her. "The hours are somewhat flexible, it pays well, and the perks are good. It involves a lot of travel, but I also work from home some of the time."

"What were Brandon's most recent jobs?" I asked.

"During the nonwinter months, he tries to find work at any of the local farms, or doing labor on construction sites. He worked at the Granger livestock farm out west of town for a long time, ever since he was a teenager, but they quit hiring him about five years ago. During the winter months, he works whatever he can find. This winter he'd been working part-time at a Kwik Trip."

"Was he still working at the Kwik Trip when he died?" I asked.

"Nope. He quit the job so he could focus all his time and energy on whatever this new job was. He seemed quite dedicated to it, disappearing for long hours every day and even some weekends."

"Sounds like he was a go-getter," I said.

Judith made a face. "Like I said, he worked hard. There's no denying that. But he was never going to get very far without a college degree or some type of apprenticeship training. I kept trying to talk him into going to school, but he always had an excuse for why he couldn't do it." She paused, looked out a side window, and sighed. "And truth be told, he had a bit of a drinking problem. That held him back as much as anything did."

"He never mentioned what this new opportunity was or told you anything about it?"

Judith shook her head. "He'd get short with me if I started asking too many questions so I finally gave up and figured he'd tell me when he was ready."

Rita said, "I'm curious, did you ever tell the police you didn't think Andy had anything to do with Brandon's death?"

"I did," Judith said. "They didn't seem impressed. I'm sure opinions don't matter much to them in the long run. It's more about the evidence."

"Which was all circumstantial," Rita said. I could tell she was getting defensive, and I put a hand on her leg to calm her.

"I hope things work out for him," Judith said to Rita. "Maybe your PI here can find the evidence needed to exonerate him."

"I'm not a PI," I said.

"Oh. I thought you said you were investigating Brandon's death."

"I am, but as a cryptozoologist."

"A what? What is that? Some kind of puzzle expert or something?"

"Not exactly. A cryptozoologist is someone who hunts for cryptids, creatures rumored to exist even though there's no proof to support it."

Judith looked both amused and puzzled. Then both her eyes and her mouth opened wide, and she said, "Oh, I get it. I heard how Andy tried to claim a Hodag killed Brandon and now you're here trying to prove it true by finding one?"

"Essentially, yes," I said.

Judith laughed. "Well, that's a fool's errand," she said.

She wasn't going to get an argument from me on that count. Though I couldn't resist one last remark in my defense.

"It might not be a Hodag, but there's something out there. I saw it myself."

"Right." She made a point of looking at her watch. "I need to get back to work, so if there's nothing else I can help you with . . ."

"There is one more thing," I said. "You mentioned that you sell pharmaceuticals. Do you keep samples here in the house?"

"Sure. Some. Why?" Judith's voice had turned prickly all of a sudden.

"Any chance Brandon would have had access to the drugs?"

Her face darkened. "What are you implying?"

"The police found a rifle made for firing darts, like tranquilizer darts, beneath Brandon's body. And he had darts in his pocket filled with something. I thought maybe whatever was in those darts might have come from your stash."

"That's absurd," Judith said, but there was something in her expression that told me she was frightened. "I don't have a *stash*," she said, sneering the last word. "I have samples of certain medications that I give out to the appropriate health-care providers. And police came here and looked around the house after Brandon died and they never said anything about any darts." She then made a point of looking at her watch again and said, "If there's nothing else, I need to get back to work."

Clearly, we'd worn out our welcome. "I appreciate you taking the time to see us," I said as Judith showed us to the door and stood by as we put on our coats and boots.

Judith said nothing more but her brusque closing of the door behind us—just shy of an outright slam—communicated plenty.

"Well, that didn't go quite like I'd hoped," I said to Rita once we were in the car. Newt was nuzzling my neck with his cold, wet nose to let me know he was glad I'd returned.

Rita didn't respond and remained quiet during the entire ride back. As I pulled the car into the motel lot, I asked her if she was okay.

"I'm fine," she said. "But I'm beginning to think your idea of me going back home was a good one. I'm not accomplishing anything here and I think I'd be more help to you if I was managing the store."

"Maybe it would be best," I said. "This case is a lot more complex than it seemed at first, and with the murder of Ulrich Liebhardt, I'm worried things will get more dangerous. I can look out for myself, but I can't always watch out for you."

Rita nodded. "I'm going to go pack and head home this afternoon."

"I'm going to give Newt a quick potty break and then I'll be in."

It was with mixed feelings that I watched her walk to the rear side door and card her way inside. On the one hand, I did think it wise for her to leave given the events of the past few days. On the other hand, her slumped posture and slow stride made me realize how sad she was with the way things were unfolding. And I felt helpless to do much about it.

CHAPTER 27

W hile walking Newt, I thought about whether or not I should
go home, too. I didn't have anything else to do in Rhinelander for
the time being, and assuming Detective Hoffman wasn't going to
make me stay in town, I might be able to accomplish more from the
store.

I'd more or less decided I would follow Rita home when my
phone rang, and I saw it was Devon.

I answered with, "Whatcha got for me, Wonder Boy?"

Devon chuckled. "What I got is maybe some answers or maybe
a lot more mystery. I did some lurking about on some of the dark
web conspiracy sites and found some talk about someone named
MS in conjunction with EDDNA. I don't know if MS is our Margaret Smith, but it seems likely. There's one primary conspiracy
theorist who posts under the username doT red—all lowercase

except for the T—and he or she claims MS dropped most of EDDNA's original studies in favor of a secret plan to build the perfect mercenary army, one they could rent out to the highest bidder. Dollars to doughnuts doT red is Ulrich because it definitely seems as if the poster had inside knowledge."

"Building a mercenary army certainly doesn't seem in line with what EDDNA was supposedly about."

"I know but bear with me because there are several crazy theories involved here. doT red claims MS was using genetics and environmental science to create an army of venomous, deadly insects immune to pesticides that could then be released on an enemy."

"Insects are something Rick knew about. If he was trying to develop insects with resistance to—" I stopped, hearing myself. "Oh, wow, that's it, Devon. That mystery caller I had told me to look for the resistance. I thought he was saying to watch out for the resistance and that he meant a human group of folks opposed to what I was doing, but now I'm thinking it was about this insect research and a resistance to pesticides."

"Makes sense," Devon said. "Except there was a big problem with the bug research, according to doT red's posts. They didn't have a way to ensure the insects would go after only those people considered to be enemies. They tried to instill some kind of kill switch into the bugs to make them die immediately after they attacked, similar to how some bees die after stinging. But apparently they weren't able to do it with enough certainty to ensure their mercenary insects didn't end up wiping out all of mankind."

"Wow, there's a nightmare scenario," I said, imagining it.

"Here's another interesting piece to this conspiracy as it's being discussed on the dark web. doT red claimed MS had decided to expand the research and use pigs as, well, guinea pigs by splicing genetic material from the venomous insects onto pig DNA, hoping to eventually get it to translate to humans. doT red claimed that MS said obtaining chimps was too difficult and pigs were a close-enough match to humans to make the results reliable. Also, chimps have gestational periods of around two hundred and twenty-six days whereas a sow's gestational period is half that and they typically produce multiple offspring, thereby increasing the number of generations and the time period for their experiments. The deciding factor was that there was a nearby farmer ready and willing to sell EDDNA as many pigs as they wanted at a reasonable price."

"Interesting," I said, seeing some of the puzzle pieces start to fit together. "I just came back from talking with Brandon's girlfriend and she told me Brandon had worked on a livestock farm every year since he was a teenager. I wonder if it's the same farm your conspirator is talking about."

"If it was the Grangers' farm, it might be because it's close to Rhinelander, about twenty miles outside town."

"That was it!"

"I can send you the address if you want."

"That would be great."

"You'll also find this interesting. Several types of highly venomous insects were purportedly used in the EDDNA labs, including giant Japanese hornets, fire ants, and bullet ants, presumably for their toxins. But they also used flesh flies in their genetic manipulations. Want to guess what distinctive feature flesh flies possess?"

"Of course! They have bright red eyes!"

"Correctamundo! And there's one final thing our conspiracist had to say about this insect research. Apparently the genetic alterations in the insects triggered some changes in the pigs who survived the bites and stings. They became extremely aggressive in their behavior, to the point they were nearly impossible to handle safely. They also started to show changes in their skin, changes that were attributed to the insects' chitin."

"You mean the stuff a bug's exoskeleton is made from?"

"One and the same. The ingestion of chitin, or an injection via a bite or sting, can trigger an immune response similar to an allergic reaction. The thought was this reaction might prove fatal but in the pigs it did something different. It led to them developing scaly skin and split hooves that look like claws. These characteristics were heightened in the offspring of the pigs that reproduced."

"Wow. That's some scary stuff."

"And I'm not done," Devon teased. "I saved the scariest claims for last. doT red said MS was mating the experimental pigs and keeping them in a special barn pen designed exclusively for them. Many generations of piglets have been born and grown to go on and mate themselves with resultant mutations. And even though EDDNA supposedly went out of business a decade ago, this MS character is still conducting these experiments years later."

"Yikes."

"Yeah, but remember it came from a conspiracy site on the dark web and while I'm ninety percent sure much of the insider info was coming from Ulrich, I can't be certain."

"Does the username doT red mean anything to you?" I asked.

"I did a quick online search but didn't come up with anything."

"Okay. This is great information, Devon. Thanks so much."

"I see a bonus in my future."

I laughed. Devon was always teasing me about getting more

money. He was invaluable to me and knew it. I dreaded the thought of losing him. He was young and had a sense of adventure that I feared would one day lead him to move on.

"Your fortune-telling talents are spot on," I said. "By the way, Rita is on her way home. Be nice to her. No teasing for a while. She's a bit raw right now."

"Got it. Later, boss lady."

After ending the call, I carded my way into the motel and went straight to Rita's room. She was packed and seated at the table looking at something on her tablet.

"Ready to go?" I asked.

She shut down the tablet and nodded.

"You okay to drive?" She looked pale and had dark circles under her eyes, but no sooner did I question her ability than she sprang to life.

"Don't coddle me, Morgan. I'm fine. And if I'm not, I'll let you know."

"Okay. Fair enough. Want to grab some lunch before you go?"

"Thanks, but I want to make use of the daylight. I hate driving in the dark. Make yourself useful and carry that bag out to my car, will you?" she said, gesturing toward a large tote.

"Sure."

She stood, whirled her wheeled suitcase into place behind her, and led the way to the parking lot. At the car, she was eager to hop behind the wheel once the cases were loaded and she'd given Newt a quick pat on the head and me a brief, stiff hug. Rita has never been very physical with her shows of affection.

After I got her to promise me she'd text or call me as soon as she arrived home safely, I waved goodbye to her and watched her drive off. When she was gone, I looked around for any cars that looked like they didn't belong or that might be holding a stalker, but all the vehicles I could see were empty.

"Come on, Newt. We're on our own now." I went inside and carded into my own room, wanting to do a computer lookup of the address Devon had texted to me for the livestock farm. First I scribbled down the username doT red on a motel notepad as a reminder to look at it again later, though if Devon hadn't found anything relevant about it, odds were I wouldn't either. After opening my laptop and finding the farm's address on Google Maps—it was twenty-two miles outside town—I sent the directions to my phone. It was lunchtime and I was hungry, but like Rita, I didn't want to waste the daylight. There was too little of it right now, though we were getting a little more with each passing day.

"Up for another road trip, Newt?"

He wagged his readiness. When I got up, I knocked the notepad off the table. As I bent down to pick it up, I suddenly saw the doT red username in a whole different light.

"Clever devil," I muttered, making Newt tilt his head and eye me quizzically. I tossed the notepad onto the table and texted Devon my revelation. Then off I went, Newt tailing behind me.

I was feeling quite good about the way things were coming together and it put an extra spring in my step. Too bad it didn't last.

CHAPTER 28

It took me half an hour to get to the Granger farm and I spent the bulk of that time checking the rearview mirror every few minutes, convinced I'd seen someone following me. There was only one incident of a car staying behind me for any length of time and I pulled off onto a side road just to see if they'd stick with me. They didn't, and I breathed a sigh of relief as I pulled back onto the highway.

When I got to the farm, I saw that the house and most of the outbuildings, which were surrounded by fields, sat atop a small hill and were set some distance back from the road. There was a long drive leading up to the buildings, but it hadn't been plowed. However, I noticed there were tire tracks in the snow, and I switched my car into four-wheel drive and gave it a shot, staying in the existing tracks the best I could. I managed to get to the top with only the occasional minor slip and slide. The tracks ended in front of a large barn near the house, and whatever had made them had then made a three-point turn and apparently been driven back down to the main road.

I parked my car and trudged through virgin snow to the house. It was a typical farmhouse: white, two stories, small front porch, and in need of some paint. I knocked twice at the front door—there was no doorbell—and then went around to the back of the house and did the same thing on the door there. No answer, no sound, and a brief peek into the ground-floor windows revealed no signs of life and a heavy layer of dust.

From the back of the house I could see another barn, much newer looking, and a large trailer situated higher up on the property about a quarter mile away. They sat at the edge of some woods and if there was any road leading to them, I couldn't see it. I wasn't about to try to tackle that much high-drifted snow and unknown landscape to get to them, besides which, they were fenced off with barbed wire.

I trudged over to the closer barn instead, which had a sliding door that was unlocked. It took some effort and snow kicking to open it a couple of feet and then Newt and I slipped through the opening. A strong aroma of hay with a subtle undertone of manure hit me, and I thought I smelled hints of engine exhaust, too. Newt immediately put his nose to the floor and conducted his own olfactory exploration. I couldn't find a light switch, but between cracks in the walls, holes in the roof, and an open door in the loft I was able to see well enough despite the gray skies outside. There was a tractor that looked well used, some hay bales scattered about, and some attachments for the tractor. Miscellaneous tools were hung on the walls or from the ceiling. There was no ladder or other means to access the loft and other than the occasional mouse or mole hiding in one of the bales stacked along the walls, there were no signs of life.

Back outside, I checked the other nearby buildings—a silo, an equipment shed, and a livestock trailer, all of them empty—and then looked once more at the barn and trailer off in the distance. A faint hum carried through the air from the direction of this second barn but as far as I could tell, there were no vehicles anywhere near it, nor roads leading to it.

Frustrated, I scanned the surrounding countryside in the other directions and spied another white farmhouse with a nice big red barn beside it about half a mile away on the other side of the road. I slogged through the snow to my car and drove back down the driveway, the slight incline just enough to make things hairy at times even with four-wheel drive.

The second farm was closer to the road and easily accessible via a recently plowed, level driveway. Here there were many signs of life: a dog who came barking but wagging its tail to greet us, a boy and girl who looked to be about four or five building a snowman in the front yard, both of them sporting rosy cheeks and runny noses, and a woman in a parka standing on the front porch eyeing me with classic, friendly Midwest curiosity.

I parked, told Newt to stay, and got out. The woman's smile turned a bit tentative as I approached, but once I was safely past her kids she appeared to relax. She was as rosy-cheeked as the children, and I wondered if it was natural coloring or a result of the cold.

"Hi there," I said with a wave. I stopped at the bottom of the porch steps, letting her have the height advantage, hoping it would make her feel more comfortable. "My name is Morgan Carter and

I'm looking to find out some information about the farm across the road from yours, about a half mile to the east. The Granger farm?"

"Are you a friend of the family? Or are you looking to buy it?"

"Neither. I'm looking for someone." I dropped my voice and leaned toward the stairs. "An old boyfriend," I said with a nervous giggle. "He used to work for a company that bought pigs from the Grangers. I know it's a long shot but I'm trying every lead I can."

The woman considered me, her smile never faltering, but I knew she was weighing my sincerity and the level of danger should she talk to me. I must have passed muster because she suddenly started spilling like a full-open tap.

"That's sweet, looking for an old love. But you won't find any Grangers in the area to tell you anything. They packed up and moved somewhere warmer. Rumor has it they went down to Florida, but I can't verify that. The old man said they were tired of the Wisconsin winters and the labors of farming." She sighed, looked beyond me to the open fields, and added, "It's a hard life, farming. And not one to make you rich. Heck, these days you're lucky if you can afford your house and put food on your table unless you grow it or kill it yourself. We thought we were being smart going the route of dairy farming, but I don't know how much longer we'll be able to hold out. And now I've got another one on the way." She smiled grimly and rubbed her hand over her tummy.

"Old man Granger did the smart thing with the pigs," she went on. "He lucked into a deal with that company and never looked back. Good thing, too, because he was in dire straits back then and worried he was going to lose the farm. That deal saved him. They must have paid a pretty penny for old Franklin to be able to retire and just walk away after only a handful of years with them."

Her eyes grew larger, and she leaned a little my way. "But we'll never know because the whole deal from beginning to end was very hush-hush," she said in a low, conspiratorial voice. "Franklin said the folks buying his pigs wanted it that way or they'd walk. Lord knows we tried to get more details out of him, but he never did spill. It's unfortunate because we'd love to make an offer on some of that land so we can expand our enterprise, but they left without any notice or forwarding address. Someone is managing the pig herd up in that high barn, but everything else has gone to seed. Even the house."

"When did the Grangers leave?"

"Aw, it's been four, maybe five years now. It was right after the escape."

"The escape?"

"Heck yeah. A half dozen of Granger's sows broke out of that fancy barn at the back of the property and ran for their lives. They disappeared into the woods and two of them were caught after a couple of days. But the other four were never found. We figured a bear or maybe some wolves got them. Poor pigs. Here they thought they were escaping the slaughterhouse only to end up getting eaten anyway. The whole thing was an awful mess for Granger. He said the people paying him for the pigs threatened to walk away from the venture over it. Seems they were quite angry . But they must have worked it out because a few months later, old man Granger retired, and he and his wife moved away."

"Did they have any kids?"

"No, the good Lord didn't see fit to provide for them in that manner. My husband, Kurt—that's with a K, he always has me say— has had his eye on that property for nearly fifteen years now.

Though we're pinching pennies as it is, so I don't know how he thought he could buy it, but he was kind of hoping he could talk Franklin into selling it to him given that Franklin was getting up there in years and didn't have anyone to pass the farm on to. But once the pig people showed up, Franklin had no need to sell. We were kind of surprised he and Mary moved away, though. They both grew up in this area."

"Any relatives around here?"

She looked up toward the sky thoughtfully. "Not that I know of. Mary had a niece from Montana who visited once right around the time Franklin was thinking he'd have to sell the farm."

"I don't suppose you remember her name?"

She made a face and shook her head. "Sorry. I'm not sure. Mary mentioned her only briefly in passing once. If I remember right, her name started with an M also. And it was kind of an older name, like Martha, or maybe Margaret?"

My heart skipped a beat. "Do you know Mary's maiden name?"

"Sure. It was Hemingway."

Dang. I was hoping she'd say it was Smith.

"Thanks. It might be a start. You've been very kind to talk to me, Mrs.—" I let it hang out there, figuring she'd tell me if she wanted to.

"Dusseldorf," she said. "Sue Dusseldorf. Good luck finding your missing beau."

"Thanks, Sue."

When I got back on the highway, I missed a turn I needed to make, so I used the first driveway I came to and did a quick turn-around. And then my heart leapt into my throat when I glanced in my rearview mirror and saw a large, dark SUV do the same thing.

CHAPTER 29

I took out my phone and started to dial 911, thinking I'd get the first two numbers in there and then I'd have to dial only one more, if the need arose. I set the phone onto the center console and then cursed as I watched Newt put a curious nose to it and knock it down between the seat and the console.

Any doubts I might have had as to the innocuous nature of the SUV were eliminated as I watched it come roaring up on my tail, headlights bright in my mirror. When I got to my missed turn, I took it and sped up. The SUV did the same, once again coming up on my bumper. Then it did the most terrifying thing of all. It bumped into the back end of my car. The action made my car fishtail a little, but I was able to bring it back under control. I floored the gas pedal and put some distance between us, but the SUV rapidly closed the gap. With the headlights shining in my rearview, I couldn't see who was behind the wheel or make out a plate.

I crested a hill and saw a bridge up ahead crossing over what I assumed was part of the Wisconsin River. I knew Highway 17 was still miles away, but if I could get to it, it would take me straight into town, where I might find some help. But then the SUV revved its engine and moved into position off my rear driver's side bumper, and I feared I'd never make it to Highway 17 because this creep behind me was going to try to do a PIT maneuver and send me hurtling into the river.

I pressed down on the gas, trying my best to stay far enough ahead of the SUV so it couldn't ram me. I checked Newt's harness line to make sure he was buckled in and told him to lie down. He did the best he could in the limited amount of space he had, settling in sideways with his head on the console. I then hit the buttons to lower the front windows. If we were going in the water, I wanted a quick way out. Frigid air rushed into the car, the sound of it nearly deafening, the feel of it already numbing my face. A glance in my side mirror showed me my pursuer was nearly in position. Instinct told me to hit my brakes, but I didn't want Newt to get yanked hard. Still, it was the lesser of the evils I faced at that moment. I pushed down on the gas pedal once more, steered the car to the left until I was straddling the centerline, and slipped my right hand beneath Newt's collar. Then I hit the brake pedal, not hard, but hard enough.

Newt slid sideways to the edge of the seat, two of his legs hitting the floor. My hand beneath his collar kept his head from flying forward. The SUV behind me hit the brakes but not before colliding with the driver's side of my car and scraping down the side.

Then it veered hard left and went off the road, flinging up bushes, snow, ice, and what looked like part of its front bumper. I jammed down on the gas and zipped over the bridge.

Now that I had safely passed the river, I hit the window buttons to close them. The sudden silence and lack of cold, blasting air was weirdly disorienting. The road ahead took a right-angle turn to the left, making me brake hard. I'd barely accelerated again when it then turned to the right. Two more times I had to slow down, maneuver a sharp turn, and speed up again, sliding once on a patch of packed snow and ice that nearly had me spinning.

After the right-angle turns, the road curved in a serpentine fashion, forcing me to keep an iron grip on the steering wheel and my left foot poised over the brake. The SUV had disappeared from my rearview mirror, but I didn't assume they were gone. I knew they were still back there somewhere if for no other reason than because they had nowhere else to go.

When the road finally straightened out, I breathed a small sigh of relief. When I reached the intersection of Highway 17, I came to a stop and waited a few beats to let my heart slow down, watching the mirrors closely. It didn't take long. I saw the front end of the SUV, minus part of its bumper, come zooming up behind me.

I turned onto the highway and floored it. Traffic here was heavier, and I didn't know if the SUV would risk something on this busier road, but I didn't want to find out. My thoughts spun wildly as I tried to decide where to go, where I could get out of the car and be safe. I tried to remember how to get to the police station in town, but I wasn't sure since I hadn't been driving there the night we went. Not to mention I wasn't sure of my welcome there. Then another idea came to me. I started whispering a chant to myself.

Please be there, please be there!

I said it over and over again as I tore down the highway. Newt stared at me with curiosity and concern. And as soon as I saw the turn I was looking for, my heart leapt with joy and relief because I also saw a dark, nondescript sedan parked some distance ahead along the shoulder of the road.

I braked hard and swung the steering wheel around, fishtailing my way into Sonja Mueller's driveway. At first I thought my pursuer hadn't seen me turn but seconds later they came barreling in behind me with renewed energy. I think they saw my turnoff as a fatal mistake. And maybe they were right.

I laid on the horn hard and continuous as I bounced down the driveway and then I started a staccato beep. As I pulled into the clearing by Sonja's house, I was chagrined to see the door to her barn closed and a vehicle parked in front of it. I debated my options, decided Newt would be okay if left in the car—they weren't after him—and that a mad dash into the house was my wisest choice. I slammed hard on my brakes as I came even with the edge of the fencing around Sonja's front yard, hoping to bring my car to a halt right by the gate. The SUV barreled toward me, and the driver jammed on their own brakes once they saw I had stopped, making the car fishtail wildly. It slammed into the back of my car, spinning me a little and then pushing me forward. The front end of my car smashed into the Hodag statue by the gate, toppling it. I managed to keep my hand on the horn as I struggled to extricate myself from the car, but the collisions had dented my door so that it wouldn't open.

The SUV came to a halt some distance past me up the driveway closer to the barn, and it had spun around so that it was now facing me. I sat there, still punching out my staccato warning on the horn, wondering if this was it. Was I about to die? The answer came with frightening clarity as a guy exited the passenger side of the SUV. In his hand was a gun and he looked royally pissed.

He strode toward me and raised the arm holding the gun, aiming it right at my head. Though I knew I was only delaying the inevitable, I ducked down sideways and wrapped my right arm around Newt, keeping my left hand on the horn. I heard a loud *crack* and then glass was flying everywhere, raining down on me. I removed my left hand from the horn and wrapped it around Newt, wanting to hold him as the end came.

I heard another loud retort from a gun, and I glanced up to see my windshield was still intact. My driver's side window was gone, as was the back-seat passenger window. Yet my assailant had been aiming at me through the windshield. It made no sense.

Seconds ticked by and I struggled to hear anything, afraid to raise my head and look. More gunshots, seeming to come from multiple directions. Newt stayed as still as a statue, and I feared he'd been hit. But his breathing was strong and steady, and I didn't feel any wetness as I ran my hands over his fur. I unclipped his safety strap so he could escape if he had to.

I heard a car door slam. Someone yelled something though I couldn't make out the words. There was a crunch of tires on snow as a car zipped past me. The sound of the car's engine rapidly faded away but then the sound of more wheels crunching over snow closed in, stopping beside me, the engine idling. In my peripheral vision I saw a head poke through my broken driver's side window, and I twisted around, prepared to face down death.

"Are you okay?" the man asked.

I looked at him and blinked hard, thinking I had to be seeing wrong. Or hallucinating. I opened my mouth to say something, but no words came out. I became convinced I was dead. I heard Newt growl, felt his body rise up beneath my arm. The man nodded, smiled, *winked* for God's sake. Then he was gone. I sat up in time to see the car disappear down the driveway. New sounds came to me: sirens, arguing voices, radio static, a holler. The sirens grew louder. I stuck my head out of my side window and came face to face with Sonja Mueller.

I stared at her, too stunned to say anything. My mind was exploding with questions, but I couldn't seem to formulate them into words.

A man materialized behind Sonja—Ian Forrester, my FBI visitor from before.

"What the hell just happened?" I asked.

"Your timing and your driving are exquisite," Forrester said irritably. "Though I could have done without the hit men you brought with you." I saw blood on his hands.

"Hit men?" I said.

"The ones chasing you," Forrester said. "The ones who were about to shoot you."

"Right." I nodded, still dazed and confused. Newt was sitting up in his seat.

"You interrupted a sting operation," Forrester said. "Ms. Mueller here was about to work a deal with a lawyer named Dunlevy for some stolen art from the war."

That was when I noticed Sonja was handcuffed.

"Adrian Dunlevy?" I said. "He's here?"

"He *was* here," Forrester said. "After I was hit, he shot the guy who was trying to kill you. He saved your life."

I looked around. "Where is he?"

"Unfortunately, he took off right after he talked to you. I got the plate number of the car, though. We'll catch him."

"It wasn't Adrian Dunlevy," I said.

Forrester looked at me oddly and smiled. "I think you're rattled from all these events. Maybe you should stay in your car until rescue gets here."

I shook my head. "No, you don't understand. The man who came to my car wasn't Adrian Dunlevy. He was David Johnson. Or at least he was for a time, though I think he's also been several other people."

Forrester eyed me with wary concern. "Stay in your car," he said. "I think you took a hit on the head."

"I'm fine," I insisted. "Though my car isn't. I can't get the door open." I tried again, shoving hard against it. Ian came up and tried pulling on it. I noticed he was limping and there was blood on his pants.

Two police cars came barreling up the driveway, followed by an ambulance, all with sirens blaring. Newt reared back his head and howled along with them. I reached past my dog and tried the handle on the passenger door. It opened and I told Newt to go. He hopped out and I climbed over the console and got out, too, climbing over the broken pieces of the Hodag statue.

An EMT approached and insisted on a cursory exam. I assured him I was okay and, oddly enough, I was. If ever there was a time ripe for having a panic attack, this was it. Yet I felt surprisingly calm. Maybe I was in shock, I thought.

Forrester talked with the arriving officers and one of them put Sonja Mueller into the rear seat of his car. She stared out the window looking shocked, lost, and forlorn. I felt for her and wondered if the things Forrester had said about her were true. Once Forrester had his leg wound looked at and bandaged, he came over to me.

"Should you be walking on that?" I asked, gesturing toward his leg.

"It's just a flesh wound. Bullet went right through. I'm hoping we'll be able to find it, but I was standing over there in front of the trees when I was hit so that bullet is in the woods, probably in the snow somewhere."

"Bummer," I said.

"Yeah. Speaking of bummers, what's with the gunmen chasing you down?"

"I honestly don't know. Something about this Hodag case has someone really worried. I just need to figure out who and why."

I walked around the front end of my car to better survey the damage. The Hodag statue sat broken on the ground, its body shattered into pieces. The head, however, had remained largely intact, with just a few bits broken off around its edges. I could tell the bulk of the head was made of a different material.

"I didn't know what artwork Sonja was trying to sell," Forrester said, staring down at the head. "Thanks to you, I do now. We'll have to have it authenticated, of course, but I believe that's Michelangelo's marble sculpture known as *Head of a Faun*. It's one of the many art pieces that went missing during World War II. My guess is Sonja's father cleverly incorporated it into a sculpture of a Hodag and had it hiding out here in plain sight all this time." He shook his head and let out an ironic chuckle. "Kind of apropos when you consider fauns are said to be protectors of the woods and the countryside."

Now I understood why the face of that particular Hodag had looked so different. Sonja's father had added some tusks and horns to it, and fleshed out the facial features a bit, but the leering ugly grin of Michelangelo's work was still evident.

"Its history is fascinating," Forrester said. "It's thought to be Michelangelo's first marble sculpture, done in 1489 when he was only fifteen years old. The story goes that Michelangelo was copying a similar piece but added certain individual touches of his own. When Lorenzo de' Medici saw the work, he had Michelangelo make some changes he thought would enhance it. For instance, Medici thought the teeth were too perfect for an old man and so Michelangelo knocked out one of the teeth and drilled a hole in the gum where it had been. If you look closely, you can see where he did it."

"Wow, you're such an art nerd," I teased, shaking my head.

Forrester laughed. "What can I say? I've always loved art and art history. I wish I possessed some artistic talent, but I don't, so it was either this work or some boring job in a museum or university teaching students who think high art is tagging an overpass."

"Hey, don't knock the graffiti. There's some amazing stuff out there."

It was Forrester's turn to give me a woeful shake of his head. "Anyway," he said, continuing with my art lesson, "several casts were made of *Head of a Faun* and they've been featured in galleries and museums around the world, but the original was stolen by the Nazis, never to be seen again. Until today."

"You think Sonja was going to sell this?"

Forrester shrugged. "I know she was going to sell something."

"What's it worth?"

"It's invaluable," Forrester said. "If someone was offering to buy it, I'm guessing they'd be willing to pay millions for it. Sonja had to know what it was worth. That's where Adrian Dunlevy comes in. He's an attorney who procures items for wealthy clients."

"Except I'm telling you, it wasn't Adrian Dunlevy who was here." The reason for David stealing Dunlevy's ID was clear to me now. If he'd convinced some wealthy patron that he could be the go-between to obtain an artwork like this one, the commission he would have earned would most likely be millions. And that's assuming he didn't keep the piece for himself to sell to other, higher bidders.

"Yeah, you said that before and I'll look into it," Forrester said. "Not sure it matters now since we foiled the sale. Thanks in part to you."

"Glad to be of help," I said, giving him a salute.

Whether or not it was the real Adrian Dunlevy here might not matter to Forrester, but it mattered to me. According to Forrester, David had saved my life. This knowledge was messing with my head in ways I couldn't deal with just then.

"We'll search Sonja's studio and her house for other artworks, but she says that's the only thing she has. She's been trying to sell it on the black market for months because she needed the money. Both her house and her studio out there in the barn are leveraged to the max, and she owes quite a bit in bank loans."

This revelation made me wonder if Sonja had been after Roger's money when they were dating as Rita had suspected. I didn't want to believe it of her. I liked the woman.

I didn't care about the ugly, invaluable artwork at my feet. All I cared about was figuring out why my pursuers had wanted me dead. Clearly I was closing in on something related to Brandon Kluver's death and the creature in the woods.

If only I knew what it was.

CHAPTER 30

The police on-site at Sonja's place called for a tow truck to come and haul my car away and then one of the officers gave me a ride to a car-rental shop so I could get another set of wheels. Damage to my car was mostly cosmetic. Technically it was still drivable if I replaced one of the tires, but I didn't want to go around in a car missing a couple of its windows in the dead of winter. Then there was the issue with the door. The garage my car was towed to said they could repair all but the body damage by the end of the next day, and I happily agreed, thinking I'd be ready to head home and could drive back tomorrow night. Heck, I was ready to go home right then but didn't want to leave my car behind.

The first place I went after getting my rental car was to the Farm and Fleet store, where I purchased a six-inch hunting knife with a sheath and a can of bear spray. I didn't want to be defenseless, and while I knew these items wouldn't do much against a bullet, they might give me a fighting chance or an opportunity to run.

Next I went through the drive-through at Culver's and got myself a salad and a side of cheese curds plus a plain cheeseburger for Newt. I figured we'd earned it. Back at the motel, I exercised extra caution in the parking lot, eyeing everyone and everything with suspicion. I didn't bother leashing Newt because I wanted both of my hands free, and I knew he'd stick close by my side. If someone wanted to complain, so be it. I approached the motel door with my key card and food bag in one hand and the can of bear spray in the other. The knife was tucked safely into my coat pocket. Once inside, I relaxed a little and managed to get to my room without incident.

The first thing I did was place a call to Devon and ask him to dig up anything he could on Franklin Granger and his wife, Mary née Hemingway, and a niece possibly named Margaret. "I don't know if there's a connection to Mary and this Margaret who was the head of EDDNA, but see what you can find."

"Easy-peasy," Devon said.

"Did Rita make it back yet?"

"She did. She's already taken over the store."

"Sorry. But you should probably let her. She needs the distraction."

"I'm fine with it," Devon said. "How are things going there in Hodag land now that you're all by yourself?"

"Kind of boring," I lied.

I wasn't going to tell him about what happened, because I didn't want him to worry. And I was afraid he'd pass on the information to Jon, who would then demand I return home immediately, car or no car. A little voice in my head said such advice would be wise to follow but I shut it down. I was angry now, angry and determined to get to the bottom of all this. Problem was, I had no idea how or what to do next.

As I ate, I couldn't shake the restless edginess I felt, and Newt sensed it. After inhaling his cheeseburger, he kept nudging me with his nose and whining. Then he'd put his big head in my lap and look up at me with those huge dark eyes until I said I was okay. He'd go lie down for a minute or two and then get up and repeat the process all over again.

I'd finished eating and was making a cup of coffee when Devon called me back.

I answered with, "You've got something for me already?"

"More like I got nothing. I've searched for any trace of Franklin Granger and his wife, Mary, but there has been nothing since about five years ago. They simply disappeared off the planet. There's no activity on their one charge card, their bank account hasn't been touched the whole time, and there's a hundred grand in it. I can't find any licenses or vehicle registrations for either of them or any home purchases. The farm remains in their names, and someone has paid the electric bill and the taxes on the property, but that's it. Either the Grangers have new identities, or they've figured out how to live completely off the grid."

"Or they're dead," I said, voicing a fear I'd had ever since talking to Sue Dusseldorf.

"If they are dead, there are no records of their deaths being recorded, no funerals, no death certificates, nothing."

"Well, if someone killed them, there wouldn't be a record," I pointed out.

I heard a sharp inhale from Devon. "This is starting to sound dangerous, boss," he said. "Maybe you should be like Rita and come home."

Even though he was probably right, I decided to deflect. "What about this niece, Margaret? Did you find anything on her?"

"Yeah, about that. Either your farm lady gave you incorrect information or you misunderstood because Mary Hemingway is an only child. According to the ancestry data, so was her mother. Her father had a sister, but she had two sons. I can't find a Margaret Smith, a Margaret Granger, or a Margaret Hemingway in the family at all."

"Crap," I muttered. "Mary Granger must have lied when she told her neighbor that Margaret was her niece. Or maybe the neighbor has the name wrong. Either way, somebody was hiding something on that farm." My phone buzzed with another call and when I saw who it was, I told Devon I had to go. Then I switched over to my caller.

"Hi, Judith," I said. "I'm surprised to hear from you."

"Not as surprised as I am," she said. "Something happened and I don't know what to do."

"Tell me."

"Okay, Brandon, he put up this floating shelf thing in our bedroom a couple of weeks before Christmas. It had this stupid, heavy vase on top of it because Brandon said he needed one little spot of color in the house for himself."

I had no idea why she was telling me this.

"Anyway, I've never liked the shelf because for some damned reason, Brandon put it up on the wall at the bottom of our bed. And since I sleep on the far side of the bed and my dresser is located at that end of the room, I've bumped into that shelf I don't how many times trying to walk by it. I've got permanent bruises on both shoulders from it. Brandon kept saying he'd move it, but he never did."

I looked down at Newt and rolled my eyes.

"After you left, I went into the bedroom to grab a sweater from my dresser and sure enough, I rammed my shoulder into that shelf again. I got so pissed, I turned around and started slapping the damn thing. Not a great idea because it's hard as a rock and I knocked the vase off and broke it."

Okay, Judith had some anger-management issues. Understandable given what she'd been through, but I wasn't much in the mood for playing grief counselor.

Then she said, "After the vase fell off, the bottom of the whole thing popped open. There was a hidden storage compartment in there and it contained a notebook Brandon was keeping."

Judith had my interest and full attention now.

"I've only skimmed it. There's a lot in there, like several weeks' worth. He mentions some woman named Margaret and another one named Edna and I can't make heads or tails out of it. I thought about turning it over to the police, but Brandon's notes say they can't be trusted."

She paused and exhaled sharply. "I felt really bad for that auntie of Andy's you brought along with you earlier. She looked so devastated. And it's kind of you to try to help her, to help her nephew. If he's innocent…" She didn't finish the thought. "Anyway, I thought I'd give you first crack at the notebook. Maybe it will make sense to you."

"Judith, it makes sense to me already. I think I know who

Margaret is. And Edna isn't a person; it's an acronym. I can be there in twenty minutes if that's okay and I'll explain more then."

"Sure."

"Don't tell anyone else about it."

"I won't."

I ended the call, and Newt and I were in the rental car in less than five minutes. There were no suspicious people or cars lurking about and along the drive I kept an eye on the rearview mirror for a tail. I saw none. But I kept my bear spray and my hunting knife close at hand.

Judith met me at the door looking relieved. "I thought you were someone else," she said. "That's not the same car you had before."

"Oh, right. I should have told you. Sorry. I had a bit of a fender bender earlier and had to get a rental."

Judith looked around the front yard before closing and locking the door. She held the notebook out to me. It was one of those ordinary spiral things like the kind you buy for school. It had a red cover and there was a slight curve to it, as if it had been rolled up either for carrying or maybe so it would fit in the shelf Judith had mentioned.

"Morgan, the stuff in there . . . it's scary. I don't know if Brandon was in his right mind. If what he wrote is true . . ." Her nervous anxiety was contagious, and I glanced out a sidelight window beside her door at Newt sitting in the front passenger seat of the rental car.

"My dog is out there. Is he safe?"

Judith raked both hands through her short blond hair, making it stand on end as if she'd just had the scare of her life. Maybe she had. "I don't know," she said. "The things Brandon wrote in here are bad. Really bad." She bit her lower lip. "Maybe you should bring your dog in."

I thought about Newt's hair all over the pristine white surfaces in Judith's house.

"In fact," Judith went on, "it might be good to have him in here if he's protective at all."

"He is," I assured her.

Judith's behavior had me wondering what the hell was in the notebook. I was desperate to read it but first I had to get Newt. I handed the notebook back to Judith. "Hold this for me," I said. Then I undid the locks, hurried out to the car, unhooked Newt from his safety strap, and led him inside, looking over my shoulder the entire time. Once we were in the house, I watched Judith throw all the locks again as I aimed the fob at the car through the side-light window to lock its doors.

I took some reassurance from the fact that Newt remained calm, and after taking off my boots, I followed Judith into the living room. After telling Newt to lie down, I took a seat on the couch next to Judith, still wearing my coat. She handed me the notebook again and I opened it to the first page as Judith proceeded to chew on the side of her thumb, watching me for my reaction.

Brandon's scribblings were hard to read as his writing was angular and small and the pen he'd used tended to skip. The notebook was full of his notes and some of the ink was smeared in a way that made me think Brandon had been a lefty. And some of the pages had gotten wet, in one case with what appeared to be coffee judging from the brown stain and the faint aroma wafting up from the pages. Despite all these challenges, I was able to decipher enough of the words to get the gist of things.

The beginning pages told how Brandon, while working at Kwik Trip one afternoon, had been approached by a woman named Margaret, someone he had seen years before while working on the Granger farm. Margaret had a proposal for him. She said she'd been using some of the sows Franklin Granger had sold her to conduct some experiments with a new cancer medicine prior to beginning human trials. But a few years ago, some of the sows had escaped and had managed to breed with some wild boars, creating a new hybrid animal. Margaret believed those hybrids carried the secret to this cure for cancer and if Brandon was willing to help her catch them, there'd be a huge payout for him. Margaret sweetened the deal by giving Brandon cash up front that totaled more than he could make at Kwik Trip in six months.

I paused and looked at Judith. Things were becoming crystal clear in my mind.

"The really scary part is at the back," Judith said. "Brandon wrote about this Rick guy Margaret kept mentioning, saying he was a rogue ex-employee with an axe to grind because Margaret had fired him. She told him Rick was desperate and vengeful, and Margaret feared he would try to kill her."

I read some more, and Brandon's words made it clear he was falling for Margaret. I looked over at Judith, who was watching me as I read, and saw tears brimming in her eyes. She turned her head away and said, "Yeah, so it turns out I was kind of right when I thought Brandon had found a sugar mama, just not quite the way I thought."

"I'm so sorry, Judith."

"There's something else," she said. "Something I should have told you earlier, but I don't want anyone to know because it means I'll lose my job."

As soon as she said this, I guessed what it was she wanted to tell me. "Brandon stole some of your drug samples, didn't he?"

Judith squeezed her eyes closed and nodded. "The drug sample I found missing was a new sedative and tranquilizer similar to ketamine. It's much more powerful than ketamine, though, has a really short half-life, and doesn't cause nightmares."

"Ketamine causes nightmares?"

She nodded. "And sometimes daymares. It's a well-known side effect. Ketamine was used for decades as a veterinary drug—still is—and it's only recently been used in humans. The nightmares seem to happen more in children than adults, but they can happen to anyone and be quite awful. This new drug has all the sedative and tranquilizing effects of ketamine but without the scary stuff."

"That explains the tranquilizer darts."

Judith nodded. "Please don't tell anyone. I need my job."

"Does Brandon mention it in this notebook anywhere?" Judith shook her head. "Then I think we're okay. I need to take this notebook to the authorities. Will you let me have it?"

"You can't go to the authorities," Judith said. "Brandon wrote that he was having doubts about what Margaret was doing and didn't believe everything she told him, but he didn't know what to do about it because the police couldn't be trusted. He said they were in on it."

"I won't take it to anyone local," I said. "I have some other connections, including someone at the FBI."

"The FBI?" Judith's eyes grew big. I wasn't about to tell her my

FBI connection worked in art theft. She raked her hands through her hair again and exhaled hard. "I guess you can go ahead and take it. I took pictures of all the pages with my phone, so I have a copy."

"That's good. Smart."

Judith looked pleased with my compliment.

"Let's take it one step further," I said. I tore a small corner off one of the blank pages in the notebook and used a pen on the table to write down Devon's email address. "Send those pictures of the pages to this guy just to make sure."

Judith took the piece of paper, stared at it a moment, and then nodded.

"I should get going," I said. "Thank you for this," I added, gesturing with the notebook as I got up. Newt got up, too, but he started acting strangely, staring at the windows overlooking the side yard and emitting a low, rumbling growl.

"What is it, Newt?" I said. He whined and looked up at me.

Judith said, "There's a small group of coyotes that hang out in the woods here and sometimes they come into the yard looking for food. They moved into this area a couple of months ago after some developer cut down the woods where they used to live to clear the way for a new housing development. Progress," she said with disgust, rolling her eyes.

"That's probably what has him worked up," I said. I hoped I was right. I much preferred the idea of an animal threat to a human one.

I rolled the notebook up and went to tuck it into a coat pocket but forgot I had the can of bear spray in there. Judith saw the spray and gave me a curious but worried look. I simply smiled and shoved the notebook into the pocket on the other side. Then, using the fob,

I remote started the car through the front window. Newt had stopped acting weird and his calmness reassured me. I put on my boots and after thanking Judith again and telling her to be careful, I left with Newt close by my side. I didn't see any coyotes, but I heard them. Their yips and howls echoed through the chilly night air, making Newt emit a deep-throated growl.

As I drove back to the motel, my paranoia reached a peak. I was constantly checking the rearview mirror, looking for the return of my earlier pursuers. Would they come after me again this soon or opt to lie low for a while after the exposure they'd had at Sonja Mueller's farm? I hoped it would be the latter.

A car did fall in behind me not far from Judith's house and it stayed with me all the way through town though at a reasonable distance. I desperately wanted to read the rest of Brandon's notebook, but I wanted to do it somewhere where I'd be surrounded by people, not in my motel room alone. I pulled into the parking lot of Culver's across from the motel and breathed a sigh of relief when the car that had been behind me continued on its way. I told Newt to stay, locked him in the car, and went inside. Not wanting to draw undue attention to myself, I ordered a hot fudge sundae and a soda even though I wasn't hungry. Then I settled in at one of the tables, took out the notebook, and read.

CHAPTER 31

I stayed at my table in Culver's for nearly an hour. By the time I'd finished reading the notebook, I had a good understanding of the events that had taken place since my arrival in Rhinelander. Brandon's documentation was thorough and complete and toward the end, when he got suspicious of Margaret Smith's motives, he'd done some snooping.

The crowd in the restaurant had thinned and I was debating checking out of the motel and heading home, taking the notebook with me. I could always return at some later date for my own car. Then my phone buzzed with a text message from an unknown number.

Morgan, it's Roger. Can you meet me at my cabin at eight tonight?

I glanced at my watch and saw it was already a few minutes past seven thirty. He wasn't giving me much time. I packed up and went out to the car, where Newt sniffed at my empty hands.

"Sorry, buddy," I said. "I don't have time to get you another burger right now. Maybe later."

Newt flopped down in the seat with a disappointed sigh as I pulled out onto the road and headed for Roger's place. I pulled up in front of the cabin a few minutes before eight, but the house was dark, police tape hung from the porch railing, and I didn't see any sign of Roger or a vehicle. There was what looked like a sheet of paper hanging on the front door, however, and after a careful look around, I got out of the car and walked up onto the porch, stepping over a bit of drooping police tape at the top of the stairs.

The paper was a note that had been speared by the door knocker. I ripped it loose and tried to read it, but it was too dark. I cursed myself for not buying a flashlight when I was at Farm and Fleet. I always kept one in my own car but didn't have one in this rental. Instead, I fished my cell phone out of my pocket and turned on its flashlight. A handwritten note was scrawled across the paper.

Meet me down by the river.

R

I cursed Roger and his cloak-and-dagger antics. Why couldn't he have just stayed by the cabin? Muttering to myself, I let Newt out of the car and draped his leash around my neck, hooking the clip through a ring near the handle. The notebook was on the front seat, and after a moment's debate, I grabbed it and stuffed it into my coat pocket. Roger would want to see it. I checked to make sure my knife and bear spray were also in my pockets, just in case. Then, after staring into the dark morass of those woods, I took the sheathed knife out and slid it into my boot alongside my leg instead. My gloves were old and bulky, making my grip on things tenuous, so I shoved them into a pocket.

Using the flashlight on my phone, I found the trail we had all followed a few days earlier—still visible even with the inch or so of new snow that had fallen—and headed off into the woods. Newt, happy to be off leash, sniffed along ahead of me, occasionally pausing to make yellow snow as he marked off bits of territory.

The trees were thick and the combination of a full moon and the light from my phone created a plethora of moving shadows ahead and around me. After about fifteen minutes, I reached the spot where Brandon had died. Newt was all over it, sniffing the snow and making an odd, whimpery kind of sound. I immediately veered off on the path I'd taken days before to the river. Memories of the creature I'd seen that day made me take the bear spray out of my pocket to have it ready. I held it in one hand and my cell phone in the other.

Something sent a prickle up my spine, and I stopped where I was, looking down at Newt. He seemed unbothered but my instincts were screaming at me to slow down. Where the hell was Roger?

"Roger? Are you out here?" My voice came out loud though not quite a yell and it echoed eerily around me. It was the only sound I heard. Had Roger perhaps fallen victim to the Hodag creature? Or maybe he was out here because he'd found it and killed it.

"Roger?" I tried again, a bit louder this time, but the only sound I heard was my and Newt's breathing.

This was stupid. I stood there, wondering if I should turn around and go back or continue on to the river. Roger had said in his note to meet him by the river, and I was almost there. What if he had encountered the creature? He might be hurt and in need of help. I made the decision to plod on but told myself that if I didn't see him or have him answer me the next time I called out, I was out of there.

Five minutes later I emerged from the woods along the bank of the river. Here the moonlight shone down uninhibited by trees, reflecting off the ice and snow. It provided enough light that I was able to turn off the flashlight and slip my phone into my pocket next to my gloves. I looked along the banks upriver and then down, hoping to see Roger, but there was no sign of him.

"Roger? Are you out here?"

I listened for a response and this time I heard the crunch of human footsteps behind me. I whirled around expecting Roger but instead saw a woman I recognized. She had a gun in her hand, and it was pointed at me. Newt growled and took a step toward her. The gun hand swung slightly so it was aimed at Newt.

"No!" I said, stepping in front of Newt and putting a staying hand on my dog's head. "He won't come at you."

Daisy Almay, the real estate agent who had been part of the not-so-welcome wagon that had come to my motel room, weighed my promise and lowered the gun.

"Where is Roger?" I asked.

"Hell if I know," she said. "I guessed he'd gone into hiding once I realized Rick had gotten to him and I knew he was smart enough to ditch his phone, but I also guessed he'd be in touch with you, the cryp-tow-zoo-ol-o-gist." Her voice was mocking, and she jerked her head from side to side with each syllable. "I assumed he'd be using a burner phone and that made it easy to pretend to be him and lure you out here with a text message. Obviously, it worked."

"How did you get my number?"

"A certain detective with the Rhinelander Police Department was quite helpful in that regard. You see, the Hoffmans think these experiments I'm doing are actually about finding a cure for cancer. And since their daughter has cancer, well, let's just say Detective Hoffman is willing to look the other way when it comes to me."

No wonder both Rick and Brandon had been wary about going to the police. I wondered if Hoffman had really suspected me the night Rick was murdered or if he simply wanted to find out if Rick had talked to me and what, if anything, I knew. I also realized that Rick's warning to Roger about a woman he thought was named Edna was probably Rick warning about two separate things, a woman—this woman—and EDDNA.

"You're Margaret Smith, I presume?" I said.

Her face hardened and the mocking smile vanished.

"How did you come by the surname of Almay?"

"An unfortunate and short-lived marriage. Ditched the husband but kept the name. It came in handy because I didn't want to have any remaining associations with EDDNA."

"Right," I said, nodding. "And Daisy?"

She smiled again. "A nickname my father gave me. He was French. Margaret is my christened name and 'marguerite' is the French word for the daisy flower. I needed a different name for my professional persona in the community."

"Where do you find the time? Do you really sell real estate and handle vacation rentals?"

"I have a real estate license and I've sold a property or two. But it's true that's not how I spend the bulk of my time. I have a master's in biomedical engineering."

"Impressive," I said. "What's in that nice barn on the Granger property? And the trailer? Have you got some sort of laboratory out there along with your pigs?" She didn't bother with an answer but the look of surprise on her face told me I had guessed correctly.

Instead, she said, "My men tell me there is a notebook of Brandon's that his girlfriend found? And you have it?"

How did she know this? Had there been someone outside Judith's house after all? Or did they have Judith's house or phone bugged?

"Hand it over."

The river was at my back and the steep, narrow riverbank stretched in both directions to my sides. I had nowhere to go. I had the canister of bear spray in my hand, and I considered blasting her with it, but the gun gave me pause. If I sprayed her, she'd likely fire at me and, as close as she was, the chances of hitting me or Newt were too good.

"I wouldn't if I were you," she said, seeming to read my mind. "Drop the bear spray."

I hesitated and she raised the gun back up. I dropped the bear spray.

"Good girl. Now hand over the notebook."

I thought about lying and saying I'd left it in the car, but it was sticking out of my pocket far enough to be easily seen. I pulled it out and handed it to her.

"Naughty boy, Brandon," she said, flipping the notebook open with one hand and glancing at the pages. "I had no idea he was doing this. It's probably just as well that creature got him."

"What a horrible thing to say."

She rolled the notebook up and worked it into her coat pocket. "Yeah, well, nice guys finish last in the world today," she said.

"If you're not looking for a cure for cancer, what are you doing out at the Granger farm?"

"Who said we're doing anything at the Granger farm?"

"You may have duped me into coming out here, but I'm not stupid," I told her. "What could you be doing in that mysterious barn that would justify this?" I gestured toward the gun.

"I didn't want to hurt anyone," she said. "I told my guys to simply keep an eye on you, but when you started looking into things you shouldn't have, and Rick talked, I had to get more serious. Even so, all they were going to do when you left the farm was scare and threaten you."

"They tried to run me off the road," I said.

"Did they? Well, I'm sure they wouldn't have—"

"And then they came at me with a gun when I was at the Mueller place." Her attempts to minimize what had happened irked me and my voice had grown angrier and more strident.

"They were only going to scare you by shooting out your tires. But then someone shot at them, and things got ugly."

"That's putting it mildly."

She shifted uncomfortably. "Look, you don't understand the pressure I'm under," she said. "I've made promises to several wealthy investors who come from countries that aren't known for their patience and civility. They're demanding results and if I don't produce them, they'll do worse things to me than shoot me. If Rick had just stuck with me a little longer . . ."

"Resistance," I said. "You had Rick working on the creation of insects resistant to pesticides."

Margaret looked chagrined. "Wow. He revealed more than I realized," she said, shaking her head. "Our genetic manipulations and the incorporation of certain insect characteristics into humans could eventually lead to the creation of the perfect mercenary army, men who not only have extraordinary abilities but who are also immune to the chemical and biological warfare so often utilized by the superpowers."

"And how do the pigs figure in?"

"They share a lot of DNA with us humans and their reactions to injuries, drugs, and chemicals are strikingly similar. Hell, they've successfully transplanted pig organs into humans. More importantly, they were readily available, thanks to the Grangers." She shook her head, looking frustrated. "We made a lot of progress initially. We successfully spliced certain bits of insect DNA onto parts of the pigs' DNA and produced offspring with some promising characteristics. But the piglets kept dying after a few weeks. Ulrich thought it was because of the limited life cycles insects have and that it somehow impacted their DNA. It was a setback, but we eventually found a way around it and the altered piglets survived and grew old enough to reproduce. Then, some of them escaped." Her lips compressed into a thin line, her eyes looking heavenward as she shook her head angrily.

"In hindsight, I don't think it was the accident it appeared to be. I think that's when Rick started pulling away. And I suspect he'd been secretly sabotaging the experiments ever since."

"It will never work," I said. "Your ideas are crazy. You're crazy. You can't alter human DNA with mutated bug DNA."

"We've hit some roadblocks, but it can be done," she insisted.

"Yeah, one of those roadblocks is the fact that your sows crossbred with wild boars and the end result of your genetic manipulations is the creation of monstrous creatures with deformities and aggressive behaviors."

She looked impressed. "You're right. And yes, that's precisely why I wanted Brandon to capture one. I suspect what we need can be found in the DNA of these hybrids out here. And an army of killer boars might be enough to keep my investors happy for now."

"Did you kill the Grangers?"

The sudden change of subject must have thrown her for a moment. She looked confused before her face hardened again. And apparently, this question was a step too far because what she did next came as a total surprise. She lunged at me, fast, with her arms extended in front of her. Her hands hit me square in the chest, shoving me backward. I took a step to try to keep my balance, but the momentum was too strong, and my second step met empty air. I backpedaled down the bank and out onto the river ice, my attempts to maintain my footing meeting with slippery failure. I landed hard on my butt about six or seven feet from shore.

I heard the cracks before I saw them, little *zips* of sound accompanying the appearance of crazy traveling lines in the ice. I barely registered what was happening before the ice gave way and I was plunged into freezing water. The last thing I saw was Daisy's maniacal smile as she watched me from the edge of the bank, and Newt standing a few feet behind her.

CHAPTER 32

Icy water enveloped me, and it was all I could do to suppress my urge to gasp. My swimming instincts kicked in, but my arms and legs were paralyzed by the cold. I couldn't feel a bottom and all I could see above me was a solid sheet of ice highlighted in the moonlight. Bits of debris floated by me in the water, telling me the current here was brisk but not rapid. I searched frantically for the opening I fell through, but I wasn't even sure which direction it was in. I was all turned around, completely disoriented.

My legs began to move, and I kicked as hard as I could toward the surface, only to crack my head on solid ice. Movement was coming back to my arms, too, though the muscles were not at full strength. My attempts to bang on the ice overhead were flimsy and futile. I felt the current pushing me, saw the patterns in the ice overhead change. I needed to get out of the current, find the shoreline.

The knife! I reached down inside my boot, found the end of the hilt, and pulled it out, praying my grip would stay strong enough not to drop it. I removed the scabbard and let it go. I could just make it out in the moonlight, and I watched as it drifted for a few feet and then suddenly took off, moving away from me. I headed for the spot where the current was faster, hoping the ice there would be thinner and then tried to move perpendicular to the flow of debris, hoping to reach shore.

My limbs felt stronger, but my lungs were close to bursting. I didn't know how much longer I'd be able to hold my breath. I could normally go great lengths underwater before needing to come up for air, but that was if I prepped first by hyperventilating. I'd had no time to prepare for this dunking.

I tried to kick toward the surface and use the knife to stab at the ice, hoping it would halt my downriver movement, but the knife failed to find purchase. That's when I knew I was going to die.

And then my feet dragged along the bottom! I pulled my knees up and planted both feet beneath me, using my arms to fight the pull of the current. With my last bit of energy and air I pushed myself upward as hard as I could, my hands over my head, the knife pointed toward the ice. I felt the knife take hold and then the ice above me shattered and gave way. My head burst through the opening, and I gasped in a lungful of frigid night air.

I grabbed an icy ledge and tried to hold on, my breathing hard and fast. I carefully switched the knife to my other hand and jammed it into the ice's surface. It held, and I hung on to it for dear life as I looked for Margaret and Newt. Margaret was clearly crazy, and I had to hope she hadn't shot Newt. I hadn't heard a gunshot, but would I have heard it under the ice? The shoreline I could see was vacant and unfamiliar, but it was only about twenty feet away.

My body temperature was dropping rapidly, and the weight of my wet clothes and the river current was dragging me down. I needed to get out of the water and I remembered a trip my parents and I took to Iceland to hunt for a cryptid, a giant worm known as the Lagarfljót monster rumored to live in a glacial lake of the same name. While in Iceland, a guide had told us what to do should anyone fall through the ice. Get your shoulders out of the water and then try to get your feet behind you so you're horizontal. Then kick as hard as you can while using your arms to do a commando crawl onto the surface.

The cold had my muscles screaming their reluctance at me, but I summoned all the strength I had and started kicking. One side of my face scraped along the ice, but I felt no pain. Everything was numb. I was out of the water up to my waist when I felt someone pulling on my coat near the shoulder. Had Margaret found me?

I lifted my head, which felt like it weighed a hundred pounds, and turned to look.

Newt was there on the ice, pulling at my coat with his teeth, backing up toward the shoreline.

"Oh, good boy," I said, though my voice was weak and jittery.

Something in the river hit my legs hard, pulling me back into the water a little.

"No!"

Newt tugged harder, and I prayed the ice beneath him would hold. He managed to get me far enough out of the water that I could roll over onto my back. I wanted to sit up but didn't want to concentrate my weight too much in one spot. Better to stay flat and distribute my body weight over as much space as I could. I rolled onto my side and looked at my lower legs, still in the water and entangled in something. I used the last of my energy to kick loose of whatever had them and saw one of my feet was caught in the handhold of Newt's leash that I'd had looped around my neck. The rest of the leash was caught on something else and when I pulled my foot up, Margaret's pale, lifeless face briefly appeared in the hole. I kicked the leash off my foot and then watched as Margaret's face slipped beneath the edge and drifted away.

I lay there, confused and horrified by what I'd just seen. How had Margaret ended up in the river? I looked over at Newt. "Did you do that?"

He let go of my coat and whined.

I looked in both directions, up and down the river, and saw only ice. I yanked the knife free and slowly continued my commando crawl over to the shore. Then I went on hands and knees up the shallow bank, Newt tugging on me the entire time. Once there, I collapsed onto the snow, breathing hard, my body shaking like a dog shedding water. The shaking was good, I knew. It was when it stopped that I'd be in trouble if I hadn't warmed up.

Newt stretched out on top of me, slowly lowering his body over mine, managing to stay on me despite my tremors. His warmth seeped through my wet clothes to the skin beneath, and while it felt good, I knew I had to get moving quickly or I'd be found dead here, frozen to the ground. I had to find shelter and warm clothing. Problem was, I had no idea where I was.

Newt sensed my need to start moving and got up. He stood beside me and barked. Slowly, I got to my hands and knees, and then to my feet. Newt took off into the trees and I struggled to follow him. My legs were slow to move. They seemed to weigh a thousand pounds each and I had to focus on one step at a time.

I kept it up, Newt encouraging me with the occasional bark, until I emerged into a clearing. There, just ahead, was Roger's cabin and my rental car! The sight of the car spurred me to a new burst of energy but then I stopped a few feet away, suddenly worried that I'd somehow lost the keys. I reached deep into my coat pocket and laughed with relief when I felt them along with my motel key card beneath my sopping wet gloves. I dropped the keys trying to hit the right button on the fob and wondered if the fob would even work after being in the water, but I finally got the door unlocked and opened. I tried to tell Newt to get in ahead of me, but my teeth were chattering so hard everything came out mumbled and nonsensical. I used a hand signal instead and Newt hopped in and immediately went to the passenger seat. I collapsed into the driver's seat, closed and locked the door, started the car, and turned the heat up full blast.

As the car warmed up and wonderfully hot air started blasting from the vents, I palpated the outside of the other pocket of my coat and was surprised to feel the outline of my cell phone in there. I sang the praises of deep pockets and fished it out, but my elation was short-lived. It was as dead as Margaret "Daisy" Almay née Smith.

I thought about driving to the police station but remembered what Daisy had told me about Detective Hoffman and wasn't sure how to get there. Knowing my priority had to be getting dry and warm, I drove back to the motel, a challenging task as it turned out, because I was shivering and shaking like one of those dash-mounted hula dancer dolls. I could barely keep the steering wheel where I wanted it or maintain even pressure on the gas pedal. I'm sure I looked like a drunk driver as I lurched and wove my way along the roads. I feared a cop would see me and pull me over, but I managed to make it. As soon as I was inside my motel room, I stripped naked and got under a shower spray that was as hot as I could stand. I stayed there until the water turned tepid.

I got out, dried off, put on two layers of clothes with a sweater over the top, and used the room's hair dryer to dry my hair, relishing the warm airflow. Once that was done, I brewed a cup of coffee using the room's coffee maker, walked over to the corner table, and picked up the card Ian Forrester had left with me. Then I sat on the edge of one of the beds and used the motel phone to dial his number.

CHAPTER 33

Ian Forrester was still in town and happened to be at the police station utilizing their computer to finish his reports. He didn't answer my call initially, but I left a voice mail telling him I needed to speak with him urgently regarding a matter of life and death. I left the number of the phone in my motel room, and I must have intrigued him with my message because he called me back a few minutes later.

It took some explaining and clarifying before he understood most of what I was telling him and why involving the local police was not an option. He assured me he would have an agent contact me at the motel within the hour and told me to stay put in the meantime.

As I sat waiting to hear from the FBI agent, I thought back to the craziness that had happened at Sonja's earlier. Had I hallucinated or had it really been David who'd poked his head into my car to see if I was okay? It made sense in a way if he was trying to impersonate Adrian Dunlevy to secure an artwork for a wealthy client. The question uppermost in my mind was what to do about it. Should I tell Jon? I decided yes, I should, but it could wait. After all, what could Jon do about David that Forrester or one of his cronies couldn't do?

Thoughts of Jon made me realize that if he or anyone else tried to call me on my cell, they wouldn't be able to reach me. I checked my phone just in case it had started working but it was still dead. I wished I had a container full of rice to put it in, though I suspected it was beyond that cure. I realized the people who mattered—Devon, Jon, and Rita—all knew where I was staying and how to reach me through the motel's phone. Still, I decided I would call each of them and let them know what was going on as soon as I heard from the FBI agent. I didn't want to tie up the phone yet and risk missing that call.

Then I realized I didn't need my phone. I went to my laptop and sent Devon an email explaining my phone situation and including the motel's phone number just to be sure. I also asked him to pass this information on to Rita, though I held off on having him give it to Jon. I'd decided I would call Jon as soon as I heard from the FBI.

As if my thoughts had somehow summoned the agent, my phone rang. She introduced herself as Agent Lynn Hobart, and over the next thirty minutes, I tried to explain everything that had happened since my arrival in Rhinelander. She sounded skeptical at first—no surprise there—and perhaps a bit irritated with Ian for handing me off to her because I think she thought I was crazy. But when I explained there was a dead woman under the ice in the river and at least one—maybe more—genetically altered, extremely aggressive, boar-pig hybrids on the loose in the woods that had already torn one man apart, she tuned in. Eventually she told me to stay where I was, and she would come to me to do a more formal report.

As soon as I hung up with Agent Hobart, I called Jon. He listened to me describe my visits to the Grangers' and the neighboring Dusseldorf farm. When I told him about my high-speed drive while my pursuers tried to run me off the road, his only comment was a muttered curse. When I told him about what had happened at Sonja's place, he was somewhat amused until I mentioned the appearance of David. Then he was angry with himself for not making the connection sooner. Things took an unexpected turn when I told him what had happened at the river.

"Good God, Morgan," he said. "I can't believe how reckless and careless you are. Do you know what that does to me? Do you know how hard it is for me to have to be here worrying about you wherever you are, knowing you'll put yourself in these dangerous situations?"

Apparently these questions were rhetorical because before I could answer any of them, not that I had answers exactly, he continued his rant.

"I don't think I can do this anymore, Morgan. I care about you a great deal. I hope you know that. But I don't think I can be in a relationship with someone who has such a blatant disregard for her own safety. My heart can't take another loss like the last one."

I hadn't seen that coming, though I probably should have. I wasn't the only one who had been damaged by tragedy and the loss of loved ones. It left me too stunned to speak.

"I understand you're an independent woman who's used to doing your own thing and going your own way," he went on. "But whether you realize it or not, you led a relatively sheltered life when your parents were alive. Yes, you traveled the globe and visited exotic locales, but you always had the safety net of your parents and their wealth to fall back on. I thought their deaths and the thing with David would serve as your wake-up call, but if anything, it seems to have made you even more reckless. I think I need to take some time to think about things with us."

I managed to eke out an "Okay."

"For God's sake, try to be careful during the remainder of your time there and drive safely when you come home. I'll be in touch."

And then he ended the call. I sat there on the bed numb, and not from the cold.

Agent Hobart arrived just under an hour later. She was a stunningly beautiful woman I gauged to be in her thirties with high cheekbones, light brown skin, bright green eyes, and jet-black hair pulled straight back and secured into a bun. Her looks, combined with a tall, lean body, made me think she should be modeling rather than working for the FBI.

I pegged her as one of the good guys when Newt took to her instantly and she to him. She squatted down and met him face to face, massaging behind his ears as I did the introductions. Agent Hobart was obviously a dog person.

We spent a little over three hours there in my room, going over my story several times. Agent Hobart took notes as I spoke, though she was also recording what I said to make sure she didn't miss anything. This was probably a smart move on her part because I was rambling and all over the place. My brain felt muddled, and I had trouble organizing my thoughts. I didn't know if it was because of my dunk in the river or what had happened with Jon. Maybe it was both.

Agent Hobart appeared to regard my story with a healthy dose of renewed skepticism when I told her my reason for being in Rhinelander was to try to prove Hodags were real and that a killer one was living in the woods outside town. Her eyes glazed over slightly as I tried to explain about EDDNA, and flesh flies, and Asian hornets, and how Margaret Smith aka Daisy Almay had private investors whose goals were apparently nefarious and evil. I did my best to explain genetic splicing and how Ulrich and Margaret's attempts to play God had led to the creation of genetically mutated monsters and how Ulrich had finally found his conscience and tried to warn people on the dark web posting as doT red, which when reversed read "der Tod," German for "the death."

Agent Hobart perked up visibly when I told her I suspected Margaret had murdered Mary and Franklin Granger and that their bodies might be buried somewhere on the farm, though they might also have been fed to the pigs, in which case all anyone would likely find were scattered bones. Once Hobart realized the purported dead woman in the river wasn't the only victim in this crazy charade, she wanted to take a break so she could make some phone calls. I persuaded her to wait and let me continue because the body count was still climbing.

I then told her about Ulrich Liebhardt's murder and how we thought it was Roger at first and how and why I'd been a suspect and been questioned by Detective Hoffman. Then I told her how I'd discovered Roger was still alive but he'd gone into hiding and was off the grid somewhere using burner phones and that was why I'd been duped by the text message I'd received from Margaret claiming to be Roger.

Agent Hobart then asked to see the text and I had to show her my cold, dead phone. That earned me a suspicious scowl until I told her I was glad I wasn't showing it to her with my cold, dead hand. She didn't appreciate my attempt at humor and in hindsight, I think it may have been both lame and ill timed.

Next I told her about the visit I'd had from the not-so-welcome wagon, a group that had included Daisy, aka Margaret, and Detective Hoffman's wife, Cordelia. And then I told her what Brandon had written in his notebook about not being able to trust the police, and how Margaret had explained to me her arrangement with the Hoffmans.

Agent Hobart looked both confused and excited at various points during this process. She was definitely excited about the existence of Brandon's notebook until I told her I'd handed it over to Margaret at gunpoint and it was most likely soaked and unreadable by now, assuming it could even be found because it might be at the bottom of the river. But I managed to raise Agent Hobart's spirits when I told her Judith had photographed every page of the notebook with her phone and forwarded them to my employee.

Finally, Agent Hobart asked me how Margaret Smith or Daisy Almay or whoever she was had ended up in the river.

"I honestly don't know," I told her. "Right after she shoved me out onto the ice and just before I broke through it, I saw her standing on the edge of the riverbank. Maybe she slipped and fell." I gestured toward Newt where he was sleeping on the floor. "This guy was standing behind her and the only other thing I can figure is he somehow jumped up and knocked her in after me."

Agent Hobart raised her eyebrows at that. "You never struggled with the woman?"

"Never touched her," I said. "She had a gun. My biggest fear was that she was going to shoot my dog after she knocked me in the water."

"And you managed to surface through the ice and drag yourself out of the river?"

"Yes. I had a knife and—" I stopped when I saw Hobart's eyebrows shoot up again.

"Did you try to use the knife on Margaret or Daisy? Whoever?"

I shook my head. "The knife was in a sheath and tucked inside my boot. I also had a can of bear spray in my coat pocket in case I encountered the animal that had killed Brandon Kluver. The bear spray was in my hand when I came upon Margaret, but she made me drop it. I never had a chance to go for my knife. Like I said before, Margaret had a gun pointed at me."

"When did you access the knife?"

"When I was in the water. I remembered it and dug it out of my boot. It was in a sheath, a leather scabbard, and I pulled that off and let it go in the water. Then I used the knife on the ice overhead to try to break it. Once I broke through, I used it as an anchor. Between it and Newt dragging me, I was able to get out of the water and back to shore."

"Your dog pulled you out of the water?"

I nodded and smiled. "He's pretty amazing." Sensing he was being talked about, Newt raised his head from the floor and looked at me. I winked at him, and he put his head down and went back to sleep.

"Do you still have the knife?"

"I do." I got up, fetched it from the bathroom sink where I'd left it, and brought it out to the table.

"I'll need to keep that," Agent Hobart said as I set it down.

"That's fine."

Eventually, Agent Hobart had me get on my laptop and pull up a map of the area to show her where the Granger farm was, where Roger's cabin was located, the approximate spot where I'd gone into the river, and where I'd come back out of it, though this last part was basically an educated guess on my part.

We finished up a little after one in the morning and I took Newt outside to visit his favorite field alongside the motel while Hobart made her phone calls from just inside the motel door, watching me the entire time. When I returned to the room, she told me I looked tired.

"You've been through a lot. Why don't you try to nap for a bit."

I was exhausted but didn't think I'd be able to sleep. Yet when I put my head on my pillow, the next thing I knew, it was six thirty in the morning according to the alarm clock, and Agent Hobart was gone. Or so I thought. Turned out she was right outside my room in the hallway. When she heard me flush the toilet in my bathroom, she let herself back in with my key card, which she'd hijacked from the table.

She handed me a cup of coffee she said was from the continental breakfast the motel had set up in the lobby. "I wasn't sure how you'd take it, or even if you liked coffee, but I saw you'd been hitting up the stuff in your room, so I gambled. I didn't get you any cream because I saw you had half-and-half in your mini fridge here, but I do have some sugars if you want." She fished into her pants pocket and pulled out four packets of sugar.

While I was a bit disturbed by the fact she'd been snooping

about in my room while I slept, I was so grateful for the coffee, I forgave her. Newt was asleep on the floor and hadn't bothered to get up, so I was in no hurry to take him out. I swear he has a bladder capacity the size of Lake Michigan.

"I have some things to tell you," Hobart said. "Let's sit." She gestured toward the corner table, and I took one of the seats after removing my half-and-half from the mini fridge. She took the other seat and leaned forward, elbows on the table.

"Your story struck me as bizarre and I admit I had my doubts as to the veracity of parts of it, particularly after Ian Forrester informed me you were also involved in his investigation."

"Not involved per se," I said, adding the creamer to my coffee. "More of a peripheral interest, I think."

She shrugged and continued. "We contacted Judith Ingles, and she did have the pictures of the notebook pages you mentioned. Those photos are now in our possession and are being analyzed." She paused and her expression turned serious. "We also obtained a search warrant and conducted a surprise visit to the barn and trailer out at the Granger farm during the early dawn hours. There was an access road you couldn't see from where you were because it was on the other side of the trailer. Our people are still there. The trailer contains a state-of-the-art laboratory, though no one was there at the time. Do you know of anyone who was working with Margaret Smith?"

I shook my head. "Just Ulrich before he defected and Brandon at the end. I know she had some hired goons who were watching and following me. They tried to run me off the road and I'm betting they're the ones who killed Ulrich. But I have no idea who they are or where they might be."

Hobart nodded. "The barn contained some interesting findings. There were close to forty pigs contained inside, most of them demonstrating some disturbing anomalies."

"Like what?"

"Odd growths on their bodies, deformed feet, and several had weird red eyes."

"That's the flesh flies," I told her. "Red eyes are one of their hallmarks. I'm not sure why Ulrich was using them other than for their short life cycle and simple genetics."

"These pigs weren't overly aggressive toward our agents, but we did find a well-stocked armory in the barn that suggests they could be at times."

"Maybe," I said. "Or maybe those guns were for nosy people."

"Like you?" Hobart said with a sly grin.

I couldn't help but chuckle. "Yes, I suppose so."

"There were some tranquilizer darts out there, too, similar to the ones they found with Brandon Kluver."

"Yeah, I think Margaret must have developed the tranquilizer because she wanted to catch the hybrids alive and potentially mate them with the barned pigs." I hoped this explanation would direct attention away from Judith Ingles and her missing inventory. I didn't want to get her in trouble, and it was certainly feasible to think Ulrich and/or Margaret could have formulated a tranquilizer on their own.

"You said hybrids, plural," Hobart said.

I nodded. "There were six genetically altered sows that escaped five years ago and only two were recaptured, at least according to Mrs. Dusseldorf at the neighboring farm. The other four could have been impregnated by wild boars, assuming other animals didn't kill them first. Pig-boar hybrids are quite common. Given that these pigs escaped five years ago, that they're able to reproduce around the age of nine months, that their gestation period is only a little over three months, and that they frequently give birth to multiples, well, you do the math. We know there's at least one creature out there but there may be more. Maybe they aren't as aggressive. There's no way to know unless they're caught or killed." I paused and frowned. "While it's probably the best solution, I hate the idea of them being killed. It's not their fault they are the way they are. It's all rather sad."

"I suppose it is," Hobart said. "I'm sorry this trip has turned into such a disaster for you."

I nodded, but then said, "Actually, in one way it's been a huge success."

Hobart tilted her head and gave me a quizzical look. "How so?"

"I'm a cryptozoologist and I finally found a kind of cryptid."

CHAPTER 34

After giving Agent Hobart my address, my cell number (though I reminded her I would have to get my phone replaced), my store's phone number, the landline phone number in my apartment, and promises to turn over my firstborn, I was allowed to go home that same day. The broken windows in my car had been replaced, the tire fixed, and the dents pounded out enough to allow me to open and close the driver's side door. I happily handed in the rental car and prepared to drive home. But first I made a stop at Sonja Mueller's place, where, with Sonja's permission and Ian Forrester's help, I loaded Wally into my car so I could take him with me.

I thought Jon might get in touch a few days after I arrived back home. Agent Hobart had asked for his contact information, and she told me she planned to speak with him to verify certain aspects of my story, so he had to know the case had been resolved and I'd come home. But when I still hadn't heard from him a week later, I felt panicky, then depressed.

Rita kept reassuring me. "Give it time. Give him time," she said. Devon stayed quiet and just watched me mope around the store with my hangdog face and slumped posture. Newt, sensing I was upset, kept trying to reassure me but initially he was busy guiding Wally around the store, trying to keep him from bumping into things.

Agent Hobart called me after I'd been home for nearly two weeks to let me know Margaret Smith, aka Daisy Almay, had been found by some ice fishermen who'd caught a bit more than they'd bargained for. Brandon's notebook wasn't found with her body, but it didn't matter since Judith had had the foresight to photograph the pages.

Devon was able to find a record of someone named Margaret Smith who had a master of science degree in biomedical engineering from Northwestern and had graduated around the time our Margaret Smith would have. When Margaret had initially founded EDDNA, her plans had been more altruistic, but when the government contracts dried up and her business started going under, she apparently latched on to offers from some less savory funding sources and switched her focus. Ulrich Liebhardt had been part of that deal because he'd developed a problematic online gambling habit while in college and owed a lot of money to some people who didn't take kindly to unpaid debts. Maragaret had initially been able to lure him away from medical school and his mounting debt with promises of a good-paying job because she was interested in his work with insects, but when the EDDNA business floundered, and Ulrich still owed a significant sum, he couldn't resist the much bigger paycheck Margaret could offer thanks to her foreign investors. Hobart said she thought he'd used the Michigan address of his old friend to hide from his creditors and ultimately to disappear because not all his creditors played nice.

In addition to the large trailer on the Granger farm that housed the state-of-the-art lab, there was also a smaller trailer nearby that served as living quarters. It was hidden just inside the woods behind the larger trailer and Hobart said it appeared Ulrich and Margaret had been playing house. In it they found the makings for the tranquilizer darts Brandon had on him the day he died. They also found several hidden diaries Ulrich had been keeping over the years. The entries had started out as a record of his experiments, but later they had grown more uncertain, heralding the guilt and paranoia he'd developed near the end. Though there was no way to prove it, the FBI's working theory was that Brandon had been in the trailer and had read Ulrich's diaries, prompting the beginning of his own doubts about what Margaret had him doing.

Agent Hobart also informed me that the bodies of Mary and Franklin Granger had been found inside two freezers in the basement of their home Both had been shot in the head, though there was no way to prove who had done the killing. It was hard to develop an accurate time of death because they'd been frozen so long, so it was estimated based on the time of their disappearance not long after the six sows had made their escape.

Agent Hobart said there were a lot of unknowns, but they believed Margaret had approached the Grangers when Franklin was thinking he'd have to sell the farm, offering them enough money so they couldn't refuse. Or perhaps she'd made them a different type of offer they couldn't refuse. Maybe it was a combination of the two. Margaret likely told the Grangers to tell anyone who asked that she was a niece who had come to visit, though as far as anyone could tell, the only person the niece was ever mentioned to was Sue Dusseldorf. The Grangers and Margaret had managed to play nice together for several years, so it was anyone's guess as to what had happened to change things.

Margaret's two goons were tracked down and arrested thanks to Ian Forrester's capture of the license plate on the vehicle that had chased me and security-camera footage that Sonja had set up outside her barn and home. Though I hadn't noticed the cameras any of the times I was out there, it made perfect sense. If I had an invaluable work of art sitting in my front yard, I'd probably want cameras watching it, too. The goon twins both denied killing anyone at first but the security footage from the restaurant where Ulrich had been murdered clearly showed both goons in a car pulling into the lot right around the time of Ulrich's death. This evidence prompted one of them to take a deal and start talking.

The talking goon revealed that Ulrich had fled about a month before he was killed, driving away in the old car he'd kept but hadn't registered for nearly a decade. The car had been stored in the Granger barn down by the farmhouse. Margaret was the one who had ordered Ulrich killed. She had set up his cell so she could track him when she began to suspect he was growing more and more dissatisfied, but she hadn't counted on the strength of Ulrich's paranoia. He had turned the phone on only twice: once when he'd called me in my motel room, and the second time when he called and asked

Roger to come back to the restaurant to meet with him. The first of Ulrich's calls had alerted Margaret to me though it hadn't enabled her to find Ulrich, because he'd turned the phone off right after the call and moved on. But the last call Ulrich had made had enabled the goons to track Ulrich and murder him. I wonder how Roger felt when he found out how close he'd come to being killed had it not been for a slow waitress. I'm guessing he probably doesn't care, now that Andy has been exonerated and released.

I turned over the claw piece I'd found at the site where Brandon had died and feel certain it will be matched to one of the creatures in the woods, assuming they are captured. To date, they are still out there somewhere, though I've been told there is a special group of hunters looking for them.

Of course, both Roger and Rita are delighted with the way things have turned out and Rita told me Roger is thinking of retiring and will be looking at properties elsewhere in Wisconsin as soon as he and Andy return from the vacation they embarked on right after Andy was released. Hopefully, they'll be able to get in some good father-son bonding time.

I've learned that Detective Hoffman retired from the police force in Rhinelander shortly after I shared my story with Agent Hobart, but so far there have been no other repercussions for his role in what happened. Nor have there been any for the real Adrian Dunlevy. His impersonator remains at large.

The good folks of Rhinelander have not only taken all these events in stride, but they've also tried to take advantage of the news stories about the possibility of living Hodags lurking in the woods around the city. While I can't prove it, rumor has it there's significant reward money being offered for the live capture of one of the beasts, though none have been found yet. At least not that anyone is admitting to.

Sonja Mueller was arrested, processed, and put in jail. I paid her bail, had Roger get her out, and then drove Wally back home. Sonja's trial is coming up and there's little doubt she'll do some jail time, but for now she's in the process of liquidating her assets to pay for her legal expenses. I bought six of her Hodag sculptures—one for each of the escaped sows—paying considerably more money than she was asking because I wanted to help her out. She'd broken the law, but I couldn't help but feel sorry for her. And I like her. Rita has tutted a few times over the assistance I've given Sonja, but she hasn't come right out and condemned my actions.

I'll likely never know for sure who all the shadowy figures I saw were. No doubt some of them were Ulrich—for sure the one at the restaurant had been—and the goon twins said they'd spied on me a time or two, but I couldn't rule out the possibility that David had been watching, as well. That whole episode out at Sonja's place had me stymied.

Now that I've been home a while and have had time to think—too much time, if you ask me—I'm struggling to figure out where to go from here. I miss Jon with a ferocity that surprises me. I never minded the times in between our get-togethers, even when weeks went by, but that was because I knew we would get together at some point and we often conversed or texted. With this lengthy silence and the thought that I might have lost him from my life forever, I'm truly miserable.

Rita has grown tired of my sulking and even Newt seems to be avoiding me of late. So I've decided it's time to put on my big-girl panties and take the ferry over to Washington Island to see Jon and try to talk things out. I only hope I can somehow persuade him to stay in my life.

After all, for someone who's spent a huge portion of her life trying to capture cryptids, how hard can it be to capture the heart of a single police chief?

AUTHOR'S NOTE

The history, rumors, and theories surrounding Michelangelo's creation of *Head of a Faun* and its subsequent disappearance during World War II make for fascinating reading. I encourage readers to check it out on their own, if for no other reason than to picture this creepy sculpture as the face of a Hodag.

The kindly folks of Rhinelander are very protective of their Hodag, and they don't like suggestions that the creature might be anything but friendly. So to all the residents of Rhinelander who embrace and protect the Hodag's reputation with impressive vigor, my apologies. I meant no harm, only to entertain.

The genetic engineering of living creatures is an ethical quagmire bound to become more prevalent as scientific abilities in this arena advance. Animals like pigs and goats have already been genetically engineered to make their meat (in the case of pigs) and their milk (in the case of goats) healthier for human consumption. Genome alterations in insects to make them more or less susceptible to pesticides have already occurred. While many countries have laws that ban genome editing in humans and genetic experiments on human embryos, the idea of designer babies is not as far-fetched as one might think. Gene editing of human embryos for nonreproductive purposes, while questionably ethical, is legal in many countries. This area of science and research will undoubtedly be at the forefront of legal, ethical, and moral battles in the future, particularly given that there might be unintended consequences. And there are no current laws I could find banning germline gene editing if it's paid for with private funds.

For those who find the combination of insect DNA with human DNA to create an army of hybrid soldiers far-fetched and unbelievable, you might want to read a 2017 article using the link below that highlights attempts to combine the DNA of a tardigrade—an intriguing little creature that can be boiled, baked, frozen, crushed, or blasted into space and still survive—with that of a human:

popularmechanics.com/science/animals/a43509580 /tardigrade-dna-human-stem-cells-super-soldiers

You should also know that we share as much as sixty percent of our DNA in common with some insects. In 1984 it was revealed that a fragment of a gene common to humans, chickens, frogs, earthworms, and flies is suspected of playing a critical role in the development of vertebrates, including humans. And finally, the abilities of CRISPR (an acronym for "clustered regularly interspaced short palindromic repeats"—a process of gene editing) are advancing daily. Search the term and go down the same rabbit holes I've spent days in! It has enabled us to turn certain genes on and off, to find miniscule bits of DNA inside cells and alter them, and to develop promising new advances in the treatment of human disability and disease. The speed with which these technologies are progressing is both frightening and exciting. The arena of gene editing, genetic engineering, and cloning is full of promising applications in many areas, including medicine and the availability and safety of food. It is also rife with abuse potential, and that gives writers like me lots of plot potential. And Hodags.

Stay tuned.

ACKNOWLEDGMENTS

While the many thanks I give out with each book I've had published can be a bit repetitive, my sincere appreciation for the people who are part and parcel of my writing life grows with each book. Writing feels like a solo process much of the time, yet it is anything but. All the people who support me bring different things to the table. So bear with me while I express my gratitude to these people yet again.

I have to start with my indomitable agent, Adam Chromy, who has been the best cheerleader, commander, and adviser a writer could ask for. Our journey together has had its ups and downs, but it has never been boring! I look forward to being together for any adventures the future may hold. A heartfelt thanks to my amazing editor, Tom Colgan, whose keen eye and years of experience have been a supportive and guiding light for me. I also owe a huge debt of gratitude to all the marketing and other support staff at Penguin Random House I've had the pleasure to work with. Just because I don't mention you by name doesn't mean you aren't integral to the success of the team. And of course, I wouldn't be thanking anyone at Penguin Random House if not for Michelle Vega, who was willing to take a chance on me with the very first Monster Hunter Mystery.

As always, the love and support of my family are crucial. Without them this journey wouldn't have been possible, and I can't think of anyone I'd rather share the ride with.

And finally, to the readers who have shown such inscrutable faith and devotion to my craft through reads, reviews, attendance at events, book buys, word of mouth, and participation in my social media . . . you are the reason I do this. I am forever grateful! Thank you from the bottom of my heart.